Leave it to the extraordinary author LK Kelley, she has written yet another brilliantly executed classic spellbinder! The saga continues with the supernatural world of werewolves, elves, elementals, and vampires, the legend of the White Wolf Prophecy continues into the "Hall Of Records" and is not only historical, but a riveting and fascinating read. While love flows freely from all the mates, and new understanding and knowledge is acquired, the evil Zanack has got to be reckoned with. They need to put an end to this evil for once and for all! I can't wait for the next trilogy!

Author Anita Meyer
The Primordial Language – Confirmation of the Divine Creator
And
In Search Of The Holy Language

Criminologist Religious Procurement Specialist

~~~
~~~

Reviews

LK Kelley has created an engaging second book. I didn't think the second book would be as good as the first but I was wrong. The writing itself draws beautiful pictures and the story is one that you can not put down. The characters are well written and the mystery continues. I kept turning pages to see what would happen next and the ending as madding because I wanted to know what was next. Can not wait to read the third installment and see where it leads us. Knowing my friend, I will be surprised and probably left wanting more.

Martha Cochenour
Administrative Assistant

The Law of Mount Everest: As the challenge elevates, the need for teamwork escalates.

~~~
~~~

Other books

The White Wolf Prophecy
~ Mating ~
Book 1

The White Wolf Prophecy
~ Hall of Records ~
Book 2

L K Kelley

DragonEye Publishing

Dedication

"To my husband, Wes, who has been very patient as I wrote, and believe me … he has been! To my daughter, Laura, without whose help and support I could never have made this dream of mine possible!   And, to my many friends who have helped me develop the characters, and helped me refine the book through their wonderful support and patience! And, especially, my dear friend, Anita Charlet Meyer, who, without her, this would never have been possible. Thank you so much, dear friend!

(Check out her books)

http://anitameyer1.wix.com/anita-meyer-books

Thanks to these wonderful people!

I want to thank all of the best people in the world who have been so gracious to help me with my book. I have the best group of people in the industry!"

Photographers:

ElleKelle Productions
http://www.ellekelleproductions.com/

Erica Boniface

Matt Mcclenahan
http://www.razorbackfoto.com/

Special Thanks to:

Curtis Meyer

Jennifer Lamb

And, of course, my publisher, Michael Kiser, whose patience and guidance has been appreciated throughout writing the Trilogy.

~ PROLOGUE ~

The location of The Hall of Records is rumored to be under the Sphinx in Egypt. It is said to hold all known knowledge of the Earth. Its true age is a mystery, and who built it, even more so - if it actually exists. A handful of the races on Earth do know it exists. But, where it is would be a surprise to all. And, who had put it there even more so.

Within the Hall of Records exists the real scroll of The White Wolf Prophecy. But, where, is the question. With the fate of Earth at stake, there is little time left to find it. But, there is far more to all of this than meets the eye.

The White Wolf Prophecy is no longer a fairy tale, but reality. And, unknown to all, are two who will interfere in the future of the world.

"It is time, love. Did you put the scroll into the Hall of Records?" a quiet voice asked.

"I did."

"Where they can be found easily?"

"Yes, but only the Prophecy, love."

"So, now we sit back, and watch."

"No. We sit back and hope that the Elementals discover it in time."

"Hope? We don't have time for hope. They must find it. And, I have made sure that they will."

<u>*The White Wolf Prophecy*</u>
(Lost Scroll)

When the White Wolf appears,
All that once was,
Will yet again be,
Beware that danger is not past.

Four there were,
Four were cursed.
Four there are,
Four are blessed.

Evil still present,
Will cause to suffer,
That which is,
To not last.

The one who cursed our worlds returns,
From the beginning and to the last.
For if he wins, the second time,
Our fate, forever, will be cast.

And, The White Wolf Prophecy continues …

~ 1 ~

When it takes thousands of years to acknowledge love, well, you have a problem

"I need them here tomorrow, Kaitlan. You cannot allow them to mate before they arrive here - even if they finally wise up, and recognize that they are mates! But, I wouldn't hold my breath on it! And, I don't give a flying flip what you tell them. Just make sure they are here ASAP! I'll explain everything to them when they get here. They may be our only hope to save us all."

"Cordone is *not* going to like it!" Kaitlan exclaimed. "And, just how in the hell am I supposed to get them there?"

"Duh! You are *Alpha*, are you not? Everyone has to obey your orders just like Cordone! Now, get going girl!"

"Well, there is that. OK. I'll get right on it. Oh, crap! Your brother just walked in, and heard me!"

Kaitlan darted her head toward Cordone who was walking toward her with his eyes narrowed, and his hand held out for the phone.

"Kaitlan! Is that Anita about that ridiculous idea, again?"

"Uh, I'll call you back." She quickly hung up the phone, and smiled at him innocently.

"Kaitlan," Cordone warned.

Dan wrapped his arms around Anita.
"Well?"
"My idiot brother came in, and stopped her from talking! Honestly! Sometimes he can be such a dic… " Dan

interrupted her with that gorgeous mouth of his, and like always, it worked to shut her mouth.

"Tits, Cordone is the last person I want to talk about! Hell! I don't want to talk at all!" Dan covered her mouth, picked her up, and took her back to bed.

"Kaitlan! I still cannot believe you are going along with this idiocy! They are *not* mates! How many times must I say it?"

Cordone stared at her. Anita was driving him crazy! Then, the vision in front of him calmed him down. It was the sight of his mate nursing their daughter that did it. He could never get over the most beautiful thing he had ever seen, and he never tired of watching her nurse their children - her swollen breasts filled with life-giving milk for them served to calm the beast within his chest. This last week had been challenging, but rewarding. Kaitlan had almost totally healed within three days after birth, surprising them both. He came back to reality with Kaitlan's next words.

"Cordone, I understand how you feel. But, really. What part of *any* of the things that have happened to us make sense? Especially since I turned into The White Wolf?"

Damn! She had him there! And, the real truth was that he didn't really have a reason not to send Lynne and Richard to Anita. How should he know if they were mates? There had been no sign of mating on the girl's side at all. No one had ever seen it.

"Look, I know how it must sound to you, but Anita is brilliant, right?" Kaitlan asked him.

He nodded once. Yes. His sister was brilliant. But, sometimes she lacked in common sense.

"OK. This entire thing is horribly serious, Cordone. Anita is convinced they are mates. You even told me *you* saw his eyes glow, right?"

Another nod.

"Well, then?"

"But, hers have never glowed, Kaitlan. Doesn't that tell you something?"

"All it tells me is that she was out of it when his glowed. We don't know if hers will glow, or not!"

She glanced down at Tara. Her tiny mouth was moving, but she was sound asleep. Before Kaitlan disturbed her daughter, she looked up at him, again.

"Your sister knows what she is doing. If there is something on your land to help to break the curse fully, why would you not let her do what she must? How long did she work trying to find an answer for the vampires? This could very well take years as well, but maybe not, since she has real time technology. If she had that when she found the almost cure for the vampires, it might have gone much faster."

"Our land," he corrected her once again, reminding Kaitlan that it was her land as well. He sighed. "And, you're proposing that we do what Anita wants?"

"Our land. Right. No. I'm saying it is what Anita *needs*, my love."

Kaitlan grinned as she saw him slump his shoulders, and knew she had won! YES! She looked down at her nursing daughter, again. They had named her Tara Seneca O'Hara Valon after her Mother. Kaitlan smiled gently. Tara was sound asleep. She gently detached her daughter from her breast, stood up, and carried her back to the sitting room they had made into a little nursery. It was next to their bedroom making it easier for Cordone to get up in the night to give their children to her to nurse. She gently laid Tara down, kissed her little black fuzzy head, and then, checked on their son, Canaan O'Hara Valon, named for her Father. He was sucking on his thumb. The warmth she felt for these two little miracles was overwhelming. Kaitlan had never been happier. She only wished her Mother and Father could share in their joy. She smiled, covered him up, and kissed his blonde fuzzy head goodnight, too, then returned to her Father's office where Cordone was writing his next best seller.

When Cordone was announced as the new President and CEO of the Seneca Publishing House, it had caused a huge sensation in the publishing world. Being run by the most famous science fiction writer in the world was gigantic news, and the news media had been all over them! Their main question? Would he continue to write his best sellers? Cordone had confirmed that he would, and his next book was a science fiction thriller called "Thunder on the Loose". But, he had admitted, writing came a bit slower with the twins. He had laughed along with the reporters.

The cloud of Zanack seemed so far away while in Kaitlan's Father's house. The four of them had moved there right after the twins were born. She had grown up in it, and she had been so happy there as a child. There were so many things a child could do, and a huge yard in which to play. The bonus was that it was only fifteen minutes from work. However, with a werewolf child advancing in age two years for every one, human year, they reach full growth in about ten years. No matter what, this would be noticeable in a big city like St. Louis. Therefore, Kaitlan and Cordone reluctantly decided that they would move to their "cave" home in Colorado permanently, designating a Vice President at the St. Louis branch of the Seneca Publishing House.

Cordone only wrote late at night when the babies were asleep with Kaitlan curled up on the sofa across from her Father's desk editing a book for one of their other authors. For the time being, everything seemed to settle down.

Kaitlan quietly slipped out of their semi-dark sitting room after feeding the twins, and fell into bed next to Cordone. He grabbed her tightly, and kissed her thoroughly. He couldn't wait until she was in shape for him again. Anita told them it would be at least another week, even though she appeared to be totally healed. It was convenient being a werewolf. They healed many times faster than their human counterparts.

Kaitlan felt him grind his hardened cock against her bare thigh.

"I can't wait for you, either!" she told him through their mind link.

He looked down at her remembering last night when he had brought his son in for her to nurse. Their vision of Cordone suckling her breast at the same time their child suckled the other one, finally came true. She fed Tara first, then Cordone took Tara back to her crib bringing Canaan to her who begin to greedily suckle her right breast, and then, Kaitlan had looked at Cordone. She had very quietly asked him to suckle her other breast. He had not needed any coaxing, and had latched onto her other breast suckling gently just the way their son was doing. Kaitlan had never been as happy as when both of her men were suckling her. She was totally content.

What did surprise her was how much milk she had inside of her. She was never empty, yet never in severe pain from her breasts that were heavy with milk. Kaitlan chalked it up to the fact she was a werewolf, and a breast pump was not needed, thanks to Cordone, who drank whatever the children couldn't. When they were alone, he drank his fill of her sending her into waves of ecstasy. No. She couldn't wait until she was ready for him again, but they were able to give each other orgasms with their mouths and hands. And, for the moment, that would have to be enough.

Anita had asked to send her two subjects - well, really, they were her guinea pigs, again - to her the same day Kaitlan had gone into labor, and Anita had decided they could wait a week, or so. She was still awed that Cordone had delivered both his mate and their children! What were the odds of that? But,

Anita didn't really mind the reprieve. She and Dan were perfectly happy where they were at Cordone's house, and they went out daily for research. Still, they had found nothing. Maybe it was the location? A configuration of the land? It was as if the entire place was magical in some way, but it refused to give up its secrets.

Dan would make love to her when she didn't expect it, and hold her afterward telling her he knew she would discover the causes in time. They both talked about which way making love was better - human, or wolf form. It was a toss-up, so they alternated. They never did make up their minds, but that sure didn't keep them from experimenting!

The phone rang. Whoever it was had really bad timing. Dan was moving inside of her slowly, and growled at the phone. Anita shushed Dan, grabbed her phone, and slid the slider to answer while feeling Dan's mouth descend to suckle her nipples.

"Kaitlan? Is something wrong?" Anita asked trying very, very hard not to groan aloud as Dan continued to pump into her. It was so hard to concentrate when he was doing that! Dan's face had a huge, wicked grin as he began to move much faster needing to spill into her. Her channel tightened around him as she lifted her hips to make it easier for him.

"No. This is your brother."

Anita groaned. Their orgasms were approaching fast. Cordone didn't notice.

"Can I call you back later?" she asked almost breathlessly.

"No! This has to be settled immediately!" Cordone demanded.

Oh, hell!

~ 2 ~
Why is it that whenever your involved, someone always calls?

His voice was that of her Alpha. She motioned to Dan who grinned even more with evil at her, and pulled out. Then, he flipped her on her stomach quickly, pushed her to her knees, and plunged right back into her slick wetness. Anita wanted nothing more than to pay full attention to Dan's throbbing cock plunging into her! Cordone be damned! Dan was about to come into her, and he was not about to stop, now! She knew it, too, as she felt her tighten around his diving cock that was plunging in and out of her depths with rapid movements.

"OK. Look, Cordone, are you going to send them or not? We can't wait any longer. I have to do the research, now."

She thought she was doing a great job of pretending nothing was going on - until a louder groan exited her mouth as Dan's cock pounded into her faster and faster. Again, Cordone didn't notice. She bit her tongue to keep quiet.

"OK, I will. I still don't get how they can be mates. I've never seen his eyes glow, but you have. Never seen Lynne's glow at all. So, I don't know why you would think it."

"We've been over this before, Cordone. The answer hasn't changed, so why do you keep asking?"

She was impatient, and annoyed with her brother. Trying to deal with her mate's imminent release, and trying to keep Richard and Lynne's real secret from Cordone, was trying her patience. Dan won out, and she push against him. Anita heard nothing from her brother as she shut her eyes in ecstasy, biting her lip to keep from crying out when she felt Dan flooding his hot, wet seed into her womb. Then, he slowly removed his hardness from her. He gave her a kiss on her ass, then another kiss on her neck with the unspoken promise that they'd resume their coupling when she was finished, and left the room. Dan had no intention of stopping until his mate was pregnant with their child.

Anita sighed. She had avoided telling Cordone the truth for a very long time, even though Canaan had known for a great many years. It wasn't her secret to tell, but it seemed that she would have to tell Cordone after all.

Anita clearly remembered when Canaan had insisted Anita tell him the truth about Lynne when he had found blood stashed in her office. Now, it was the only way she could make Cordone understand why he had never seen Lynne's eyes glow. She had been hard-pressed to get to Richard when Cordone had told her Richard's eyes were glowing. Luckily, Richard had kept his head lowered so no one else could see them.

She grinned and stretched. There was something wild and wicked about having sex while on the phone! Anita flipped onto her back feeling their liquid spill from her onto their sheets, and closed her eyes in ecstasy as it flowed from her. Yes! Wild and wicked!

"Anita? Did you hear what I said?" Cordone bellowed.

"No, I didn't, brother. I'm too busy with my sex after-glow!" she thought with irritation.

"I heard that, Tits! Don't worry. I'll be back to put my cock inside of you. I'm standing here, naked on the deck, and I'm still hard! So hurry it up, will you?"

Her womb tensed at the thought of Dan outside naked! She stretched her deliciously sore muscles, then turned back to the phone.

No! Stay there! I'll come to you! Wolf mating! I'll be off in a minute!" Anita promised Dan.

"There's a reason why you never saw her eyes glow, Cordone. No one has. She wears special contacts I invented for both Lynne and for Richard. I've refined them through the years, and they are extremely effective hiding their real eyes."

"What are you…HEY!" Cordone yelled when Kaitlan grabbed the phone from his hand.

"What? I'm putting it on speakerphone. You don't think you get to listen and I don't, do you?"

Kaitlan laid the phone on the table, and said, "Go on, Anita."

Cordone glared at her in a huff.

"Now that I decided to butt into this," Kaitlan just grinned at him, "Anita, what are you talking about? Their real eyes? Contacts? Why would they need to wear contacts?"

"Whatever. As I said. It's not really my story to tell, but Canaan knew. And, it was totally an accident that he had found out years ago. As my Alpha, I guess it's your right to know, now, but I am really at war with myself."

Puzzled, Kaitlan looked up at Cordone who shrugged.

"I guess I can understand that," Kaitlan told her. "But, if what you do know can clarify it for Cordone, and he is your Alpha, it's probably a good idea. He would never coerce you into telling a secret, but we are asking you to tell us if it is, in any way, relevant to why you need Richard and Lynne. We won't tell anyone, you know."

"Yeah. I know. OK. Here goes. I've used them so many times for my guinea pigs, I guess it won't be anything new." Anita sighed as she realized she lost the argument. "Did Richard ever tell you how he found Lynne?"

"No. Never," Cordone answered.

"Well, it's a really sad story, actually. Richard was on his way to his kingdom after the Vampire Wars. He'd lost many dear to him as had all of us. He had to go through the Enchanted Woods to get home. And, by the way, I still think it is a damn, stupid name for a forest! Who the hell came up with that name, anyway?" she complained, getting off the subject. Shaking her head, "Anyway, Richard heard a cry. A child's cry, and he followed it. He found a young girl of about twelve covered in blood. Her clothes were torn giving little coverage, and her hair was matted with twigs, mixed with blood and grass."

Kaitlan took a very deep breath. The worst was coming. She just knew it. She watched as Cordone fisted his hands at his side.

"Richard said he stooped down to put his hand on her shoulder, and she jerked away from him. He tilted her face to him, and moved back several feet at what he saw. She growled at him with her bloody face, revealing her bloody fangs. Her mouth was full of blood. Her eyes were wild - and red." Anita paused.

Cordone's mouth dropped, and Kaitlan slapped her hand over her mouth.

"It was Lynne? Oh, God! No!"

"I didn't think they turned children?" Cordone was horrified.

"Well, the rogues turned anyone, apparently. Something we didn't know. Give me a minute, bro. This is still hard for me to tell." Anita took a deep breath. "OK. And, I'm moving on … Richard glanced around him, and saw a huge moose that was torn to shreds. Its body was partially eaten, and blood drained. Then, he turned back to the girl. He couldn't believe a vampire turned a child. She had tears running down her cheeks - bloody tears as they mixed with the blood on her face. He slowly approached her, again. She was a vampire, and a brand new one by his calculations. He pulled her hair out of her face, and then he said he almost lost it. Vampire law forbid the turning of any child under the age of fourteen which was alright in those days. Yucky, I know. Lynne had the bad luck to be in her village when a few rogues attacked. But, even more than that, it was more horrifying because of what she was."

Kaitlan just had to ask. When would she learn not to ask?

"What she was?" She reached out to hold onto Cordone's hand.

"Lynne was an Elf."

Silence. Dead silence greeted Anita through the phone. Cordone dropped into a chair, stunned. Kaitlan was speechless. Lynne was a vampire Elf? Cordone had never heard of such a thing. He was as speechless as Kaitlan!

"No questions from the floor? Right? Good. Well, Richard picked her up, and carried her with him until he found a stream. He waded into it to wash her. She was in shock, and it was impossible for her to bathe herself, so he took over. He cleaned her hair with mud, and washed her body. He pulled out clothing from his pack, and dressed her in them, even though they were obviously way too big."

To Kaitlan, she explained. "Camping was big in those days, Kaitlan. Villages were few, and far between, and there were few inns in which to stay. But, even if there were places to stay, he couldn't risk her being around others. Not in her condition. He built a fire, and pulled her to it so that she could warm herself. Sometime in the night, he found her trying to bite him."

Anita closed her eyes. She didn't know if she could tell them the complete truth, but knew she had to do it.

"There is just no easy way to say this," she stated flatly. "Lynne succeeded."

Cordone was a statue. He couldn't move nor speak, so Kaitlan asked.

"Wait! Do you mean by 'succeeded' that she … I mean … that Richard … is… ?"

Cordone saw Kaitlan slap her hand over her mouth, again, to keep the cry from coming from her.

"Yes, Kaitlan. Richard is a vampire Werewolf. But, the vampire overrides the werewolf, just as it overrides Lynne's elf."

Cordone looked at Kaitlan in mute silence, listening as Anita continued.

"Lynne was horrified by what she had done. It had shaken her into reality. Even though she was just a child, because she was an Elf, her mind was far beyond the age of twelve. She took care of him while he turned, and afterwards, he took her to his castle, set her up as his daughter, and Princess of the Vikings. Lynne had been so terrorized by what she was, she vowed to never feed from a human being, but only from animals." She stopped, then began again. "Look, Cordon. Richard has always thought of her as his daughter. Everyone knows this. But, that can no longer be allowed to continue. He cannot change into a werewolf. His vampire blood prevents him from doing so. Like Richard, Lynne has no use of her Elven powers. You know what it would mean if she could use them. And, remember, it was because of Lynne and Richard who volunteered to be my guinea pigs, that I found a partial cure for vampirism. They are my first success. My potions worked to a point, but both still need some blood about once every month, or so, to survive. But, the most important thing that happened was that it keeps them from biting any creature. Sometimes, in times of stress, they may need an extra boost with the donated bags of blood. Both of them always have a stash of blood in their possession."

"You say my Father knew the entire story?" Kaitlan asked.

"Yes. And, so did your Grandfather, for it was he who put Lynne in her position as protector to the Alpha. The Council members do not know that Richard is the guardian of the Council. The two, deadliest people in our midst guard the Alpha, Cordone, and the Council Members."

Cordone's head just shook side to side to side running his fingers through his hair. How did he not know this? What else had Canaan never told him? Kaitlan just sat without blinking, and then her head came up.

"You said you are the only one to ever see his eyes glow?"

"Until the day she was poisoned, yes. His contacts melted from his eyes, and that's when Cordone saw them. Good thing I always keep spares in the office, and both carry extras with them as well. The glow dissolves them."

Cordone had been beaten, and he knew it. Kaitlan reached out to stroke her mate's cheek. Cordone looked at Kaitlan, and she nodded.

"They'll be on the jet within the hour, Sis. Do whatever it takes!"

"I'll do my best, Brother of mine."

She hung up the phone, and turned to look at Dan.

"It's time to prepare."

Five hours later, Sam stuck his head into Cordone's office.

"Cordone? I contacted them as you wanted. The answer was yes."

"Did you convene the Master Council?"

"Absolutely! I've put it on the calendar for next week."

"Good. Thank you, Sam."

Sam left, both of them remembering the last time the Master Council met. It was before the Vampire Wars. And, look how that turned out! Damn!

~ 3 ~

"A lie is doomed in secret." ~ LK Kelley

Lynne jerked her head up at Cordone's words.

"*WHAT* did you just say?" she yelped.

Lynne was always cool, calm, and collected. She never showed emotion at work, and she had just shot that all to hell!

"I said you will report to the jet in one hour."

"And, just why should I do that?" She was really angry at being ordered to abandon her duty to her Alpha.

"I am your Alpha, Lynne. It is a request. However, I will make it an order if you don't obey me."

Cordone was standing tall, every inch her Alpha. Lynne had seen Canaan do it rarely, and always because there was some dire emergency. It appeared she'd see it with Cordone as well. But, what possible emergency could include her? She had never dreamed that *she* would be the recipient of any Alpha!

"But, I can't go. I, mean, I have a lot of work to do!"

Lynne waved her hand over her perfectly clean desk. She was his protector, even though he didn't know it. He couldn't send her away. Both he and Kaitlan would be far too vulnerable.

"Then, it would seem I have to make it an order, Lynne. Go home, pack, and be on the company jet in one hour," Cordone ordered, and walked into his office slamming the door.

Cordone rubbed the back of his neck - a habit he had acquired long ago when he was frustrated. He always hated to use his powers on others, but now that he was Alpha, he hated it even more. He heard all kinds of banging going on as he heard Lynne slam drawers, hit the desk, and finally slammed her office door as she left. He shook his head, his mouth turned

16

up in a snarky grin.

"*What else did you keep from me, Canaan?*" he thought to no one, but he received an answer.

"*I'm wondering that myself,*" Kaitlan thought back to him.

Lynne stormed out of her office slamming the door behind her. She had *NEVER* been so angry in her life! How dare he order her! Her thoughts were still murderous as a driver dropped her off at her apartment to wait while she packed, then they continued on to the airport. Once inside the company jet, Lynne plopped down in a plush seat tapping her foot. She was there to protect the Alpha. That was her entire job. The secretary stuff was just a side job that she just happened to do well. She clenched, and unclenched her hands, digging her nails into her palms, causing them to bleed. She healed quickly only to do it again.

She couldn't sit still, and got up to pace. She was very grateful to Anita, even if she had been Anita's guinea pig, because she could live almost as a normal being. She didn't even need blood, but once a month - unless she was under stress. And, she was under plenty of stress right now! Reaching into her tote bag, Lynne pulled out one of her many blood packets, downing it fast. But it did nothing to quell her anger! Why would he do this? What was the reason behind it? Her entire job had always been the secret protection for the Alpha, and his mate, and family, if there was one. The bad part was that Lynne knew he could order her to do anything as her Alpha, and she had no choice. She and Richard had vowed to the O'Hara Clan to be obedient to the Alphas. Luckily, that had only happened once with Canaan's Father, once with Canaan, and now, it was Cordone. But, with the current danger, Lynne felt as if she had involuntarily deserted her post, and she didn't like it one, damn bit!

Lynne thought back to what she wasn't. This vampire affliction kept her from being as powerful as she should be. Elf power was terrifying to all who dared to inflame their anger! Damn it! If she had that power, now, she would use it against Cordone!

Huffing, she crossed her arms, and fell back down into her seat. She was paralyzed by her vampire blood, and that just made her more furious! She reached into her tote to grab another blood packet, downing it just as fast as the other one.

Hearing a noise in the plane, Lynne jumped back up, and swung around ready for an attack. Richard entered, and she stopped in surprise.

"What are you …" demanded Lynne at the same time.

"… doing here?" demanded Richard at the same time.

This was what came from two people who knew each other a long, long time. Finishing each other's sentences. They really had been around each other way too long, Lynne thought.

"Cordone had the nerve to *ORDER* me here!" Lynne's voice was furious.

"Really? Interesting. He ordered me here as well!"

Richard was angry as hell, but nowhere near as angry as Lynne. He dropped his overnight bag on the floor, and pulled a blood packet from his pocket.

"WTF is going on?" Lynne demanded. Yep. They had both picked up some bad language habits from each other, too.

They both turned in preparation of an attack as they heard steps coming up behind them. It was Timothy Matthews, the Clan Pilot.

"Good afternoon, Mr. O'Malley. Ms. DeVane. If you will take your seats, and buckle-up in preparation, we will get under way in about five minutes."

"Really, Tim! You shouldn't sneak up like that! And, just *where* the hell are we going?" Richard demanded.

We will be landing at DIA, and from there, Mr. Dan will collect you. You will continue to Cordone's home in the Rocky Mountains, Mr. O'Malley. Now, if you'll both please buckle up," he repeated again, and turned back to the cockpit.

Lynne and Richard looked at each other.

"It appears we are being ordered to the backwoods of beyond!" Lynne griped, and plopped down in her seat, again.

OK. So. Maybe it wasn't the backwoods of beyond. And, it was an incredible house, and a great place to go - when she had her friends with her. But, still….

"I guess it won't be too bad since Anita is there!" she thought. Lynne hadn't seen Anita since she and Dan had mated.

Two hours later, they landed at DIA. Their plane had been delayed circling the airport. They grabbed their hastily packed carry-on luggage, and proceeded to the arrival area where Dan was waiting to pick them up. He'd only had to circle the airport three times since it was forbidden for anyone to park and wait to pick up passengers. DIA was pretty strict about it, too.

Another four hours spent catching Dan up to speed, and they arrived at Cordone's "mansion". Their anger had dissipated somewhat by the time that Cordone's house was in sight.

The door opened, and Anita stood there.

"Lynne! Richard! So glad you guys got here safely. Come in!"

She stood back to let them through, then Lynne grabbed Anita in a big bear hug.

"I missed you so much! How's the mating life?" Lynne smirked knowingly.

She was so happy for Anita. She deserved happiness. Anita had made Lynne's entire life the best it could be, and she wished nothing but the best for her.

"It's unreal, Lynne! You need to try it!"

"Yeah. Right. I'll get right on that," Lynne snorted at the very idea of Anita's suggestion that she needed a mate! "As if!" Lynne muttered under her breath. Anita just pretended she hadn't heard it.

"Richard! It's good to see you!" Anita gushed giving him a big hug.

Dan came back into the main room, and they all sat in the overstuffed leather chairs that surrounded the fire pit that was blazing happily in the center. It was still cold in the mountains even though it was Spring, and snow still lingered in the higher elevations.

Lynne's long legs stretched out in front of her, as she demanded, "OK. Spill, Anita. WTF are we doing here?"

Lynne had always been blunt and to the point. But, Anita wouldn't have her any other way. She liked that she knew where she stood with Lynne. Made things so much easier!

"I'd like to know as well, Anita. Why *are* we here? Why did Cordone not ask us, but order us to come?" Richard echoed.

Anita looked at Dan, and he nodded. "Would you two like a drink?"

Both of them shook their heads, but Dan wouldn't have it.

"Believe me. You *will* want that drink. Cordone had me place a supply of blood in his frozen locker."

Cordone had warned him why, but what he didn't know was that Dan already knew about Richard and Lynne.

Richard shot up out of his seat, and was on Dan in a split second with his hands wrapped around his neck.

Anita was horrified, and Lynne grabbed Richard's arm as she shouted, "Richard! Let him go!"

"No! How the hell did you know about us?"

Dan just grinned at him. "Canaan."

Richard gritted his teeth, while Lynne's powerful arms forced him to release his hold on Dan. She managed to drag him away, and coaxed him into sitting back down. Richard slumped into his seat in shock. Canaan? Canaan had told Dan? What the hell?

Anita had not even known that Dan knew about them, and her face also registered surprise. But, then, Canaan was always full of secrets! After there was calm, Dan brought their blood cocktails - his own personal recipe - and gave Richard and Lynne a glass. Both of them tasted it, and they gave Dan a thumbs up. They were delicious! Dan kissed Anita on the head, nodded to the others, and then made himself scarce by sauntering into the garage to tinker with one of the cars taking his wine with him.

"OK. Lynne, here's the scoop. It has to do with matings, and the Prophecy. You already know the basics of it. Such as we would be able to mate in our wolf forms and get preggers. Kaitlan, Sarah, and I have already found our mates. Sarah had an idea, without proof, of course, but her belief is that because the three of us, and our wolves, have mated, there may be a correlation between the four of us. Even though the Prophecy has been broken, it's only partially broken. She said that logic dictates there is a need for four women to mate to break the curse completely. When the fourth mates, then all weres will be able to mate in both forms, and become pregnant everywhere. The only one of the four of us who has not mated is you, Lynne. Now, your case is a bit different, and Richard cannot turn into a wolf just as you cannot use your Elven powers. This means that the curse may very well be completely broken once you and Richard have mated."

The faces of Richard and Lynne changed instantly.

"This is a joke, right? Where are the hidden cameras?" Lynne quipped.

When they didn't see Anita smiling, their fangs descended, they shot out of their seats. Their contacts melted as their bright red eyes glowed at Anita in anger.

Anita wasn't afraid of their anger, and sat back in her chair sighing in triumph. She grinned widely. She *had* been right.

"Cameras? What cameras, Lynne?" she laughed out loud.

~ 4 ~

The Hardest Thing for Anyone to Admit to Themselves is the Truth

"OK. Patient confidentiality time. I am doing what I have to do to save our Clan females. This is going to be hard for me to say, but even harder for the two of you to hear, let alone understand. I hope the both of you forgive me for what I'm about to ask you to do."

Lynne and Richard looked at her skeptically as they both sat back down. Richard protested.

"Patients? We aren't patients!"

Ignoring his outburst, Anita continued.

"The first thing you need to know, Richard, is that Kaitlan is The White Wolf of the Prophecy."

Lynne already knew this, and just frowned crossing her arms across her chest.

Richard, however, was floored. Kaitlan? The White Wolf?

"Impossible!" he exclaimed. "That is a total myth!"

Lynne looked up at him. "It's true, Richard."

Richard looked at her as if she was nuts. Lynne shrugged, and just nodded.

"How do you know?" he demanded.

"She showed us when we were here the day of the funeral."

Richard's mouth dropped. And she didn't think he, as well as the Council, needed to know this? Anita followed Lynne's statement.

"When Cordone and Kaitlan mated, they discovered that they could mate in both forms. Tara came from the human form while Canaan was the result of their wolf form," Anita explained.

His mouth dropped open - again.   He moved to speak, and Anita forestalled him.

"There's more. Sarah is human. You guys know that. But, when she and Sam mated, Richard, she developed fangs. We all saw her turn into a red wolf. They, too, were able to mate in both forms. Moreover, Dan and I can mate in both of our forms as well."

"What are you getting at, Anita?" Lynne cocked her head, but she was afraid she knew what she would say.

"When Kaitlan became The White Wolf, the curse, or whatever you want to call it, was partially broken. How we once mated, part of it has reversed. This is why we can mate in our wolf form."

"And, that has to do with us how?" asked Richard.

"It's rather simple. No other were has been able to mate in their wolf form, as I have said. If true, and the fourth couple is the key, we need to test this theory. And, I have to find out what is causing the breaking of the curse. Children of weres, as you know, are rare any longer. Yet, there have, now, been three pregnancies. Even though Kaitlan is The White Wolf, the only wolf matings, and pregnancies have happened here. If the Prophecy is correct, all will be able to mate without being here at some point. That leaves the two of you. We don't know what is effecting the reversal. Whatever it is must happen on Cordone's land first."

"Anita. You're wrong. There have not been three pregnancies. Only two. You can't count Kaitlan's twins," Dan interrupted as he walked into the room.

Anita looked up at him, and Lynne knew that look! Anita was the third! She looked at Dan who really didn't get it, and smothered a laugh. Even Richard looked puzzled. No wonder men were always the last to know! They were so damn dense!

Still Dan frowned, and shrugged. He didn't get it.

Anita put her ear to Dan's head, and tapped it with her

finger.

"Heeelllloooo! Anyone in there? You do know it takes four months to have a baby with weres, right?" she laughed.

He looked at her really weird. Suddenly, understanding dawned. Anita just looked at him, and nodded. No wonder her wine was still sitting in front of her!

"*YOU* are the third?" Dan's mouth dropped open.

"Yep! You betcha!"

He swept her up in his arms kissing her as if he would never let her go. Whatever was happening, it *was* possible that the werewolf lines could continue!

A round of "congratulations" was heard in the room.

"I'm so happy for you, Anita! I get to be another auntie!" squealed Lynne.

"Congratulations, Dad!" Richard said patting Dan on the back!

Lynne hugged Dan. "You stud you!"

Lynne laughed at his faux, outraged expression, and Dan laughed, too.

Dan brought some wine for himself, water for Anita, and another round of blood cocktails for Richard and Lynne. The four toasted together.

But, more was to come, and Anita had to shoo Dan out of the room once again. Once he was out of sight, Anita continued.

"OK. Coming back to the subject. There is only one way to test the theory, and I need someone to help me zero in on what is causing the change. A couple that will mate while letting me monitor their surroundings."

"And?" Richard asked, looking at Lynne's shoulders shrug.

She didn't understand what Anita wanted, either.

Anita just shook her head. Honestly! These two really were clueless! She took a giant breath. They were just going to make her spell it out, weren't they?

"I need two volunteers, who are ready to mate, and

willing to let me tag them with sensors. And, the mating must happen here on Cordone's land."

At first, Richard and Lynne still didn't understand what she wanted. And, then … Anita watched their faces go from blank looks to surprise, to shock, to outrage as they both realized who it was she was talking about, and they both jumped up.

"Are you fucking crazy, Anita? You mean us?" Richard's face was red with anger as he pointed to Lynne and himself.

Anita just stared at them without answering. Lynne's face told Anita she agreed with Richard.

"Anita, we are not mates! Where in the name of all that is holy did you ever get that fucking idea?" demanded Lynne, her face red with anger and embarrassment.

Anita shrugged, and leaned back in her chair calmly.

"You are both hybrids. Richard is a were-vampire; you are an elf-vampire. Need I remind you that while it is extremely rare, hybrids do find mates in all three species?"

"So?"

Anita rolled her eyes. These two were as dense as a dwarf star! Seriously? Yep. She had been right. She really was going to have to spell it out for them?

"Richard, remember when you ran Lynne to the clinic when she was poisoned? You barely got her to me in time."

Lynne turned her head in surprise to look at Richard. No one had told her that he had saved her.

"You saved me?"

Richard's head was hanging down, remembering he almost lost her. It still scared him that he could have lost her due to Zanack. He raised his head to look at Lynne.

Anita was hoping this would push them.

"I have to ask you both something."

Lynne didn't turn her face away from Richard while Richard nodded to Anita still staring into Lynne's eyes.

"If there were ever two people meant to be mates, it is

the two of you. You have been together a very, very long time, and I doubt you even realize that the possibility of the two of you as mates is probable. The same happened with Dan and me, remember? I am sending you to talk. Take your time. But, just in case, I also want to inject you with one of my newest inventions. It contains sensors that will record your heartbeats, blood, toxicity, as well as monitor your respiration, etc. It's similar to nano-technology, only far more advanced. It also monitors the air and earth around you. There will be no one watching, or hearing you. I'm not interested in those details. I'm only interested to find out if the sensors can detect anything out of the ordinary."

Lynne was just shaking her head as if she couldn't believe she was hearing this. Richard just stared at Anita.

"Now, if you do mate, the information will be invaluable, and the two of you could be the very ones who could save all of us. Look. You two are my good friends, and Lynne, you are my bestie. I know what I'm asking of you. But, I'm also asking this as your doctor, and clan mate. And, I'm asking you to help our species. Remember, this is completely confidential. No pictures, or words are recorded. I hate like hell to ask you two to be my guinea pigs, again, but do you trust me enough to ask you to help our Clan? However, should I learn something important through the sensors, I will be reporting to Cordone and the Council."

No answer. Anita took a very deep breath.

"I know mating is intensely personal and private. This will not, in any way, detract from mating, if it occurs. And, even if it doesn't, perhaps the sensors might pick up an anomaly. But, we have a danger out there from Zanack. He is trying to destroy all of us by killing off our females. We have just learned this. The Elves have already experienced this long ago when they were targeted. I didn't want to have to tell you this, but if it helps your decision, I must. Cordone called Stefan and Ali'on. The vampire females were also being poisoned, and some have died from Wolfsbane. Cordone has convened the

Master Council, because of this threat."

Richard shot up! "Stefan? Ali'on? He didn't tell us? Why?"

This was far more serious than Richard and Lynne had known if the MC was being called. Only in the case that there was a serious threat to the supernatural world would it be convened. The very last time the MC had been called had been about the Vampire Wars. If Cordone thought there was a threat, then this was, indeed, serious.

"He just found this out today, and called the Council for a week from now. This is why it is imperative to find out whatever is causing the reversal. If Zanack finds out that the Prophecy has come true, and has erased the curse, we don't know what he would do. I can't even promise that he doesn't know already." Anita looked at them with a frown. Lynne had never seen Anita this worried as long help."

Lynne took Richard's hand in hers. He turned to look at her. She gave a short nod.

"OK. Do it." Richard agreed. "Inject your toys into both of us."

Good thing Anita was worricd. Otherwise, the "toys" comment would make her really mad! Anita ledas they had known each other.

"I desperately need your help. The Clan needs your help. The entire supernatural world needs your them into her makeshift office, and injected each of them with yet, another of her inventions. She just hoped it was going to work. These two had served her as her guinea pigs for other tests in the past. They were brave. Only this time, it might save all of them.

And, then, Richard took Lynne's hand walking out of the glass door without looking back.

Anita stood in the window watching them leave.

"Do you think it will work, love?" asked Dan placing his hand on her abdomen where their child grew.

"I don't know." Anita looked up at him shaking her head. "I guess we have to leave it to the Creator, now."

He nodded, and they watched as Richard and Lynne disappeared into the woods.

~ 5 ~

Sometimes, you must be forced with the truth to proceed into the future

Silently, Richard and Lynne walked hand in hand, as they had done so many times when she was little. But, she was no longer a little girl. Hadn't been in a very, very long time. But, still, she was his daughter - adopted, perhaps - but his daughter none the less. Yes. He knew she was his mate, but she didn't, and he would never force that on her. It was the only reason he had agreed to this preposterous idea! Perhaps Anita knew what she was talking about, but Richard didn't believe it.

They reached a bluff, overlooking a vast, forested valley, and just below them ran a large, unknown stream that was more like a small river. It ran through the valley just below the bluff. The evening was cold, and cloudy. Winter snows were still on the ground high in the Rocky Mountains. These things didn't bother supernaturals. They were immune to temperature. Heavy clouds were rolling across the sky, signaling a thunderstorm of monstrous proportions.

Richard looked up at the sky. Mating was private, personal. Did he have the right?

"A storm is coming, and it's going to be a bad one." he stated, uninterested.

Lynne nodded. She, too, could feel it.

Richard let go of her hand, and walked away from her his head hanging down. Their contacts having disintegrated earlier, Lynne frowned when he detached himself from her, but when he sank to the ground on his knees burying his head in his hands, she felt a wave of love crash over her. How had Lynne not known that she had loved him for a very, very long time?

29

Her heart had known, but her mind wouldn't accept it until now. Thank God Anita hid this fact for it was only Anita who had seen her eyes glowing when Lynne looked at Richard. Few people knew who he really was, let alone his name. But, she did. She still carried guilt for turning him into what she was. Richard had been so wonderful when he had found her. He showed no fear, but helped to wash all the blood that was encrusted on her body from her first kill. Later, hunger drove Lynne to bite him low on his neck while he was sleeping. Those marks were long gone, but he had turned. She had cared for him until his turning was over, but it didn't ease her soul as he found her crying her heart out at what she had become, and what she had done to him.

Because of her, Richard could no longer phase into his werewolf form. She had done that to him! She had taken his werewolf life from him, and guilt had consumed her since that day. But, his control made her envious. He hadn't seem to suffer from being a new vampire. His werewolf fangs that curved at the ends, changed into the straight fangs of a vampire.

Richard and Lynne had traveled to his home - a castle in the mists - or at least it seemed that way to Lynne in those days. A Viking King he was, without a doubt. His kingdom consisted of all species of werewolves, humans, and vampires for he was a kind, and just King. Elves had always kept to themselves, but with the addition of Lynne, he had relented, and allowed homeless elves to reside in his kingdom. His people would follow him into battle, and would die for him many times over in order to protect their home.

The day he entered his castle with Lynne, he gave orders to have her placed in one of the largest rooms, and treated as their princess. Richard dressed her in the finest clothing, and declared her his daughter in front of all. He taught her that before one can lead, one must be humble, learn to serve others, and follow orders.

Years progressed. Lynne stopped aging at around the age of twenty-two, and she had full control of her vampire nature. Lynne loved exploring the castle with all its secrets. She spent hours with Richard hunting for the blood they needed, and they never bit any human for blood. Just animals, and only taking what they needed. Their eyes were only red just after they ate. The rest of the time, their eyes reverted to normal.

But, Richard was fun. He taught her to fish, hunt, and fight with swords, bows, and arrows, becoming proficient in the cross bow, her favorite weapon.

A few years passed, and their lives changed forever. They had been hunting on their land, and heard a noise. Richard drew his sword, and Lynne had grabbed her crossbow. Even though it was night, they found two young werewolves being attacked by rogue vampires. The werewolves were outnumbered, but they fought like veterans. Richard and Lynne dashed into the meadow. Lynne's arrows flew with absolute precision into the vampires, the wood in the arrows killing them instantly as they pierced their hearts turning them into ash. The four fought side by side, and those rogues that had been thought gone after the wars, were finally defeated. The Vampire Wars were finally ended.

At the time, they had not known that they fought side by side with the heir to the O'Hara Clan called Canaan, and his personal guard, Sam. Canaan had been grateful beyond measure, and asked them to please come, and meet his Father.

Richard and Lynne were honored, and protocol demanded that they meet the leader. In those days, honor was everything. Dillon Canaan O'Hara, leader of the O'Hara Clan, was grateful for the two who had saved the life of his son and guard, so he honored them with a huge dinner and ball. Although they only stayed a short time, a permanent friendship was created. Richard and Lynne thanked him for the honor they had been given. Richard was told that if they ever wished to dispense with their duties, or if their duties were removed from them, Dillon would be honored if both he and Lynne would join them in the Clan. The Clan was totally unaware that they had two vampires in their midst. Richard thanked them, and they had left.

When Richard and Lynne returned home, their kingdom had been destroyed. Very little remained except a burned-out village. Neither Richard nor Lynne knew what could have caused it. Only a few subjects who still survived had told them it had been attacked by rogue vampires. The same rogues that Richard and Lynne had helped Canaan and Sam fight. But, Richard had nothing left to rule or to protect. So, he and Lynne gathered up all those still alive left in their kingdom, and returned to the O'Hara Clan. Both he and Lynne accepted his offer, and pledged their allegiance and loyalty in exchange for his people being permitted to live within the Clan. Canaan's Father had agreed. Richard, however, wanted there to be no misunderstandings, so in secret, Richard had told the Alpha what both he and Lynne were.

While Dillon had been surprised, Richard and Lynne had already proven themselves to him. So, Richard was installed that very day, given the left seat to the Alpha, and a place of honor, while Lynne was installed as his personal assistant. There were a couple of weres on the council who protested that one of them should have the seat by seniority, but Dillon had used his Alpha powers to subdue them. Richard and Lynne's duty was to defend the Alpha, Beta and Third with their lives. He never told his son the truth about them because, less than a year later, Canaan's Mother died by Wolfsbane poisoning, and Dillon followed her in death. Since she was the first ever to die by that method, no one ever thought that it was murder. Now, Lynne wondered if it was Zanack, then, as well. The new Alpha, Canaan, and his Beta, known as Cordone Valon, were installed after Dillon's death, and Richard still sat at Canaan's left hand.

Many years passed. One day, while Lynne was gone, Canaan accidentally found a stash of blood in Lynne's office looking for a scroll. He confronted her, and it was then, Richard told Canaan the truth.

It was at that time that Anita Moore, the Clan doctor, discovered that Richard and Lynne were also vampires when a couple of bags of her blood supply had disappeared. The incident was small, but Anita accidentally found Lynne taking blood from a squirrel. Richard was terrified. The more who knew, the more chance others would know. However, instead, Anita found a blood supply for them in their own stock, and began breeding the stock for their supply. Anita took an interest into trying to reverse the side effects of the vampire life. Many vampires refused to give up the blood of humans. But both Richard, Lynne and others wanted it as well. So, Lynne and Richard were selected to be her guinea pigs. There were unexpected side-effects of the potion she gave them which caused their eyes to remain red permanently, and the reason the two of them used contacts to this day. Anita eventually discovered that an allergy to a root in the potion was the culprit that caused their affliction, and even while she was discouraged, she found a breakthrough which resulted in an almost cure. It consisted of eighteen injections of a mixture of roots and herbs that took away the cravings for blood, and gave them the ability to go out in the sunlight. She continued to try to find a full cure, but she hadn't as yet. Once discovered, vampires no longer had red eyes at any point. The injections that had been given were all they ever needed, and were permanent once all the injections were finished. However, the injections could only be given once, and Richard and Lynne were stuck with the red eyes.

There was another side effect of the injections, causing an unexpected benefit. The vampires remained strong without blood, and they only needed a blood booster every month or so depending on their activities, and emotions. The humans that they did know were glad to donate to them. And, even with that, most of the vampires chose animal blood instead. In time, they were even able to eat some human food.

Anita became their doctor as well. Anita found herself, on the rare occasion, flying all over the world to treat werewolves and vampires. It was this incredible breakthrough, though, that changed the course of their entire supernatural world. This earned Anita the highest honor among all supernaturals, and they still honored her to this day.

Today, Richard and Lynne still protected the Alpha. Unfortunately, Canaan had been out of their sight when he had been killed by Zanack. Both of them felt guilty, but no one ever held them at fault. Zanack was very clever.

While Lynne thought about their past together, Richard had been doing his own reminiscing.

When Lynne had been poisoned, he had realized that she was his mate. And, this was why he was on his knees, now. He was ashamed of it. She was an innocent person, and his daughter! How could he even think of her that way? Why would the powers decide that she was his mate? After everything they had been through, why now? What kind of a pervert did that make him? Oh, he knew Cordone had felt the same towards Kaitlan, but this was different. Lynne was HIS daughter! He had fought it since that day, but he knew it was a losing battle within himself. He could not look at her, because if he did, his eyes would glow. He needed to put them in before she saw. He sure had used a hell of a lot of them in recent weeks. But, this was against everything he had ever believed. He reached into his coat to retrieve another set. Damn! He was out!

Lynne knew his thoughts as if they were her own. She approached him knowing he wouldn't look at her unless she forced him to do so.

"Eric, please? Look at me," she said. He kept his head down.

She was beside him. "Eric! Look at me!"

This time it was a demand. He still refused. He couldn't allow her to see his glowing, red eyes. He was out of contacts, and he knew if she saw them, now, she'd run from him.

Lynne sighed, and kneeled before him as she had done as Princess to her King. She gently took his face in her hands bringing it up so he could see her face. He kept his eyes closed, but couldn't resist her.

"Please, Eric? Look at me?" she begged.

He gave up, and opened his glowing, red eyes expecting to see disgust in hers staring up at him. His mouth dropped when she smiled at him.

"Linora? What the fuck?"

He grabbed her face looking into her matching, red and glowing eyes!

"You, my dearest and oldest friend, are my mate." She smiled widely at him.

"How? I mean. It's not possible. I mean … oh, hell! I don't know what I mean!" Eric exclaimed in confusion.

Lynne almost laughed at his reaction. He was so adorable when he was all flustered - if it had ever happened at all! She always lifted his spirits when he was down as did he for her. She was shaking with the wonder of it all. Both of them had also fallen into their old habit of calling each other by their original names. The same names they had used while living in his kingdom. While it was nice before, their names, now, took on a more intimate sound. But they didn't realize that - at first.

"Anita was right about us, Eric. She knew when you brought me into the clinic. She must have seen your eyes glow, before you had to leave me."

"Both she and Cordone saw, Linora. I don't have the right! You are my daughter, for the Creator's sake! What does that say about me? It makes me some sort of cradle snatching pervert!"

"Cradle snatching pervert?" Lynne laughed out loud, clutching her stomach. "In case you haven't noticed, Eric, I haven't been a child in a very long time!" She gestured to her body. "Cordone mated with a newborn baby. Is that any different?"

"You bet your fucking life it is! You are *my* daughter! I chose you! I gave you the title of daughter and Princess!"

"Well, let's look at facts. Technically, I bit you first, turned you, so that actually makes you my son!" She was still laughing gently at him.

He looked at her as if she had taken leave of her senses.

"What are you taking, Linora? What drug is it? You have to be taking something pretty damned strong to even suggest that we are mates!"

"Then, you explain this!" she demanded pointing to her glowing eyes, then at his.

"I … I … I … Oh, fuck! I can't!"

He stood up, and grabbed both of her arms shaking her while staring down at the glowing eyes that looked into his.

Oh, God! Lynne thought! He was glorious! Strong, handsome, and every inch a Viking god. From his neatly cropped strawberry blonde hair to his strong, massive physique that he kept in perfect form with abs that would make any woman die to touch let alone having them over their own bodies! His skin was fair, yet still tanned. A conundrum. He stood no less than six feet, five inches. His red eyes were a perfect compliment to his hair - at least to a vampire woman. In the old days, his hair had been past his shoulders. She felt wetness begin to flow between her thighs. Oh, DAMN! She was in such trouble! Such incredible, glorious trouble as she felt her womb clinch tightly in anticipation!

Richard stared at Lynne, and if he was still breathing, his breath would have stopped at her beauty. He now saw that her glowing red eyes were heavy with desire for him. For the first time, he saw no child, nor did he see his daughter standing before him. She was the most beautiful woman he had ever seen. His groin tightened as desire raced through him, and whatever blood he did have, flew south at supersonic speed to harden his member at the sight of this beautiful woman. His woman.

Her hair was coal black, shining and sleek. Always pulled into a very long ponytail out of her way. Loose, it would probably fall to her waist, and the idea of that hair falling around him as he lay beneath her just made him harder. Her face was the white paleness of the Elves. But, combined with the vampire in her, it was also perfect and transparent. She was exceedingly tall as all Elves, yet she was petite against Richard's stature. Standing six feet, her body was sleek and long. Perfectly proportioned, her body moved as if flowing. Her breasts were smaller by the standards of other women, and her waist slim. Her hips were also slim, yet rounded, and her legs very long. She carried herself with royal grace. What was at the apex of her legs was not really a mystery as he had seen her naked many times when they swam when she was a child. However, he was perfectly willing to find out what that area looked like as a woman. And, he would. She was his mate, and he knew it. Even though he still tried to think of her as his daughter, it was getting more difficult by the second.

Her red eyes glittered and glowed as she realized he had accepted she was his mate. But, he had put a barrier between them almost as fast. She decided that she would have to figure out a way to force him to get past the idea she was his daughter.

The storm had been building around them, and now, lightning lit up the sky followed by thunder, which was increasing in intensity. Rain started to pelt down on them, and yet, they still did not move. They stared at each other without speaking.

It was the hail that knocked them out of their staring game. He held out his hand, and she put hers in it. They began to run. It didn't really bother them, of course, but it was really dumb to stand around in it. But, that wasn't the immediate danger.

"Are we going back to the house?" she yelled over the thunder and rain.

"We'll never make it back in time! Look!"

She turned, and saw a tornado forming. Even they were not totally immune to the forces of nature. And, certainly not a tornado!

"Oh, shit!" she yelled. "Where do we go?"

"Cordone has a fishing cabin on the river bank, below the bluff. We're jumping!"

They both ran off the bluff, and dropped one hundred feet below landing as if it was only a step into another room. Richard turned, and saw the tornado gaining on them. What the hell? Was it following them? That was crazy! But, this one sure seemed as if that was exactly what it was doing! The cabin would provide the protection they needed from the rain and hail, but not from the tornado. The small, but deep stream that was beside them, flowed over rocks. They darted along it hearing what sounded like a train behind them. They were just not going to make it!

~ 6 ~
Even a vampire can't Outrun a Tornado!

Richard changed directions toward the stream pulling Lynne with him. They splashed into it diving to the bottom. Luckily, the center was about five feet deep. It was his imagination that the tornado was following them. It just happened to change directions. At least that's what he told himself. They sat on the bottom waiting for it to pass over them. Looking up, they could see the vortex sitting on top of them even through the muddiness of the water. It took some of the water up into it, but the river was too deep for it to reach them. They waited until the tornado was no longer over them, and then surfaced to see nothing but rain pounding the ground. Soaked, and wet, they dashed down along the stream until they reached the cabin under the trees, and ran inside.

The cabin reminded Lynne of the one-room cabin that they had used for fishing so long ago. It was primitive and basic. Little furniture, other than a simple bed with a mattress, and a small chest was at the end of the bed, sealed tightly for clean linens. At least that's what Lynne surmised. Cobwebs were here and there, and a small fireplace was in the corner, and looked as if it hadn't been used recently. Ashes remained from the last occupant. A box on the side of the fireplace held plenty of dry wood to start another fire. Two, hand-made wooden chairs, and a small table with a half-full oil lamp sitting on it was across the room. A tiny, pot-bellied stove with one burner for cooking sat in another corner with a rickety, two-tiered table holding a pot, tin plates, and cups, as well as some canned food on the second shelf just in case the hunt didn't go well.

"You know, Linora, I feel at home here. Even after all the marvelous inventions that have been discovered in this technological world, I still prefer simplicity," Richard reflected with a smile.

Lynne nodded.

"I know. I feel at home here as well." She looked at Richard, rolling her eyes. "OK, so, as nice as this is, there are still comforts I prefer in this time."

"What's that?"

"Indoor plumbing, and my 60" widescreen TV!"

Lynne made a point of looking at Richard who was standing in his wet, designer suit. Richard looked down. They both had high-end tastes. They looked at each other, and both burst out laughing.

"OK, maybe not ALL of this time period is bad! I admit it. It does have its pluses!" Richard said in amusement. "I'm going to start a fire. Linora, why don't you serve us up some…what is over there anyway?"

Lynne looked over their "stash" of canned food.

"Well, let's see. A can of beans. Oh! And, another can of beans!" Then, she held up the prize she found, and turned.

"And, look, Eric! MORE beans!" She couldn't help it. She started laughing so hard her sides began to hurt.

Richard tried to smother his laughter, but failed miserably. How long had it been since either of them had laughed this hard? He couldn't remember. In fact, this was probably their first actual "vacation" in a few thousand years.

Lynne lit the stove, and placed the pot on it. Then, she opened the can of beans with a manual can opener she had found laying on the table, and dumped them into the pot. She could have used her nails, but she wasn't going to ruin her manicure. She heard Richard say he would hunt a couple of deer to go with the beans. Neither had blood with them, and he knew they would be needing it after the marathon they had just run.

Richard pulled off his wet jacket and shirt. They were both destroyed. Didn't bother him. He treated clothing as if it were something to be discarded anyway.

Lynne sucked air into her lungs as she turned, and saw his bare chest. Nudity had never bothered either one of them, but then, they did try to maintain protocol as Lynne had aged. In the past, seeing his chest, she never thought a thing about it, but this was something entirely different! As his mate, she looked at him with entirely different eyes. Creator! He was beautiful, if that word could even be applied to him. No hair on it at all, and shoulders as broad as the day was long, exuding strength. Even if he wasn't part vampire, and all werewolf, that strength would still not diminish his body! And, he was completely oblivious of the fact she was staring at him! Damn! This cabin was too close for comfort! If she could have panted, she would, and her tongue would be hanging out - and drooling, too!

He opened the door to leave, and stopped when Lynne called to him. He turned with his eyebrow up in question with a little hint of a smirk on his face.

"See if you can find me a mountain lion, or a tiger instead, will you?"

He made an elegant and regal bow from his waist.

"I shall endeavor to do so to the best of my ability, your highness," Richard smiled, and shut the door behind him.

Oh, she was so in trouble! But, little did he know, he was in worse trouble! His hunt would take about an hour, she reasoned. Why was it that women had to force men to realize their real feelings? Well, she knew she had time enough to prepare for him. She smiled as she danced around the cabin making her preparations for the shock of Richard's life!

Dan held Anita tightly after making love to her. Her head was on his chest. He couldn't believe how he loved this woman, and why it had taken both of them so long to realize they were mates. And, now, she carried his child! His hand automatically covered her stomach, and hers rested on top of his.

"I love you, Dan," whispered Anita.

"I love you," and kissed her gently. "You think they have figured it out by now?"

She turned to look into her mate's eyes. "I don't know, but they haven't returned. I'm hoping that is a good sign."

A sound was heard downstairs on her computer. It was the sound of the sensors picking up something from the two as if they were moving fast.

Dan smiled at Anita as she smiled back.

"I think we just may have a winner!" Dan laughed as Anita pulled his lips back to hers while the storm inside put to shame the storm raging outside.

Lynne stepped back to look at her handiwork. She hadn't forgotten anything. Neither of them liked soft beds, so they had always slept on the floor - even today. She had arranged a large quilt, and four pillows she had found inside the chest, piling them up on the quilt facing the cheerfully crackling fireplace. Neither of them felt the cold, but they enjoyed the warmth.

She also had taken the pot off the stove. Lynne wasn't hungry at all, now. The throbbing and wetness low down was a testament to what hunger she really craved. She heard him long before he ever came into the cabin. About ten minutes left. Pulling the band from her ponytail, her long, black hair cascaded over her shoulders, and now, it was time for her shock factor. She grinned.

Richard returned with that mountain lion Lynne had wanted. He stepped onto the porch, and found a bucket sitting on it. He rinsed it out in the pouring rain, then slit a juggler vein in the animal with his fangs, letting the struggling lion's lifeblood drain into the bucket. After filling it with enough blood for both of them, he took the carcass, and ran it back up the bluff side for the scavengers to eat. They never wasted a kill.

He picked up the bucket when he returned, opened the door, and walked to the pot-bellied stove setting the bucket down next to the stove. He preferred his blood warmer than body temperature.

Darkness had fallen, but the rain continued. Shaking his hair of the rain, and brushing off the water that soaked his body, he looked around for Lynne, but didn't see her. The only light in the room came from the fireplace. He had done a lot of thinking while he hunted. He had decided he needed to talk her out of this mate business. Not because he didn't want to take her as his mate, but because of what he viewed as a betrayal against his daughter. It was a matter of honor. But, there was more. Lynne did not know the rest of his secret, and he couldn't tell her. He had forgotten how long he had withheld it from his own mind. He had ignored it for a long time. In truth, it actually frightened him if she reacted badly, so he had never told her. What if she did not like the truth? No. He could not mate with her. His groin tightened with his decision telling him that he did want to mate with her even to the point that he actually felt his wolf demand it. But, Richard was using his brain instead of his heart. What he didn't realize was that the heart is far wiser than the brain, and had a tendency to take over when faced with a sudden shock. And, that shock was just about to hit him - hard.

"Linora?" he called. "We need to talk."

"Over here, Eric," came a soft voice from the fireplace.

He had never heard Lynne's voice so soft. His brain was trying to send him a warning. Richard was extremely cautious as he slowly walked over to the fireplace. He saw a pallet in front of it. Terror gripped him inside. Not because he was scared, but from what he might find. His brain kept telling him to stop, but his heart kept his legs walking.

Eric approached the fireplace coming to a sudden halt as he reached the edge of the quilt, his red eyes widening in surprise at the sensuous sight that was before him.

Lynne lay totally nude on the pallet, her elbow propped

up with her head in her hand. Her long hair streamed down her body, framing it while covering her breasts, but nothing covered the curls at the apex of her thighs. He hadn't seen her hair down since, well, forever. He did not know it was that long! His fingers suddenly itched to grasp it in his fingers, and that same vision of it draping over his body with her on top of him as he moved inside her was explicit in that moment! Their eyes met. Hers were filled with desire. Richard was rock hard in an instant. No! He couldn't allow this! But, he also couldn't ignore his hard-on, while his brain kept telling him to stop.

"Linora, what the fuck are you doing?"

Richard's voice was tight with wanting her, he felt his resolve eroding every second he stared at her beautiful, nude body. He couldn't take his eyes off of her. And, then, she smiled sexily at him. That was his undoing.

"Hmmm. Interesting word choice, Eric. Very appropriate for once. We are mates. You know it, as do I."

She sat up, flipping her luscious, long hair behind her revealing her breasts to his hungry eyes. It only increased the hardness of Richard's cock. Lynne made no secret as she looked down at his hard member that was straining against his pants, then back up at him. Good! Wetness flowed heavily from her, and she smiled even wider.

"You know, Eric. Your pants won't last long with that huge bulge pushing at your zipper," she laughed up at him. She got on her knees, and gently brushed her fingers against that bulge watching him flinch. She saw Richard watch her breasts gently bounce with her movement.

Then, more serious, "We are meant to be together. This was inevitable, and is exactly what was supposed to happen when you found me so long ago. Now, come to me, mate, and complete the mating bond."

She cocked her head, and gave him her sexiest grin.

Richard's eyes narrowed. When she had brushed against his hard-on, he realized that he was losing the battle with his brain as his body took over right along with his heart. His red eyes glowed even brighter as he finally admitted to himself that she really was his mate. At that point of realization, Richard ceased any thought that she was his daughter forever. She was all woman, and she was his! Everything ceased in his mind. Even who he really was. He had yet to take his eyes off of her body, and she continued to smile at him with that damn sexy smile! It was time to move forward - together. In that moment, the primitive urges he thought bottled up inside him due to civilization, were released. They surged through him, and he wasted no time stripping his pants and briefs from his body. He stood for a minute letting Lynne view his hard-on growing in front of her eyes showing her that he no longer considered her his daughter. He preened, and a sexy grin spread across his face as he watched Lynne's eyes widen as they swept over his body.

Lynne's eyes were large in her face as she stared at his beauty. It had been one thing to view his naked chest, but the hardness standing straight and tall - and pointing directly at her? How was she going to keep from attacking Richard before the mating?

"THIS is mine? OMG!! That's what the girls would be saying. ALL OF THIS IS MINE?" she thought as she felt her body speed to its release. Was she going to come just looking at him?

Lynne couldn't stop staring at his cock! It left her with no doubt that he didn't look upon her as a child. She licked her lips as she felt wetness flow from her sex beyond anything she could have ever imagined. She didn't even know it was possible to have that happen! She was so ready for Richard to take her! She looked back into his eyes, and they were no longer the eyes of a Father for a daughter, but the eyes of a lover. She sank to her knees, sitting cross-legged in front of him revealing her wetness to his gaze.

Richard slowly lay down beside her. He propped his head in his hand staring at her gorgeous, naked body. His eyes traveled from her beautiful face, to her perfect small breasts with the hardened pink tips, and then to the medium brown fur at the lowest point of her torso. He just hoped his dick, that seemed to have a mind of its own, could wait till they had mated to bury it inside of her dark fur. He felt it throb, causing it to bounce. And, she saw it! Good! He could smell Lynne's arousal for him. Richard was dying to wet his fingers at the entrance to her womb, stroke her clit with his fingers, then plunging them into her slick channel! His tongue wanted to taste the sweet nectar from its source! The thought of plunging into her body was pushing him to take her. Richard's urgency was growing with every passing second. His control was seriously in trouble of breaking. He gave her a wolfy grin, fangs extended, as his eyes met hers.

She gulped, and jerked with desire as his hand gently brushed her breast. It almost broke Lynne's control. She didn't know if she would make it through the mating before she took him inside her body. She closed her eyes as she laid back down beside him, lengthening her long, lithe body for his view.

Without fancy words, Richard declared his claim - but with an added twist. He opted to make it as quick as possible. He was throbbing with desire that wouldn't wait much longer. For the first time since he'd been turned, he wished that he would be able to manufacture semen to spill into her body. They could not have children, thus there was no need for vampire males to make semen. To see her swell with his child would be ….

"My beautiful, Linora. I, King Eric Richard Morton O'Malley, King of the Viking Nations, declare you, Linora Lynne Victoria DeVane, to be no longer Viking Princess of the Viking Nations."

Lynne's head jerked back. He hadn't claimed her? He had stripped her of her title? She wasn't prepared for that, and tears began to form as he reached for her hand placing it over his heart, and with his other hand tilted her head to look into her tearing eyes. He, then, placed his hand over her left breast and heart. His left hand gently brushed her left nipple causing it to harden even more as he continued.

"I, King Eric Richard Morton O'Malley, claim you, Queen Linora Lynne Victoria DeVane O'Malley, as my mate and wife. I will love and protect you forever. I will fight at your side as I always have done, and die when you die. Will you accept me as your mate and husband?"

His words had the ability to cause her to cry. Tears in her eyes, running down her cheeks, one drop fell onto her right nipple. Before she spoke, Richard's head dipped, and his tongue licked the tear off of it. He felt her shake when his mouth stayed to suckle it for a few seconds. He raised his shining red eyes to hers again. His mouth had sent her body into spasms of desire for him, and he just smiled in triumph. Lynne pressed her right hand over his left hand as it rested on her breast. Touch was everything in mating. Stroking each other's bodies as they mated with their words was part of it. When finished, their bodies automatically sought refuge in each other quickly. The idea of clothing during mating was abhorrent to them, and to keep clothing on was to insult each other.

"I, Queen Linora Lynne Victoria DeVane O'Malley, accept you as my mate and husband, King Eric Richard Morton O'Malley. I, too, love you, will protect you, and fight by your side as I always have done. I give to you my heart, my love, and my body."

She lay on her back with her breasts jutting upwards, so that he could see her entire body. His hand began stroking her breast. She had never felt anything as wonderful as this! Richard leaned down shaking with what he was about to do. Once done, he would never be able to go back. Looking at his mate's body, he knew he never would want to return to their prior life. Richard took her lips, brushing his fangs across them. Lifting his head, she turned her neck to him. A vampire mating was slightly different, because neither had a pulse, and neither had blood to sip. Their bite established their bond. To keep to tradition, unlike many other matings, as King, he was first to bite his mate.

Richard brought his head down quickly sinking his

fangs into her neck fully. Complete surprise hit him when a small amount of blood flowed from her carotid artery. It tasted like smoked meat. and he sucked greedily. Then, he retracted his fangs from her neck. Neither of them needed to worry about healing the marks. Mating bites would remain forever visible to all supernatural beings. Human eyes would never be able to pick up the wounds. Their eyes were not as evolved as supernaturals.

He raised his head, and she turned hers back to look into his eyes. He saw her eyes widen when she saw a tiny bit of blood remained on both of his fangs as he dipped to kiss her.

Richard whispered to her when she noticed the blood on his fangs. "I don't know why blood came from your artery, Linora."

Lynne's head shook as she acknowledged his words letting her pink tongue lick the blood from his fangs. His cocked jerked hard. It was an erotic feeling! It was such a turn on, he prayed to the Creator to hold back taking her right now until the bond had been finished! He had no idea that fangs were an erogenous area!

Taking his head into her hands, she smiled into his eyes. She pushed him over, and lay her upper body on his. His hand slid down to her curls, dipping his fingers beneath her to stroke her wetness. Something was wrong about it, but he was too far gone to try and figure it out.

"I, Queen Linora Lynne Victoria DeVane O'Malley, claim you as my mate, King Eric Richard Morton O'Malley. Will you accept me as your mate and wife?"

Without hesitation, Richard repeated, "I accept you, Queen Linora Lynne Victoria DeVane O'Malley, as my mate and wife. Today, I give to you my heart, my love, and my body."

Her fangs were extended as she kissed him, raking them across his lips. Then, Eric turned his neck to her. She dipped her head fast sinking her fangs into his neck. She was stunned to taste about an ounce of blood from his carotid artery that tasted just like smoked meat! She had tasted the same taste when he had kissed her after biting her. How? For a moment, she had a flash back of the taste of his blood the first time she had bitten him. It was awful. Metallic. But, this was incredibly delicious. She swallowed, then leaned down to kiss him with the same blood on her fangs. Like Lynne had done, Richard licked both her fangs of the blood. Her womb shattered when he did, and then she kissed him completing the bonding.

~ 7 ~

Death is relative … depending on your point of view

His arms wrapped around her in a vise. Finally! He would have his mate! He used the ancient words said to one's chosen mate so long ago. It was to assure her that he would protect her, give her his children (well if it had not been for their vampire nature), and love her for all time. It also secured her status as his Queen. Despite his desperate need to sink his swollen cock deep inside of her, his respect for her overrode that desire.

"Come, mate," and gently rolled them over with him on top, his legs between her thighs, his hardness just outside her sex. He kissed first one hard, pink-tipped breast, and then the other. He looked up at her.

"My Queen, wilt thou spread thy legs for me, and allow me inside thy body? Wilt thou except my seed?"

Lynne's heart sped up at the words. Respect for her was his most important desire right now. That is why he asked her. He would not take it. She must willingly give herself to him. They were the simple words used so long ago when men took their mates and wives. They were so beautiful, yet she never thought to hear them from her mate let alone even have one. It was right. It was a great honor asked by a great man.

Lynne stretched her arms over her head, linking her fingers with his, shedding tears of love as she answered him.

"Oh, my love. I give my love, my heart, my life, and my body to thee. I accept thy offer and thy seed within me."

With those words, he entered her with one, single, hard thrust letting go of all the passion and love he had for her as was her right as his mate and Queen.

Vampires could neither procreate nor experience

orgasms. All knew this. Richard's words of love combined with his movement inside of her took her to a place she thought never to feel in her life.

Richard panted as he increased his speed pounding within her. Lynne cried out his name. Then, something happened that startled, and shocked them both, yet they could not stop. Richard felt his balls suddenly fill with liquid. So fast, and so much that they distended much larger than normal. He was in sudden pain from them? And, then, he felt his release. It came out of him in a huge burst of power flooding within Lynne. Their screams echoed inside the cabin.

"Not possible!" Richard yelled as he drove his cock hard into her releasing what he had not felt in a very long time. "It's not possible!"

Lynne gasped hard, taking him deeper into her by lifting her hips meeting thrust for thrust. She already wondered how she could have been wet, but she felt something build within her that made her eyes fly open as Richard began his release. Lynne cried out his name as her walls tightened, and throbbed around him, squeezing him, and draining every drop from his body.

They were panting, Richard still hard inside of her. Richard raised his head in shock and surprise. He saw these echoed in Lynne's face.

"What the hell was that?" Richard's shock and surprise evident on his face.

Stunned beyond belief, he still couldn't believe that he had felt his testicles fill with semen just before he spilled himself into Lynne.

"I don't know. D-d-did I just feel - semen - released inside of me, Eric? Did I just experience an orgasm?" Lynne was stunned.

Richard looked at her. How did this happen? That was impossible for vampires. Completely impossible!

"I don't know how, Linora. I have no idea! I felt my balls fill quickly just before I felt my seed pour from me into you!"

"But, that's not possible, Eric! It's not! What the fuck!?"

They were both completely thrown off guard. More than that, he had still not removed himself from her, and she felt a rising of desire for him again. The same thing was happening to Richard. She was very wet, and very sensitive - another thing she shouldn't be feeling. Sex wasn't a source of release for vampires. It was just fun.

But, so much more was happening here. Richard placed his head on her breast against the onslaught of the desire that was building, and she held him to her. He shook, and his head came up fast.

"Oh, my God! Your heart! Linora, YOUR HEART!"

"What?"

"It's beating!"

Lynne entire body jerked hard at his words. What was he saying? Then, she felt it. A low beat becoming stronger with each beat. Richard placed his hand just above her breast feeling her heart beat.

"Eric…if-if mine is beating, then, could it … is it possible … that yours is as well?"

Richard rolled them over without leaving her body, and straddling him, Lynne placed her ear to his chest. Her mouth dropped open.

"Eric! So is yours!" Shock was apparent on her face.

They looked at each other not understanding at all.

"Let me test something else." What if? Richard removed himself from her, and stood up moving to dip a tin cup into the bucket of blood. Then, returned to her, he placed the tin to his lips.

"I'm going to drink the animal blood, and then I want you to do the same."

She nodded, and watched as he tipped his head upward drinking the blood. He yanked the tin away from his mouth, put it down, and ran to open the door out into the rain vomiting up the blood.

Lynne looked at the tin, then up at Richard. She was shaking as she reached slowly for it, and took a drink. One sip was all it took. The iron taste made her sick, and she, too, ran out into the rain. She threw up the blood she drank.

And, there, standing in the rain a miracle happened. Richard extended his fangs. They were werewolf fangs. Lynne tried to extend hers, and…and she couldn't!!! They were gone - totally and completely gone!!! She could feel her Elf again!!!

Richard's eyes went to his mate, and in a second, the black hair she had was gone, replaced by the Elven white!

"Your hair, Linora! It's white! And, your eyes? They're silver!"

Lynne stared at Richard in disbelief, then ran to the river. She looked at her reflection in the water, and saw that her hair had reverted to white. She touched her face gently, staring into eyes she had not seen since she was twelve years old. She turned her head to Richard behind her, and bewildered, and saw a wolf! A strawberry blonde wolf with an incredibly large member! Richard had phased for the first time in thousands of years!

"H-how is this possible?" she asked the wolf kneeling, and taking his head into her hands. "We're alive, Eric! I'm an Elf again! And, you're a werewolf!" And, then, she realized the truth. "Kaitlan. White Wolf Prophecy. It really IS true! Sarah was right!"

Lynne realized that Richard's wolf eyes were a brilliant blue - the color he had before he was turned into a vampire. Lynne could drown in those eyes! She pulled the wolf's head to her breasts, and he let his fur tickle her nipples, then he stuck out his tongue to lick them.

"We have to get to Anita, now," Lynne giggled at the tickle.

Richard's wolf head nodded as it almost agreed, then he phased back.

"No. Not yet, Linora."

He swept her up into his arms standing in the pounding

rain.

"Wrap your legs around me, Linora. I want to make love to you as a living being!"

Lynne did what he asked, and he entered her right there. He moved slowly inside of her, until he roared as his semen flowed inside his mate. He grinned at her, and watched her face as his seed exploded into her body. She threw her head back as she felt the hot liquid flood inside of her.

They were no longer vampires. Why, they had no idea. It was really a miracle. Richard carried her back inside the cabin, and laid her on the pallet still within her. He knew they should go to Anita, but he wasn't about to stop this amazing miracle that had happened to them. Not for twenty-four hours! He wanted to impregnate his mate if it were possible, and he was not prepared to stop until he did!

"Before we run to Anita, I think we need to complete our twenty-four hours of mating, don't you? And, let's keep this secret between us for a little longer. I want to FEEL again! And, more than that, I want to feel my balls fill with semen, and to spill into your womb, Linora!" He began to move inside of her again.

"So do I, Eric! I want to feel your warmth, and your hot seed flow within me! I never thought to feel it!"

She screamed his name at his release, tightening her throbbing walls around his thrusts. She sucked him dry as she felt the hot liquid flow into her body, yet again, straight into her womb.

Suddenly, she had a thought. *"Can I, now, get pregnant?"*

Richard answered her thought. *"If it is possible, I will be the happiest man in the universe. To watch you swell with our child inside of you born by love would be the ultimate dream."*

Aloud, he said in wonderment, "And, we can feel, now, Linora. FEEL!! The next hours are going to be very active," he laughed. And, then, "Oh, by the way, are there enough beans over there?"

She laughed out loud. "All that we can now feel, and you are asking about beans? Silly! Right now, the last thing I would ever want is food! I'm content just to eat you!"

And, Richard took her to the heights of the gods!

Lynne dressed, but Richard did not. Both knowing they had to return, their time of mating over, and knowing their bond sealed forever, it was time to go confront Anita with their new lives.

"Ride me, Lynne."

He laughed uproariously as he saw her stunned face.

In another context, that would have all kinds of implications! And, well, it already had. But, she would have no problem accepting it again - and again - and again!

He took her in his arms before he phased.

"Did I tell you how beautiful you are as an elf? Not that you weren't before, you understand, but God, Linora! Your white hair and silver eyes are magnificent!"

His mouth devoured hers in a mind-drugging kiss before he phased into his wolf. Laughing and turned on by his amazing kiss, she climbed onto his furry back, and he ran with werewolf speed back to the house.

When they reached the house, he phased back, and they retreated to their room so he could dress quickly.

For the first time since she was twelve, Lynne was shuddering with cold despite the fact that Elves felt no cold. Richard's arms wrapped around her, his warm body giving her the warmth she needed.

"Anita! Where the fuck are you?" he yelled.

Anita's computer had been showing her very odd readings from the monitors, readings indicating two life signs right outside her room! Heartbeats? Whose heartbeats? Anita stood when she heard Richard yell, and darted into the room from her makeshift office, Dan joining her from the garage, also having heard Richard yell. They both stopped when she and Dan saw them, mouths gaping at the sight that Lynne had WHITE HAIR? Neither of them had RED eyes any longer?

Before she said anything, Richard demanded, "How in the FUCK are we alive, Anita?"

In a dark alley, a figure was leaning against a brick wall with arms folded across the chest, scowling. He was supposed to have been here an hour ago. The figure just couldn't stand him, but he could help with the greenbacks, and it was needed - badly. Loss at the track and bad bets on games were what drove the figure to make a deal with the Devil.

When he had come along, and offered the money, the figure refused to touch it. Now, it was needed, and fast. Reluctantly, contact had to be made.

The figure turned as the sound of footsteps approached. It was him. He stopped.

"You'd better be alone."

"I told you I would be, and you're late! I've been waiting for you for over an hour, Zana…Arrrgggg!" and the voice was shut off by a hand that had grabbed at the throat, and shoved the figure against the brick wall.

"Do NOT say my name! You do NOT speak! You WILL listen! Do you understand, or I will break your neck! Nothing more to say?" Zanack waited for an answer he knew wouldn't come. "Good!"

Zanack opened his hand, and the figure dropped unceremoniously to the ground, on the butt with legs splayed outward.

"Now. Let's get to business. I will say this only once, and if you so much as cross me, remember … I love eating fear for a midnight snack! And, I suck the flesh off their bones. And, you smell," he sniffed, "of great fear! Delicious! You make me hungry!"

The figure shakily stood up in front of Zanack, but

nodded.

"You will go to this address, and obtain three vials that will be waiting for you," he ordered holding out a slip of paper. "Then, you will proceed to make sure that Sarah Knight drinks the first one, knocking her out, but she will recover. Two days later, you serve her the second vial. This will cause her to go into early labor, and miscarry. And, finally, you will put the third vial in her IV bag, making sure the bag empties, and is not replaced. Do. You. Understand?"

The figure started to speak, thought better of it, and said nothing.

"At least you learn quickly. You will not betray me. If I do not hear that Sarah Knight is dead within five hours after it is administered, there is not one place on this planet you can escape me!"

He extended his claws, and swiped the figure across the chest. Blood spurted from the chest onto Zanack who swiped his finger in the blood, and licked it off his finger.

"I-I-I'll make sure of it, Za ... uh, sir."

"You had better! Count to 10 before you leave. I'm watching you!"

Zanack fled into the night. No one knew his face. No one had ever seen it. He always met his contacts only at night, and only in the dark.

Painfully, the figure tried to wipe the blood off the clothing with the back of a glove, finally giving up, and held the coat closed walking painfully out of the alley into the dim light of the porn sign hanging above the business it proudly displayed. Zanack was a demon. He wasn't were, vampire, or anything else. But, *what* was he? Evil incarnate. The figure was doomed. Death would surely come whatever happened to Sarah Knight. But, the money was too much to pass up. In order to stay alive, Sarah Knight would die.

Zanack stood watching as the figure slithered away. He hated dealing with amateurs, but he needed someone who could get close to Sarah Knight. That evil, filthy, human bitch *dared* to become pregnant on his watch? It was bad enough that Kaitlan had not one, but two! And, now, a second bitch was pregnant? This should not be happening! Why? He ignored it for the moment. That fucking bitch was going to die, and so would that "thing" she had spawned in her womb! He would not allow it! He wanted to reach up inside her, with his own hands, to rip the thing out of her body, and eat it right in front of her as he watched her bleed out! That sounded so good to him, it was almost tempting to kill her himself! But, that would compromise his cover. He was having a hard enough time, now, maintaining his human and werewolf appearance!

Zanack worked himself up into a fury, and stomped off to find his midnight snack. He glanced around with wild eyes, fangs out, and hatred in his dead heart. Long ago, he had made sure that none of his prey had family. No one would miss them, and the best place had been in the red light districts. But, as of now, he was willing to break that rule.

His anger was so great, he desperately needed to tear out a woman's womb, eat it, drink her blood, and then eat her flesh! His mouth watered deliciously at the thought of her pain as he ate her alive! Glancing at his watch, it was time for her to walk home. Ahh!   *"There's the whore now,"* he thought.

A waitress from the local diner. No one would miss her! And no one would dare lift a hand to help her anyway, knowing the consequences. They would glance away as if they saw nothing. Everyone in this neighborhood was terrified of him, and well they should be. Then, he had another thought. He knew his accomplice might chicken out, so he decided to strap his dinner down to the table. And, then, he would bring that figure down to watch as he fed on his dinner. Yes. The person would not *dare* to disobey him if forced to watch what he would do if betrayed! And, so what? Death was coming anyway. He just didn't know, yet, how he wanted to kill his accomplice.

Zanack streaked to his dinner, threw her over his shoulder, and fled to the basement where he left his scraps of human remains for the rats. After all, they needed to eat, too.

He was such a generous man!

~ 8 ~
Life goes on in the face of danger

Kaitlan and Cordone still had a business to run. That meant, occasionally, they had to meet with a top writer on their own turf. She didn't have to worry about her top writer of all time, of course. She was still amazed that despite everything that was happening - running a Publishing House, being Alpha of a huge Clan, and her mate still made time to write! His next book, she knew without a doubt, was going to blow the rest of the Publishing world out of the water! But, right now, Mort Farley, who lived in Australia, and one of their ten most popular writers, was insisting on meeting the new head of Seneca Publishing. He had also asked Kaitlan to come as well to give credibility to the new CEO. He distrusted everyone and was a bore, but his books on political satire were lucrative to the company.

Kaitlan was highly amused when she had asked Sarah and Sam to stay at their home to baby sit Canaan and Tara.

"You may as well get used to taking care of babies!" Kaitlan patted Sarah's tummy, which was getting larger every day. "I can't wait till this little one comes! They can all play together!"

"And, who knows? Maybe we might be in-laws one day!"

Sarah smiled as Kaitlan put Canaan into her arms, then watched Cordone as he dumped Tara in Sam's. Sarah's face softened as she looked at the little baby boy. Watching her face, Sam's heart knew that she would make the perfect Mother. But, looking at the tiny little girl in his huge arms, he wasn't exactly sure if he would make a good Father despite how many times Sarah had reassured him. Sarah shook her head, and laughed at her mate. He couldn't wait to be a father even though he was very nervous about it.

Cordone slapped Sam on the back.

"You're next, old buddy!"

"Yeah. But diapers?" Sam screwed up his face.

Cordone laughed out loud picturing Sam changing a dirty diaper.

"Sarah, did I give you all the numbers?" Kaitlan asked trying not to laugh at Sam's face, and failing miserably!

Sarah and Kaitlan looked at each other, and gave up as they burst out laughing.

"You did," Sarah answered as soon as she could get her laughter under control. Everyone delighted in teasing Sam. He was really a trooper, and took it all in stride. He rolled his eyes.

"Kaitlan, relax! You're only leaving for what? Two days?" Sarah poked Cordone in the ribs while Sam waggled his eyebrows in amusement. It was about time Cordone had the tables turned. "I promise, we won't let them watch!"

Kaitlan looked at her in mock horror. Cordone looked at his watch with a grin. He wasn't going to walk into that one!

"Babe, we gotta go!"

"OK, coming." Cordone was really a pushy Alpha!

It was her first time away from the children, and it was extremely hard to leave them. She kissed both of them. Luckily, Katilan had been slowly switching them from breast milk to formula so they could leave town if needed.

They were growing fast. Too fast, but as Anita had reminded Kaitlan, again.

"They aren't human, Kaitlan! They are weres! From other babies I have delivered in the past, though extremely few and far between, they are developing normally. Werewolf babies grow very fast. Well, except for you. You're the only one in our records who grew at a human pace."

With one last kiss for each baby, Kaitlan and Cordone got into the SUV driven by Dan.

Sam sniffed at Tara while Sarah held Canaan using her stomach as a boost. Tears formed in Kaitlan's eyes as she saw Sarah help Canaan wave "Bye-Bye" to them.

"Uh, diaper time for Tara! Here you go!" He shoved Tara at Sarah, and ran!

Anita was still upset since Richard and Lynne had come back to the house announcing they were breathing, and their hearts were beating. They were stunned, shocked, and thrown off guard at the fact that they were no longer vampires. Anita's legs, literally, morphed to water, and Dan had to grab her to keep her from falling down.

When her legs had some sort of strength to them again, she had conducted several tests on them, but she just didn't have the equipment she needed. They had to go back.

While Dan contacted Tim to get the jet ready, Anita whipped out her cell phone to contact Cordone. She didn't know about their trip to Australia, but apparently, they were already on their way back. Holy Hell! It was one thing for all the other weird stuff to happen to them, but this?

"Cordone!" squeaked Anita when she heard him answer. "I need Sam and Sarah to do some research for me, now!"

Cordone listened, his face becoming more stunned by the second, and the expression on Kaitlan's face told him that she realized it.

She mouthed, "What?" As he hung up.

He shook his head in disbelief. "Lynne and Richard have completed their mating."

Kaitlan was sure that there was a "but" in there somewhere, and she wasn't disappointed.

"But, they are no longer vampires, Kaitlan."

"NO! S-shit!" Kaitlan stammered.

Kaitlan's eyes widened in total shock, and her mouth dropped. She just looked at Cordone as if he had grown two horns, and a tail. All he could do was nod.

Gathering himself together, he called Sam with Anita's instructions. Trying to explain was a whole different matter!

Sam hung up the phone, and stood like a statue looking out the window. Did he actually just hear what he thought he heard? He stared down at the phone as if it had sprouted a tail, and was breathing fire as he dropped it on its cradle! Sarah sat across from him. Sam turned to look at her, not really looking at her. Just a few people had known about Anita and Richard being vampires. It had been a closely guarded secret since Dillon had put them in their positions. The girls had been let into the secret as well.

"Sam? Sam! Are you OK?" Sarah asked.

Her voice startled her baby, and it kicked. She patted her belly soothingly.

"Sam!!" she yelled at him knocking him out of his reverie.

"You are NEVER going to believe it, Sarah! I can't believe what Cordone just told me! It just isn't possible!!" The frozen look on his face returned.

Sarah stood up, and walked around to him grabbing him by the lapels of his gray suit coat. She shook him gently. When he didn't respond, she shook him harder. His head turned to look down at her without seeing her. Drastic action was needed. Sarah slapped him across the face - hard. Slapping a werewolf across the face was usually not a smart move, but there wasn't anything else she could think of doing.

Sam jerked, and his eyes refocused.

"What the fuck did you do that for?"

"Sam! What. Did. Cordone. Say?" She enunciated loud and slow.

He stared at her, again, shaking his head as if trying to come out of the trance. He just knew Sarah would fall down when he told her.

"Sarah, sit down, first - please. I don't want you and our baby to get hurt if you fall down."

Scowling at Dan, she sat down in his chair, and swiveled it to face Sam.

"OK. I'm sitting. What is going on?"

Sam rubbed his hands together as if he was trying to figure out what to say.

"Sam, just spit it out!"

Looking her in the eye, he spoke in monotone.

"Richard and Lynne are mates."

Sarah's smile lit up her face!

"But, that's great news, Sam!"

He waved at her to zip it. Sarah scowled at him.

"Sorry, Sarah. There's more."

More?   There's more? She had been told all about vampire anatomy. She knew Lynne wasn't pregnant. What could it be?

"Lynne and Richard …," he struggled for the words. "… how do I say this? Lynne and Richard are no longer vampires."

He waited for Sarah's reaction, and he got it in spades.

First, her eyes widened in the same frozen shock he had experienced. Second, her mouth opened, and closed half a dozen times pretending to be a fish! Third, her eyes lost focus as she processed everything. Finally….

"HOW THE FUCK DID THAT HAPPEN?"

She jumped up fast, and whipped around to stand in front of him. She had not even noticed how fast she had moved.

"*Sarah didn't cuss, EVER,*" he thought shaking his head.

"I know the answer! And, the question is 'What is the White Wolf Prophecy'?" OK. So. One of her favorite shows was Jeopardy. And?

Sam smirked at his mate's reference, and rubbed the back of his neck.

"You really think it's because of Kaitlan, Sarah?"

Nodding her head emphatically, "YES! Of course it is! It's all due to your Prophecy, Sam! It has to be! From what I read of it, when Kaitlan's white wolf appeared, everything began to change just as the Prophecy said. More babies will now happen, and they won't need to be on Cordone's land ."

Sam nodded slowly. Sarah was right. She had to be.

There could not have been any other explanation. Nothing was making sense any way, and to a rational warrior like Sam, that was unacceptable. But, lately, he was beginning to question his entire belief system - big time!

"Dan is getting the four of them back here ASAP, and Cordone and Kaitlan should land in about two hours."

It was a definite plus when the Seneca Publishing House finally bought a secondary jet. Made life so much easier!

"Anita has a task for us, if you're up to it?"

"Whatever it is, you bet! Nothing would please me more than to help out in whatever way I can, Sam! Especially since I'm so big, and can't do anything physical, right now. "

Sam leaned down kissing her belly, then stood back up.

"OK. Here it is. There are only a few who know about The Hall of Records. Most mainstream scientists, and some archaeologists, think it is myth. But it isn't."

Hall of Records? Where had she heard that before. Her eyes narrowed in thought.

Then, "Wait a second! The Hall of Records? Like in THE Hall of Records some think is located underneath the Sphinx!? Are you saying we have to go to Cairo, Egypt?"

He laughed. "Of course not! It isn't there. That was disinformation we spread around on purpose, because we didn't want anyone else to know where it really was. Richard moved them here a few thousand years ago long before America was founded, obviously. The Hall is about three stories just beneath your feet under the building! In fact, the Seneca Publishing House was deliberately built over The Hall to throw everyone else off the track!"

Again, Sarah imitated a fish.

Then, "Ah … I get it! Like in 'Keep location secret. Put under contemporary building'. I call that two thumbs up!"

Sam sighed. "Yes. The vampires once were allowed, but after the war, they were banned."

"Why tell me, then? Doesn't that compromise the location?" Sarah asked completely ignoring his mention of the vampires.

"Not really. Anita believes you are right about why the curse was broken. Cordone has asked us to do some research for Anita. See if we can find out if there are scrolls that will tell us what happened prior to the curse. Anita feels it may help her figure out how the curse was reversed. So far, not even her newest sensors injected into Richard and Lynne has turned up anything."

Sarah frowned. "Two things. One, is it that important for us to know, and two, you trust me that much?"

Sam pulled her to him. "One, yes. Two, there is no other I trust as much as I do you."

As his lips met hers, he felt their child kick him. He groaned. He wanted her, now.

"I'd rather strip you right here, and take you right now," he whispered against her lips.

She smiled, and wrapped her arms around his neck, holding on as he took her lips again. So would she, but they had a job to do. He let her go, and nodded.

~ 9 ~
The Hall of Records - It really exists?

Following Sam, Sarah realized she was about to enter an entirely different world. Watching as Sam inserted a "key card" into a slot in the elevator, he pushed the "C" button.

The doors opened into a small room. Sarah followed Sam to a door opposite the elevator - and into another elevator?

A secondary "key card" was inserted, but no buttons? Hmmm. Down they went again. Out into another small room, crossing to another elevator, and another "key card"? She glared at Sam.

"Are we there yet?" then, suddenly laughed.

Sam turned to look at her in amusement at the old child's question when on a trip.

"Did you *really* just *seriously* say that?" and laughed. Sarah had barely said "Yes", before the door slid open into ….

Sam stepped back with a grin, and let Sarah enter all by herself. He followed her, and then stood with his arm around her waist to watch her reaction. Her mouth gaped open. His reaction had been much the same when he saw it for the first time.

She stood on a high platform, surrounded by three metal rows of rails keeping one safe from falling. A vast cave was before her eyes, seemingly having no end! No less than ten levels of platforms with rows upon rows upon rows of shelving held books, scrolls, paper, and even priceless treasures. There were small areas scattered on every row with overstuffed furniture, library tables, and Tiffany lamps for reading. Anything, and everything, one needed for reading or studying. Computers and printers dotted the landscape of the room. A secret she never told anyone except Kaitlan and Sam was that she was an avid book reader, and researcher. Her job with Seneca Publishing House allowed her freedom to research to her heart's content.

Her eyes traveled up into Sam's who was smiling widely at her. He made a gesture with his arm sweeping The Hall.

"Like?"

Sarah could only nod. Like, nothing! She *loved* it! The floor underneath her started moving down, and she grabbed Sam. She looked down, and realized it was a lift.

They rode the lift down at least six levels until it reached floor level, then they stepped off.

"Holy freakin' cow!" she exclaimed. "How many of these are here?"

Sam laughed. "There are lifts every one thousand feet. It's overwhelming, but The Hall of Records holds all the history of the Earth - well, that which hasn't been destroyed. While you know about it, now, you also need to know that we maintain a staff of the most trusted people in the world - including humans."

An older man approached Sam and Sarah.

"Sam! It's good to see you again, my old friend!"

"Hello, Johnson, it is good to see you as well."

Sam and Johnson clasped forearms instead of shaking hands. Sarah wondered why mankind didn't do this now. It would save a lot of problems when colds and flu were around.

"Johnson, we have added one more to our group. This is my mate, Sarah. Sarah, this is Major Nicolas Johnson."

Johnson gave her a slight bow, then held out his hand. Sarah almost giggled when he kissed her hand.

"It is, indeed, a great honor, Sarah. We have all been very excited to find all our four highest have found their mates."

"Thank you, Johnson. I am honored to meet you as well," Sarah answered.

Secretly, though, she was surprised that his touch gave her the creepies. It was clammy, and sweaty. Ick! Maybe she was just being overly sensitive. But, it explained her urge to wipe off her hand after his lips had touched it! Who does that any more?

"Johnson is our Librarian, so to speak. It's what we call him, but it's really a misnomer. His job is so much more than a librarian! He and his staff maintain the entire complex. It is a calling, and once taken, a lifetime job."

"Really? For life?" asked Sarah, already fascinated. Turning to Johnson, "Do you like the job, Johnson?"

"It's a researcher's dream, Sarah. When I was approached with the offer thousands of years ago, I thought they were joking. I remember the overwhelming feeling when I first saw it. It's a lifetime appointment. Only those who are strong enough can become a Librarian, or a staff member. We give the outside world up forever."

Seeing her surprise, he continued. "Truthfully, we choose this life. I have never regretted it once! The knowledge down here is so massive, one can never learn it all."

She nodded.

"I'll bet! I am also a researcher," Sarah explained.

"Really?" At her second nod, Sam put his two cents worth into it.

"And, she's really, really great at it, Johnson. She has been known to find answers others could not. My mate excels at research for many of our best writers. And, Sarah has been allowed to be on the list of those who know about The Hall of Records."

"Then, Sarah," Johnson said to her, "you have been accorded one of the greatest honors anyone in our world can receive. We keep our group relatively small in order to keep the secret. If the outside world knew about it, it would be divided up all over the world, and that would stop us from being able to cross reference anything without traipsing across the world."

Sam got to the point of why they were there.

"Johnson, can you point us to where we might find our most ancient of histories?" Sarah added, "What I need, Johnson, are the histories of the supernatural world that have specific mentions of The White Wolf Prophecy, and anything written - no matter how small - written by anyone at all."

Johnson nodded. "Those are all the way to the back, and in the left-hand corner of The Hall of Records, but there are only a handful about the Prophecy, and there just isn't much."

He led them to a golf cart. Seeing her surprise at using a golf cart, he told her, "The library is no less than five miles wide and eight miles long, Sarah. For the weres, it's a skip and hop, but for humans like some of us, it would be a virtual impossibility. Quite frankly, I have to admit that even the supers find it a great help. Most of them don't like to expend energy just to look at musty old books."

"Ah, I see. Hence, the golf carts!" Johnson nodded.

After they entered the cart, Sarah discovered that they were powerful golf carts! Their speed equaled about thirty miles per, so it didn't take long to get to where they needed to be! He drove them past knowledge upon knowledge of the world, pointing out a few interesting places she might like to look at some day. She filed that away in her head.

Finally, they reached the left-hand corner of the Hall. Johnson pointed upward.

"Our histories comprise all ten levels in Section 3126 XZYX, and are all to the left of that lift," he pointed to the right. "All to the left are prior to ten thousand B.C. All to the right are after ten thousand B.C. Ten levels contain our history all the way back to thirty-thousand BC which is on the top level. Each level contains three thousand years of history, beginning with floor level, with the tenth level being oldest. Many of the documents have been copied and recopied over the years. And, now, of course, we are making them digital, but it's going to be a really long haul to get them into the computers. We do have a much smaller, and older, section that contains much of our history prior to thirty-thousand B.C., and you will find that in section 4000 XZYZ through that door to the back."

He pointed to a doorway, and continued.

"These are kept in a climate-controlled room, for obvious reasons, since all of those documents in there are originals. Now, to clarify three thousand B.C. begins on floor level. Then, six-thousand B.C. begins on the second floor, and on. The higher you go, the older the history. Anything to the right of the lift deals with anything after ten thousand BC as I said earlier. Unfortunately, we have lost a great deal, as you can see by this smaller space, prior to ten thousand B.C. I know it seems confusing, Sarah, but truthfully, once you get the hang of it - and all sections are marked well - you can look it up on what is in the main computer database. We have few people here at a time, so it's like having the whole place to oneself. And, that's how we like it."

"Ah. So, ten-thousand B.C. would be on level four, right?"

"Yes."

"Then, that's where we will start."

Sarah was totally overwhelmed by excitement! She couldn't imagine what she could learn! Holy Cow! She couldn't wait to get started

"I will have Jeffrey provide you with coffee? Cola? Snacks?"

Sarah patted her belly, and grinned.

"How about a lemon-lime soda, and some snacks? Oh, and I have to ask this. I hope there's a bathroom close?"

Johnson laughed. "First, congratulations on the baby. Second, there are bathrooms on all floors to the right of each lift every 600 feet. No one wants to lose valuable research time looking forever, or walking forever, to get to a bathroom."

Her eyebrows went up at how close they were. Well, that works out well for her!

"There are also vending machines every 1000 feet as well at the lifts. Drinks, candy, chips, whatever. Third, I will have Jeffrey bring you both an assortment of food. Would you like a pizza, perhaps? My wife used to get them for my sister who craved pizza when she was pregnant."

Sarah leaned over and kissed the man. "You read my mind, Johnson! Thank you. Oh, and could I get some milk, a carafe of water with a bowl of lemons, and lots of chocolate?"

Sam rolled his eyes at his gorgeous mate with her belly swollen with their child. She'd never looked so beautiful to him. She was always hungry, but that was nothing odd. His desire began to build quickly, and he'd always had this idea ….

"As you wish!" Seeing her confusion, he told her, "We have a full, working kitchen in here as well. We make all our own food, and the chefs here are world class!"

Johnson turned and left, and Sarah asked Sam, "He's human? I mean…he said 'wife', right?"

Nodding, Sam explained. "Yes. He is human. His wife, mate, was called Ter'act who was an Elf. When they mated, he took on her lifespan, and when she passed, she refused him the right to follow her to the next life, because he ran The Hall of Records. Because she forbid him to join her, his lifespan was continued. She felt he was needed, and only when his task was done, could he follow her."

Sarah nodded. "Oh, that's right! I remember, now. OK. Let's get started. I guess it looks like we have to ride it first." And, she walked to the lift with Sam in tow.

On their ride to the fourth level, Sam gently grabbed her full breasts, drawing her to him. She wore no bra, because none of them fit anyway, and she had seen no reason to spend money for such a short time on another bra. Not that Sam cared, of course, since her nipples were hard most of the time. It just made it easier on him!

"Now *that*, my dear mate, was a loaded statement! You know, I've always wanted to know what it would be like to ride my mate in The Hall!"

His mouth crushed hers as the lift carried them upwards.

Breathless, Sarah wrapped her arms around his neck, and pulled back after they reached the fourth level. The more her pregnancy progressed, the more she was insatiable for sex. Male werewolves remained hard and ready constantly during their mate's pregnancies. Anita said it was a peculiar trait of werewolves!

"OK. Sex first, research after!" Sarah grinned sexily, and wiggled her breasts at him. "We won't be disturbed?"

Sam, shaking his head, yanked off his shirt, pulled her off the lift, and then, stripped her. He picked her up carrying her to the overstuffed sofa buried between the shelves. Her bare belly and ass only served to turn him on. He loved feeling their child kick them when he was inside of her. He licked his lips, and grasped one of her nipples in his mouth.

Sarah, arched back shoving it into his mouth further. She was addicted to sex anywhere at any time, and she was so thrilled that her mate felt the same. They had had sex in some of the strangest places, and they had enjoyed every, single second of it! And, this was just another new place!

"Oh, Sam!" she cried softly. Because she was so large at this point, he sat on the sofa, his cock pointing straight up at his mate. He helped Sarah straddle his lap allowing her to take his huge cock inside of her. She looked at him as she moved up and down.

"I'm riding you," she whispered giggling.

"Wanna phase, and let me ride you?" Sam waggled his eyebrows at her, and she laughed outright as she phased.

~ 10 ~
Research is not a bore

Anita, Dan, Richard, and Lynne were picked up by another driver, since Sam and Sarah had been assigned research at Anita's request. Find any kind of reference before the curse, no matter how small, Cordone had ordered.

Now that Dan was back, he was assigned to guard Kaitlan and the babies. Kaitlan's recovery from childbirth had been rapid, and much to Cordone's irritation, she was eager to get back to the danger at hand. He had a family, now. A mate and two children. And, the children were growing fast.

Anita had said that their growth was absolutely at a normal, werewolf rate when Kaitlan expressed her concern. Within ten years, the twins would be the equivalent of twenty human years. And, they would be within mating age at nine. Their wolves would not emerge until the human age of twenty-seven, or the werewolf age of just under eighteen.

Everyone was still trying to figure out how Richard and Lynne were alive again. Anita still couldn't find an actual reason for it! But, the final proof that the curse was broken came. Other werewolves started to discover that they could mate in both forms and their mates were becoming pregnant. A fact that the entire werewolf community cheered. It was as if the mating of Lynne and Richard was the last step to breaking the curse entirely. As it had said, everything returned to the way it was before the curse. And, the first sign was pregnancies - lots of them. But, the nuttiest idea came from Sarah, as usual. It appeared she had been absolutely right! But, she still wanted proof. However, she did verbalize her theory - again.

"Perhaps, to break the curse, four women had to mate? I don't know why I am thinking that, but is it not possible since nothing happened until after all four of us found our mates? Isn't that corroboration of my theory? However, if so, why isn't it in the Prophecy? Damn! Until I have something concrete, it will just remain a theory." Sarah frowned. "You know…it's almost as if…." Sarah stopped.

"As if what, Sarah?" Lynne asked.

"Well, what kind of an example could I make. I guess …you know the old LP records? The ones that Dan collects to use on his turntable? Well, some of the LP's are scratched, and if you try to play them, they 'skip' around. Some even play as if they are in a loop, because of the scratches. That's what this feels like. As if there are 'skips' in our life. Those skips are the parts we seem to be missing."

Most everyone rolled their eyes at Sarah's preposterous speculation, and she finally dropped it. But, it did not completely leave her conscious thought. She felt, deep down, she was right.

Richard went back to his work as did Lynne. Despite the fact they were cured of their vampirism, they were highly skilled, and able to protect the Alpha as well as the council. In fact, they were much stronger in their normal forms than they were in their vampire forms. Lynne was a full-blooded Elf. She, and the few like her that remained, had full Elven powers, and they were formidable. Lynne's were returned to her when her vampire side disappeared. No one of any race in the supernatural world ever wanted to be on the receiving end of their fury. Most supernatural beings knew that Elves were not to be tested. Lynne went back to her office, but now that her eyes had returned to her original silver color, she was proud to look others in the face again. That had been another huge change for them. Their eyes. Richard's eyes were an amazing blue, and Lynne found herself drowning in them every time she looked into them. At times, though, they were like the dark blue in the depths of the ocean. Their recent transformation had not dulled their ardor for each other in any way. If anything, they were getting worse! And, they explored every way with zeal! She was wet, constantly, as they traded thoughts of sex back and forth between them during the work day. And, the nights were ecstasy spent in each other's arms.

Cordone and Kaitlan were in full parental mode. The two of them couldn't get enough of baby Tara and Canaan. They were growing fast, and had begun to crawl within two weeks after their births. Kaitlan's milk was still coming at a fast pace, but she let Cordone take care of any "extra" she happened to have. Many times, at night while she nursed, Cordone joined in the meal with his children. It was such a turn on for him, he often spent a vast majority of time inside his mate after the children were put to bed. And, Kaitlan was always ready for Cordone. They were worse than before the twins!

Sam and Sarah were in a race to get the information Anita had asked for, but so far, nothing. Sarah took another drink of the hot tea that the kitchen had provided for her.

Sarah slammed her hands down on the table making it jump, and startling Sam.

"Damn it, Sam! Nothing! Not one single thing!" She jumped up, and ran her hands through her hair in frustration. "I'm missing something!"

Sam took her hand. "We will find it, Sarah. Seriously, we will."

Sarah nodded, and plodded over to get another scroll from the bookcase. She suddenly felt very dizzy, and swooned. Sam almost missed catching her as she fell.

"Sarah! Are you alright?"

Sarah wasn't feeling right. She had never felt so bad, and they both knew it wasn't yet time for the baby. Sam was scared, and Sarah more so.

"No. You better take me to Anita fast!"

Sam sped to the elevators with Sarah in his arms, and within minutes, Anita was checking her out. Sam was with Sarah all the time, and refused to leave. The expression on Anita's face scared the hell out of him as she motioned to follow her.

Shutting the door behind her, Anita gave the news to Sam.

"Wolfsbane." Her voice was quiet with pain.

Sam's eyes bugged out! Sarah had been poisoned with Wolfsbane?

"Don't lie to me, Anita. Will they be alright?" He begged.

"Well, you got her here well within the thirty minute timeline. I gave her the antidote, and as of now, both Mother and baby seem to be responding well. But, I still don't know what might happen. And, before you ask, yes, her reaction was the same as Lynne's. The antidote, in some ways, is even worse, but it works, and that's the main thing."

Never had Sam thought he might lose Sarah let alone their baby! He fell into a waiting chair with his head in his hands. The anger and hatred poured into him. Zanack! How in the hell was he getting to them? Why couldn't they nail the bastard down? It made absolutely no sense to him! Anita put her hand on his shoulder.

"Trust me. She will be up, and OK in the next hour or so. She won't feel any residual effects. You got her here in time, Sam. But, how did she get it?"

Sam just shook his head. He was having a hard time thinking. His head jerked up.

"The tea! It had to be the tea, Anita! Sarah was drinking the tea made by the kitchen!"

Just more proof that they did have a traitor in their midst, but worse? There had to be more than one. This disturbing revelation made Sam very nervous, now. His shoulders shook with terror at the thought he might not have gotten them there in time. He gulped as he sucked air into his lungs.

Kaitlan burst into Anita's office. Seeing Sam broken, she started to cry. Cordone was on her heels. She put her arms around Sam, and hugged him. Then, asked to see Sarah. Anita gave her the green light to go into see her.

Cordone put his hand on his friend's shoulder.

"Anita says they will be fine, Sam. You were fast enough to save her."

"I know, but who gave it to her? It had to be a library staff member in the kitchen. It's the only thing Sarah has had in the last week except at home. And, she had just had a cup of tea, before she fell."

Cordone nodded, having already pulled out his cell, and called Dan.

"I'll have every one of them checked out, Sam."

Then, to Dan, "Dan. Sarah has been poisoned with Wolfsbane." He listened as Dan cursed for several seconds. "Sam just told me that she had a cup of tea in The Hall. See if you can get a hold of it." Cordone was quiet as he listened to Dan. "Right. Let me know." He hung up the phone.

Kaitlan stood over Sarah lying pale in the bed holding her best friend's hand when her eyes fluttered open. Upon seeing Kaitlan, "What happened?"

"You were poisoned by Wolfsbane, Sarah."

Sarah stared, and grabbed her belly. "MY BABY??" she cried.

"The baby is fine, Sarah. Sam got you here on time." Kaitlan put her arm around her friend, and hugged her.

Her heart was breaking as she watched Sarah crying hard at the though she might have lost her child. Sam heard her, and came into the room.

"SAM!" she cried holding her belly tightly.

Sam went to her, and took Kaitlan's place. Kaitlan left the two together. She ran into Cordone's arms, bawling like a baby.

"Cordone! She's had such a tough life in her beginning.

I can't bear the thought she could have lost her child!"

"We will find this monster," he replied lifting her face to his.

For a couple of days, Sam and Sarah stayed at home. But, Sarah was never one to let things get her down for long. She absolutely insisted on returning.

"Sam. We are the only two who can find out what is happening. We have to get back to the research."

Reluctantly, Sam had capitulated, but he placed himself in charge of her food and drink. It was almost impossible to argue with his mate when she had made up her mind. So, they returned to The Hall of Records.

Sam finished the next scroll with no results, and went to retrieve another. He sat down, and looked at Sarah sleeping on the sofa, then turned back to open the next scroll. He did a double take when he realized what he held in his hand.

"Sarah!" practically leaping out of his seat. Sarah woke up immediately.

"You found something!" she exclaimed.

"Look." He handed her a scroll. It was gorgeous, and totally intact.

"Where did you find this?" she asked as her hand spread reverently over it.

"It was stuck behind another scroll - as if someone wanted to hide it. Technically, it's not in its right place. It should be behind the door in the most ancient texts. I believe it is an original. But, look at the wax seal!"

They stared at it. It was gorgeous! And, ancient. Sarah noticed that it was quite small with silver handles on either side. Then, Sarah frowned as she turned it around in her hands. It sported an unbroken, white wax seal with a wolf impression!

"I wonder … is this meant for Kaitlan?"

"My conclusion exactly," he told her. "You think it would be a mistake to break the seal?" Sam asked.

Sarah brushed her hand over the seal. She got a tingly feeling from the seal.

"I think … Sam … I think we need to show this to Kaitlan. If the seal is for The White Wolf, you're right. Breaking it may be a big mistake."

"How do you know?"

"I don't know. I just do."

And, then, Sarah collapsed into oblivion.

Anita left the room, closing the door quietly behind her, silent tears streaming. Everyone had run to the infirmary when Anita had called them. They all knew it was serious. They looked at her with fear in their eyes. Kaitlan knew before Anita said a word, and her sobs poured from her heart. No! It can't be, she cried to herself. Cordone heard her cry, and he, too, had silent tears that streamed down his face as he held his heartbroken mate.

Anita looked up with tears.

"They are dead," she said, and joined the rest as she dropped to her knees crying as if her heart was breaking.

~ 11 ~
Death is but a door to the next part of our existence

The Clan was in mourning for their Second's dead wife and child. Kaitlan had been tranquilized. The loss of her best friend had caused her to collapse, and pass out. Anita was barely functioning, but as a doctor, she put it aside only when treating a patient. Dan was worried about his mate. She hadn't been feeling well to begin with, and now? Their baby was fine, but her mental health was not. Yet, she continued to do her job. To be fair, though, Dan knew that there was no other doctor. There was nothing he could say, or do, except be with her all day watching over her. She let him know how much she loved his concern, and gladly accepted his company. Anita just couldn't be alone, and Cordone was watching over Kaitlan.

Sam had not left Sarah's bedside for two days, and now, he lay next to his mate, dying as was werewolf custom. Anita had a bed brought in after Sam had collapsed into a coma. A mate could not survive the death of the other unless the mate forbid the survivor from following. In Sam's case, Sarah had not survived to do so. Bodies of the supernatural took far longer to decompose than did their human counterparts. Long ago, the custom was to wait until the mate had died before performing the last rites. Seven days, to be exact. The surviving mate died at the end of those seven days. They were waiting for those days to pass now. Sam would die soon, and for Sam, Cordone knew, it couldn't be fast enough. He knew it, because he would feel the same way. He could never survive without Kaitlan. She was everything to him.

Cordone was worried about Kaitlan. She had just shut down except for their children, and even then, it was difficult for her to function. She tried very hard to keep the children from knowing her pain. Putting his elbows on his desk, he dropped his head in his hands as tears rolled down his face. The Master Council was due within the week, having been postponed once already, and, now, Cordone had postponed it again. Why was this happening? It made no sense. And, then his head came up. Zanack was behind it, but why? What type of hatred could be so bad that this monster would kill not only their females, but their children as well?

Wolfsbane! It had plagued them all forever. Going over what Anita had told them only confirmed the fact that there was no longer doubt. Zanack was trying to rid himself of their species. Or, was it a diversion for something else? Both Lynne and Sarah had been targets. That couldn't be a coincidence. Someone who had access to Sarah in the library and the clinic, had poisoned Sarah, again. Dan was convinced, now, that there was more than one traitor in their midst. Only this time, with a triple dose in her water bottle - they still didn't understand how it happened unless it was switched somehow when Sam wasn't looking. To finish her off, a pure form of the drug was pumped into her from her IV bag that had been given to her after she had collapsed.

Cordone slammed his fists down on Canaan's old desk, and broke a part of it off. Apologizing to him, he called Dan and Richard to his office. They were all coming to the same conclusion. Just thinking was difficult right now. More heads were really better than one.

Pacing up and down, Richard began, "OK. Whoever administered the Wolfsbane, had direct contact, and access to The Hall of Records, as well as the clinic. This has to narrow it down. Who do we know who might have access to both?"

Dan thought a minute. He and Lynne had finally been added to The Hall of Records list. It had surprised the hell out of them, but now Dan was trying to put things together. He was a real detective. That was what he excelled at, and why he was chosen as Third. And, Lynne wasted no time at all when he asked her to get him a list.

"I asked for a list from Lynne. She's putting a rush on the list. It should help us determine who the culprit is. I just hope this is going to be the break we've been needing."

As he finished speaking, Lynne came into the office. She gave the list to Dan who looked it over quickly while Lynne stood against the wall with her arms crossed. She was glowing slightly with anger, even though she tried to hold it back. She had not had her full Elf power in a long time, and had been finding it difficult to control. Dan plopped down in his chair, and looked up at the assembled group.

"Well?" asked Cordone.

"Only one name is common to both," he paused. "Teri, Anita's nurse, was the only person who had access to both areas." Informing them of the only name on both lists.

"WHAT? How did she get on The Hall of Records list?" yelled Richard.

Dan answered. "Only one way." He looked straight at Cordone. "Zanack had to be the one who put her on the list. It means he has to be on the council."

Silence met his words.

Finally, Cordone spoke.

"Kaitlan was right. She told us this a while back. Now, we have proof. Dan..."

Dan stood up. "I'll call you when I have her in custody."

Cordone nodded only once. He couldn't wait to get his hands on her. And, Kaitlan? He stared at her. Teri would be lucky if she didn't kill her with her bare hands! He thought maybe it was better that she not be there. But, Kaitlan held out her hand to stop her mate before he could say a word to her.

"You are not going to stop me from being there, Cordone! So, don't even try! I promise I'll try not to kill her, but by God! I will if she so much as fails to answer one question!" Cordone had never seen Kaitlan like this. "Cordone, I want our babies taken to our house. I want to make sure they are safe."

"I have a better idea. I'm sending them away with two

trusted people."

Kaitlan looked up. "Who is that trustworthy?"

"Do you trust me Kaitlan? With our children?"

Looking into his eyes, Kaitlan nodded. There was no way Cordone would let them stay with anyone he did not trust. She didn't ask who, as he wouldn't tell her - at least not right now. She nodded.

Less than an hour later, Cordone, Kaitlan, Richard and Lynne had joined Dan in his office. Anita was already there standing behind Dan with her arms crossed, and murder in her eyes. Teri was handcuffed to a chair, and Dan kept her from phasing. It was a rare thing these days for that since the contemporary Clan thought it barbaric. Dan was the only other were other than Cordone who had used it in the past, and only for rogues. But, in this case, they did not see it as barbaric.

Cordone was worried. Kaitlan's eyes narrowed dangerously as she watched while Teri's head was hanging down. A bright red handprint was on her right cheek. Kaitlan's barely controlled anger was just under the surface, and one, wrong word out of Teri's mouth could cause her to lose her life at the hands of his mate. He wasn't all that sure he would try to stop her, either. And, he could see that her wolf ready to spring.

Anita was stunned beyond belief! She would never have believed Teri capable of anything like this. Teri had looked to her for help when Dan had first brought her into his office, but Anita's anger pushed her to backhand Teri. It was so hard, it threw Teri across the room where she hit the wall, and slid to the floor. Dan had not even tried to stop her. He wondered, later, whether, or not, he had done it on purpose. Didn't really matter. Anita was his hero for doing it, and Teri was dead anyway.

~ 12 ~
"To sin by silence when they should protest makes cowards of men." ~~~ Abraham Lincoln

Dan was the most ferociously ruthless interrogator Cordone had ever seen in his life, so he sat back, and let Dan take over completely. But, he found out another was far more fierce than Dan. This girl was in for an experience she would never forget. Well, what was left of her life, anyway. He folded his arms leaning against the wall next to Lynne with such an angry face, only an idiot would dare cross him.

Kaitlan, on the other hand, was drawing on all her control to stop herself from killing the woman in front of her who had killed her best friend and her baby. With Sam dying, now, it just made her that much angrier. Cordone had never seen anything like it. He knew one word, or one action, would cost Teri her life from anyone in that room. Dan pushed off the wall, and was standing in front of her. Cordone stilled his thoughts to listen.

"Teri, you are charged with premeditated murder. You know in the werewolf world, there is only one sentence for betraying your Clan. Death. You have taken not one, but two lives, and a third hangs in the balance that will die. You murdered Sam as if you had pulled the trigger yourself. Your sentence is death. Now, you can go to the Creator with a clear conscience by telling us who put you up to this, or not. It's your choice. But, I will know the truth before you are escorted for termination." Dan's voice was deadly calm. A really, really bad sign from a man who was usually jovial.

Teri just sat raising her chin, and smirked at him. She almost welcomed death after Zanack's threats. At least her termination by the Clan would be merciful. But, looking around her, the smirk quickly died on her face. Now, she was beginning to doubt it. Fear knotted her stomach.

"Teri. I've asked you before, and you have refused to answer. You have one more chance." Dan demanded.

"He will kill me. You will. So why should I answer? And, his method of death is far less preferable to ours!" Teri was defiant.

Kaitlan was just about to lose it, when, in horror, everyone watched as Lynne's form blurred. She streaked across the room, her white ponytail flailing behind her. She grabbed Teri by the neck, shoving Teri and the chair against the wall making a huge dent in it. Lynne began to choke her slowly. Teri was terrified by the look in Lynne's eyes.

"Oh. My. Freaking. God!" Teri screamed. A full-blooded Elf! Teri had no idea there were any left, let alone were in the Clan! She had just assumed her hair had been recently bleached.

Lynne's eyes had gone from their normal silver color to totally black as night consuming even the whites of her eyes! Her entire body began to glow with an eerie mixture of white, purple, and black, and her body seemed to grow larger as she towered over Teri. The office was alive with an electrical current of massive proportions. Anyone who had half a brain would be afraid of her right now. Elves rarely lost their temper, and appeared angelic, but when angered to the point of killing, there was terror. To everyone's knowledge, no one had ever seen one lose their temper in known history, but they were rumored to have no mercy for the guilty. More than that, the power they had in this form far exceeded any other supernatural.

Silently, Richard was awed and a bit nervous, but Richard was still inwardly grinning at his mate. She was, indeed, the most frightening sight he had ever seen, and he had never been as proud of her as he was right now. She was glorious! She made him look like a rank amateur! But, she was his! He desired her in that moment more than ever before. She would make him a glorious queen! He had chosen wisely!

"Listen. To. Me. Very. Carefully, Teri," Lynne's voice sounded like a sonic boom, and the others put their hands over their ears. "I am Queen Linora, mate to King Eric of the Vikings, Richard O'Malley! Most do not know that full-blooded Elves still exist, but we do. I do *NOT* show mercy. I do *NOT* hesitate. You will *NOT* be able to get away from me. I will kill you if I so choose!" she said quietly. "And, do not think anyone in this room could stop me! I am not a leader in the Clan even though I am mated to one of the council members. But, *I will choke the fucking life* out of you, then snap your scrawny neck like a chicken! But, that is just one of the ways I am contemplating your death. There are far more horrific ways for me to kill you! In your case, however, I will make an exception! I will torture you long and slow before I kill you! And, the last thing you will see as you die is my fucking smile!" Lynne's smile was frightening. Her whole appearance was frightening. Everyone's eyes were wide in shock as they watched something none had ever seen. Even her mate was frightened by her voice and appearance.

Teri started trying to talk through the chokehold. She had heard about full-blooded Elves. Oh, God! She really was facing a full-blooded Elf! Zanack could not have known! The decision about whether to be killed by him, or any number of the legendary and horrific ways that elves killed the guilty, let her make her decision without second-guessing. Elves were far more deadly than Zanack! She tried to talk.

"You wish to say something, Teri?" Lynne's voice boomed. So loudly, that Teri's ears had started to bleed. Teri tried to nod.

"Temporarily, I spare your life. But, I *WILL* send you straight to the Creator for judgment if you do not answer what Dan wants to know immediately! I am Elf, and I will not allow a traitor live one more minute in my Clan. Do you understand me?"

Teri tried to nod, again. She knew, without a doubt, that

Lynne would do what she said.

Lynne carried Teri in her chair back to Dan, and slammed it down hard onto the floor. Lynne addressed Dan formally.

"Dan, Teri says that she will answer your questions, now. Her life is forfeit, and she does not wish to return to the Creator without confessing what she knows. I have informed her that I, Queen Linora of the Vikings, mate to King Eric, King of all Vikings, will, without measure, kill this murderous bitch if she does not answer your questions. She will answer truthfully all questions put to her, or I will send her straight to the Creator, and let Him take of her!" She turned to Teri again. Her eyes remained black as night, although her glow receded. "I can assure you I will be far worse than Zanack!"

She threw Teri's head backward, and everyone could hear a tiny crack. Teri believed Lynne without a doubt. Tears burst through Teri's eyes at the fact she knew Lynne had cracked something in her neck. They knew about Zanack! Shit!

Dan moved in front of her again.

"Make no mistake, Teri. I'll stand back, and let Lynne dispatch you to the Creator forthwith!   And, I guarantee you, not one Clan member will care. In fact, if Lynne would wait, they would all come and watch! Unfortunately, though, Lynne would not wait for them. But, then again, maybe she would. She does love a show! Now. Last chance. Who put you up to killing our Third's wife and baby." He looked at his watch. "Name him!"

Teri tried to swallow, but couldn't. She looked at all the eyes staring at her. She was like a rabbit caught in a trap. She had been tried and sentenced. There was nothing left. But, if it came between Zanack or the Elf, she would choose the third choice of death by werewolf law. It was humane. She cleared her throat as best she could, and tried to speak.

"I…Ahem…want to state…<Cough>," her throat was hurting. Anita gave her a glass of water, which helped, but only a little. "He is evil incarnate. …<Cough>… I don't know what he is. His eyes glow red and orange depending on his mood. Mostly, red. But he is no vampire. He offered me money to kill Sarah. I had run up gambling debts. I had no choice. I was being beaten by the thugs for their money. He hates half-breeds and humans alike. He saw Sarah and her baby as refuse and filth. He wants pure bloods only, yet he wants to create hybrids for service to the pure bloods." She looked around. It was going to be so much worse. "…<Cough>… He has two others who work with him, but I have no …<Cough>… idea who they are. …<Cough>… I-I just know they are a mix of supers. He kills …<Cough>… horrendously, d-drinks their blood, eats their f-flesh, and skins others alive! There is no end to his horrible acts! I've seen his latest kill, and …<Cough>… that is why I agreed to it. He came to get me after he had told me where to get the vials. I-I swear I didn't know what was in them. I swear I didn't! He took me down into the basement of a building that reeked of …<Cough>… r-r-rotting flesh. A woman, a waitress that I had seen in the area, was tied to an old wooden table in the center of the room. He had stripped her naked, looked as if she had been stabbed on her arms and legs, and she was screaming!"

She gagged, and began to throw up. It was too late to put anything under her. They waited a while, until she cleared her throat.

"He forced me to watch what he did to her. I-I-I…," terror gripped her as she remembered what she saw. Her eyes became frantic. "H-he had her tied her to a table," she repeated, "…and…spread her legs."

Oh, it was so not what they thought as she looked at the horror on their faces. She continued with eyes wild.

"He took his fist, and rammed it up inside her. His claws ripped h-h-her w-womb from her body, and a-a-ate it!"

She saw their faces of horror. She needed to tell them just what kind of monster he really was.

"The blood was gushing! Her screams were deafening

as he rammed his fist up inside her again, and ripped out the rest of her female organs! He ate them, too! The blood flowed from her, draining on the floor! Teri lost it.

"The screams! The SCREAMS!" She yelled. "I can't forget them!"

She took a few moments to calm down as best she could.

"He hates women!"

Anita couldn't stand any more, and ran out the door with Kaitlan right behind her. Both women grabbed the nearest trashcan, and started throwing up into it.

The men's faces were masks of horror. What kind of monster were they dealing with? What had he done to sell his soul to become whatever he was?

Teri finished. "Then, he took the knife, and plunged it into her chest, reached in and ripped out her barely beating heart, and slowly devoured it. Once she was dead the blood spilled into a bucket beneath the table. He," she closed her eyes, began to gag, and she threw up on the floor, again. "He drank it! Her blood! He f-f-forced…forced me to…drink a full cup of her blood!!!!" She started to cry and scream. "He told me that it was what I could expect if I didn't do what he commanded."

She started vomiting, again.

Finally, Dan asked, "What's his name?"

She raised her head.

"He calls himself 'Alpha', but his real name…. is Z-Zanack!"

Everyone was silent. There it was. Confirmation. The terror that this girl had seen. Her vivid description making them all sick. She wanted to die, now. No one would want to live with that in her mind. Teri would turn rogue from this. Her eyes were already showing the signs, Dan thought. And, this was one time he wouldn't be able to help, but then, he didn't want to anyway. And, he was quite certain neither did Teri.

Kaitlan and Anita were still sick. Lynne had finally

calmed down to her normal appearance, and she, too, ran out of the room to vomit.

The girls held each other, and went back to Cordone's office where they sat in complete silence.

"Dan, terminate her immediately. While she saw what she did, she still betrayed, murdered, and violated the Clan. She doesn't deserve a merciful killing, but Zanack's plan for her …." Cordone's voice trailed off into nothing.

Dan buzzed his security guards who took her away. He followed them. Their Clan was humane even for the most vile crimes. Anita had developed a small amount of Wolfsbane to be used for executions of rogues, and it had made her sick to do so. But, rogues were so rare any more, the small amount had lasted well over three hundred years, which was the last time they executed anyone. But, no one ever remembered an execution for betrayal to the Clan until now.

~ 13 ~
Death is relative, depending on your own point of view ~
LKK

"Where am I?" Sarah wondered aloud as she opened her eyes, and stood.

It took her a minute for her eyes to adapt to a brilliant, blue-white light. As it cleared, the most beautiful scene she had ever seen was before her. Mountains that were so high, they pierced the white cloud mist, and thrust upward into the blue of the sky above. Green trees, soft green grass below her bare feet so beautiful she just had to wiggle her toes in it. Flowers of every known type and color surrounded her, some she couldn't even name, lay at the base of a long, low rock wall framing … what? Was that a table with a snow-white tablecloth set for tea in crystal plates and cups? To the right of the table, a crystal clear stream happily bubbled on its merry way. She followed it until it ended as it ran off into the edge of nothing. Where the hell was she? She'd been around Sam so long, his cussing had already rubbed off on her! She smiled thinking of her mate who considered her his little goody two-shoes - a misnomer, of course.

Returning to the table, Sarah realized that she was in a flowing and sheer, snow-white gown of empire design in some material she had never felt. A silver ribbon crossed her breasts in a Grecian style like the gods of Mount Olympus might wear. She was bare of jewelry, and the gown flowed lightly around her dropping to her ankles. It was so sheer, it left little to the imagination at all. Crystals were placed strategically on both the bodice and skirt, to hide her frontal nudity, but none adorned the back. She blushed heavily.

She felt as if she were floating more than actually

walking. One moment, she was floating. The next she was seated at the table. Sarah looked down at her belly. There was no baby there. She was as slim as she had ever been. Tears began to flow down her cheeks. She knew, then, that not only was she dead, but that she had lost her precious baby.

"Sarah?" a soft voice was heard.

Lifting her head, a handsome man approached with a beautiful woman with flowing, long blonde hair and green eyes. They joined her at the table. She saw ….

"Canaan?"

"Hello, Sarah."

Both were dressed in snow white. Tara was dressed similar to Sarah. A sheer white gown was bejeweled in golden crystals, and golden ribbon. Canaan wore a suit of white, a sheer, white silk shirt, white shoes, and his hair had also turned white.

What was it about the afterlife that always seemed to love nudity so much?

Sarah opened her mouth, and Canaan held up his hand. She closed it.

"First, no. This is not a dream. It is most certainly very real. Second, yes, Sarah. You are dead." He introduced the beautiful woman to Sarah. "Third, this is my mate, Tara."

Tara's smile was radiant and so kind. But, shockingly, the spitting image of Kaitlan, and her bright green eyes were staring back at Sarah! She sucked in her breath at how beautiful she was!

"You are Kaitlan's Mother." It was a statement, not a question.

Tara nodded. "Yes. I'm so happy to finally meet my daughter's best friend, Sarah."

"My … my baby is dead," Sarah stated with finality.

Tara reached over, and took Sarah's hand.

"I'm afraid so, Sarah."

Sarah started to cry in earnest, now. Tara stood up, and walked to the chair next to Sarah. Tara wrapped her arms around her, and waited until her tears were exhausted.

"Sarah," Canaan said, "We are so sorry for your loss. But, be assured your son is well cared for by the Creator. The Creator is so sorry, but in order for you to become what you must, you had to suffer loss."

Sarah's head came up. The Creator taking care of her son? It had been a boy? Tears flowed again. He had noticed her? Wait as second. Clarity dawned, drying her tears quickly. Canaan and Tara were ... dead. She was dead, because no Earthly place could be this beautiful. She really was dead. Sam! Sam would die, too! She couldn't have it!

"I don't understand. Haven't I had enough suffering in my life that my son was ripped from me as well? That my mate will join me soon in death?" She cried.

Canaan started speaking.

"I know, Sarah. You suffered in the beginning of your life, and the same at the end of it. But, we have very little time, so please listen very carefully."

"NO!" Sarah screamed.

Sarah didn't want to listen. She'd been through enough! She jumped up, and started to run, when ....

Canaan's voice became a demand.

"Sarah! I am your Alpha, and you are required to do as I ask. Stop, dry your tears, and sit back down - now!"

Sarah ground her teeth, but stopped, turned, and her tears dried immediately upon Canaan's command. Angrily, she stomped to the table, and sat back down. But, it still didn't stop her heart from breaking.

"Your suffering is a great gift from the Creator. He has named you an Elemental - a most prestigious honor, and very, very rare. You will become the water elemental. Thus, the stream at your feet. You will command the waters - all waters - on the Earth when you return."

Sarah's head jerked up. She was going back? She'd have great power? What?

"I don't understand? What's an Elemental?"

"An elemental has power over one the four elements, and is only given to the deserving. The last Elementals were born one hundred thousand years ago, and only show up when the world is in danger," Tara explained. "Kaitlan doesn't know it, yet, but as The White Wolf, she is the Earth Elemental. You are water. Anita will follow as the Air Elemental, and finally, Lynne will become the Fire Elemental. To defeat the ancient sorcerer, Odfrin, you will have to wield the powers of the elements. They can be used for good, or for evil."

Tara added more. "But, you were right. The Earth Elemental was taken from Odfrin to prevent the permanence of the curse. By whom, we know not, but we believe it was deliberate - to keep her power out of his hands, for it is the most powerful of all the elements. We also believe that the one who took her forged the Prophecy. Because of this, he was unable to finalize the curse, thus creating skips in the timeline of the Earth. The LP example, you used, was apropos. Now, it will be necessary to listen to Richard, for he will tell you the rest of the story. It is not ours to tell. But, know this. Kaitlan will need your strengths at the end, and a great sacrifice will be asked of all four elementals. She will know what to do when the time comes, and will tell you."

"Odfrin? I thought it was Zanack?" Her surprise was very evident.

"The great sorcerer merged with a human, taking his form. That person died. The name Zanack was taken from another."

Sarah waited for more explanations, but none came. Well, that was soooo not helpful! Another thought came to her.

"You said 'timeline' Are you trying to tell me that time - itself - is involved?" No answer. "Not helping," Sarah told them, but they ignored her question.

"Sarah, Sam's life will be extinguished in a very short time, and we have little time left to get you back into your body." Canaan told her. "It is urgent that you return so Sam will live."

Sarah huffed. She should have known she wouldn't get an answer to her questions. Richard would finish the story? What the hell did Richard have to do with all of this?

"One more thing, Sarah. Each of you will accept your element at the appointed times, and each of you, within a short amount of time, must learn to control each of the elements. Again, it is Richard who will bring the One chosen to help you to learn your elements." Canaan looked up into the sky, then back down at Sarah. "Remember … you and your mates will be required to give great sacrifices."

"It is time for you to return, now. Remember, Sarah …." Tara's voice faded away as that same, brilliant, blue-white light appeared around her, and she felt herself spiraling down … falling fast … straight into a brick wall.

Kaitlan's eyes were red, and Cordone tried to comfort her. But, it was difficult. She missed her babies who were with a couple of people she didn't know somewhere on the planet, and she was about to have to watch as her best friend was cremated. Anita had told them Sam would die any moment.

"Kaitlan?" Cordone placed his hand on her shoulder. He was hurting for her. "I know this is hard, my love, but you must be strong for our Clan. There is only one way to relieve your grief, and that is to turn it into anger and action. Trust me. I know. If you let grief get to you, Zanack has won. Think about it. I'll be in the living room."

Kaitlan jerked at the uttering of the bastard's name. Cordone was right. But, how could she do this? She watched as her mate turned, and walked out of the nursery where she had parked herself for the past week. Finally, realization hit her in the face, and she kicked herself! Sarah would never cop out like this! She was far braver than Kaitlan had ever been! She would have been headstrong trying to find the filth that had killed her friend! Kaitlan could do no less.

She stood up, went into the bathroom to take a shower, wash her hair, and clean up. Then, she walked into the living room with her head held high, anger building inside of her gave her the strength. They would find Sarah's killer, and he would pay by her hand. He would not live.

"You are right. I'm ready, Cordone. Let's do this."

Cordone rose, and stood in front of her searching her eyes. He smiled, took her hands, and nodded. She was ready for battle.

We rejoice in birth, and mourn in death. But, it is in death that we question ourselves and our mortality, or in this case, their virtual immortality. Lynne and Richard were seated in the council room with Dan. The door opened, and their Alphas entered seating themselves in their chairs. They were preparing for the short funeral. Anita was remaining with Sam until the end, so that she could enter their deaths in the official Clan record.

"When we cremate Sarah and Sam," Cordone began, "we will be going on the offensive. I'm tired of being defensive. We were not made that way. We will avenge their deaths, and believe me, Zanack will be destroyed!"

"Lynne and I are going down to The Hall of Records to see if we can find what Sam and Sarah were looking for, if that is alright with you? Just call us when it's over." Richard stated.

Cordone nodded. "As of now, we turn our anger into positive energy. Zanack is more powerful than we ever knew."

At that point, Kaitlan took over, and stood.

"I am the heir to the O'Hara Clan. I am the mate to our Alpha. But, Sarah was my best friend. I will not rest until my hands are around Zanack's throat. His days are numbered as of right now." Everyone agreed. "I have no experience in tactical warfare, but Cordone will teach me what I need to know. I won't sit this out, and if war is what Zanack wants, war is what he will get! If he could get to Sarah and her baby, he could get to any of us! No matter what happens, I want you to understand that Zanack is mine!"

No one is more dangerous than a woman protecting her children, and who is bent on revenge. Cordone's trusted couple had already taken their children to a safe place, but he still refused to tell Kaitlan where. It was better that she not know if Zanack, somehow, did get his hands on Kaitlan.

"It is time," Cordone said, and they all rose to go to the clinic to wait with Anita.

Richard was reaching for the council room's door when it was flung open so hard, it hit the wall, and made a huge hole in it. Everyone stopped dead as Anita stood in the doorway. Her eyes were wild, hair in tangles, skin white as a ghost, and, well, she looked as if she had actually had seen a ghost!

Dan took a step toward her, and she waved him off without a word, then stood aside.

For whatever reason, everyone held their breath, even though they didn't know what to expect. Feet were heard in the hallway. Heads were turned to Anita as her shocked face stared at the doorway.

Two people entered the doorway past Anita, and stood in front of them. There was a huge gasp as they saw Sarah and Sam who stood, hand in hand facing them, Sam holding a scroll, and they were …

ALIVE?

"No fucking way!" shouted Lynne, and fell into the chair behind her.

Kaitlan wasn't as lucky. Her knees gave out as her ass hit the chair behind her as it rolled backwards, and she fell to the floor with a loud thump.

~ 14 ~
I'm dreaming … yes. That's it!

Kaitlan awoke feeling Cordone bathing her face with a cold cloth. She had been placed on the adjacent sofa in the council room after she had passed out. She tried to move.

"Ouch! My ass!" she ground out. Laughter was heard around her.

Sarah was perched on the sofa arm, her face smiling down at her best friend in the whole world. Kaitlan's eyes flew open wide! It *WAS* Sarah! But, Sarah's eyes were so - clear! As blue as the sky! Blue as water. They undulated as if they were waves in the ocean! And, Sam stood right next to her?

Kaitlan blinked her eyes, the pain in her behind forgotten for the moment. This can't be! Sarah had been *DEAD*! For seven days, she was dead! How in the hell …?

"Nope! You aren't seeing things, Kaitlan," Sarah waggled her fingers at her in a wave. "It's little ole' me. We're alive, so get over it!"

Kaitlan slowly stood up with Cordone's help, but not taking her eyes off of Sarah. Standing a bit rocky, she grabbed Sarah's shoulders, and looked her up and down.

"You're alive? You are alive!!!!" Kaitlan squealed, then grabbed Sarah hugging her like she would never let her go. What do you say to someone who was dead, and is alive???

The two girls embraced each other tightly, and wouldn't let go.

"Why are you so surprised?" Sarah's voice was raspy with emotion. "You ought to know you can't get rid of me that easily?"

Kaitlan pulled back with surprise on her face.

"Seriously? Did you really just say that?" Kaitlan

laughed.

Her words were met with laughter, and happiness all around them as they all talked over one another, and took turns hugging Sarah and Sam! The men patting Sam on the back in joy.

"How?"

"When?"

"Why?"

"Not possible!"

After everyone hugged Sarah and Sam, Cordone had everyone sit down. Kaitlan would not let go of Sarah's hand.

"Sit down? I've been dead for seven days, Cordone, and you think I need to sit down? Thanks. I think I'll stand!" Sarah giggled. Then, another Sarah moment came out. "Besides, I'd rather be in bed with Sam! We need to make up some lovey-dovey!"

Sam dropped his head, and shook it, but was laughing silently while everyone else was laughing at his expense.

"You know about the baby?" Kaitlan whispered to her.

Sarah's happiness changed to sorrow in an instant. She nodded, and a single, silent tear slipped out of her eye, and ran down her cheek. She made no attempt to brush it away, and Sam wrapped his arm around her.

"How are you alive?" Kaitlan asked Sarah who shrugged, then turned to Anita with one word. "How?"

Everyone's head turned to Anita who shrugged, too. She had no answer as to how a person who was dead for seven whole days was standing in front of them alive. Not one. As usual, nothing made sense.

"What? You expect me to know?" Anita was sarcastic, then she sighed. "But, when I tested Sarah, no Wolfsbane existed in her body - and there should have been traces of it somewhere! Her body shows no sign of ever having been pregnant. I'm more confused than ever. I don't have a clue. Not one, single, fucking clue! The only one that could possibly be true is The Creator."

Sarah looked at Sam, then the rest of her friends surrounding her stopping on Kaitlan's face.

Then, Sam whispered. "Is it me, or does anyone else notice a recurring theme?"

"Canaan and Tara sent me back." Sarah told them quietly, shocking everyone into silence.

OK. That was soooo not what she expected Sarah to say.

"My Father *and* Mother, Sarah?"

Sarah turned to face the window. This was going to be hard, but still …. She turned back.

"Yeah. I spoke with both Canaan and Tara. It's still a bit fuzzy in places. They told me many things, but I will tell you this. Just before I died, Sam found a scroll. A very important scroll tucked behind another one in the library."

Geez, that sounded so weird! She looked at Sam again. His smile was radiant as he presented the small scroll to Kaitlan, laying it on the table in front of her. Everyone looked at it as if it would bite them! It was very small with what looked to be a solid, silver rod on either side, ancient as the Earth. Kaitlan looked up at Sarah asking a silent question.

"Bloody hell! It's not a damn snake, people!" Sarah whined. "Don't touch the rod. It's solid silver. This was, obviously, never meant to be touched by us. Look at the wax seal. It has not been broken since it was placed on it."

Kaitlan stared down at the seal. It was blurry at first, but as the shock of Sarah's being alive wore off, the blur went away, and she saw a tiny, White Wolf.

"Well, shit! Do you see that?" Kaitlan asked to no one.

"Sarah and I believe that only the White Wolf can touch the scroll, and maybe the silver rod. We think it is meant for you to break the seal, Kaitlan," Sam told her.

She looked up at Cordone. He looked back at her, shrugged, then gave her a nod.

Kaitlan picked up the scroll handling it carefully. She stroked the parchment carefully feeling its age. In here, may be the key everyone has needed for thousands of years. This was a historical moment! OK. Perhaps she was exaggerating a bit, but it was still pretty cool.

Her hand touched the silver by accident, but this silver did not hurt her at all. She knew, instinctively, that it was not silver.

"Not silver, Sarah. Platinum," she said aloud.

The wax seal was a wolf - a white wolf. It was the same mark that was on her hip. Of course, only Cordone and Sarah knew about her birthmark. Cordone loved that mark. He'd bitten it enough times. Kaitlan looked up at him, and she saw the silent amusement in his eyes as he recognized the seal. Her eyes darted to Sarah who was grinning at her knowingly. Kaitlan's eyes narrowed warning both of them to keep their mouths shut about her birthmark.

Slowly, her fingers felt a tingle as she rubbed her hand over the seal. It felt right. She placed her fingernail underneath the seal, and broke it. A howl of monstrous proportions was heard giving them all of them goose bumps.

She unrolled the scroll. It was simple. And, on it, was The White Wolf Prophecy. They all looked, but it was definitely not the one they had in their archives. There appeared to be an additional, fourth verse, but she couldn't read the words. They were written in another language she did not recognize.

Kaitlan frowned. It looked like total gibberish to her, so she gave it to Sarah.

Sarah felt honored, and she read the words silently to herself first. She realized something wasn't right, and then she knew! But, she had to explain first.

Sarah looked at everyone around the table. After reading it, her theory was confirmed, and then remembered what she had been told.

"All of you have been taught for thousands upon thousands of years this version."

When the White Wolf appears,
All that once was,
Will yet again be,
Beware that danger is not past.

Evil still present,
Will cause to suffer,
That which is,
To not last.

Find the one who cursed our worlds,
Or succeed in task will he.
For if he wins, the second time,
Our fate forever will be cast

"Is this right?" she asked again.

Everyone nodded their head. For Kaitlan it was relatively new, but the rest had been taught this forever.

"You have always interpreted it as werewolves will be able to mate in the wolf form, and children will be born, yada, yada, yada." More agreements in nods. "Apparently, you were only partially right. But," and she looked around before she continued. "What you were taught was incomplete."

Again, she paused for effect, watching everyone's face show puzzlement.

"What are you getting at, Sarah?" Cordone asked.

"An entire verse was left out, with a slight change in some existing words. Here is how The White Wolf Prophecy should read."

She pointed to the words on the parchment as Kaitlan held the scroll open for her. What Sarah didn't know was that it was written in an ancient language no one else could read. Only she could read it, and she did - silently. She gave everyone else time to read it as well.

When the White Wolf appears,
All that once was,
Will yet again be,
Beware that danger is not past.

Four there were,
Four were cursed.
Four there are,
Four are blessed.

Evil still present,
Will cause to suffer,
That which is,
To not last.

The one who cursed our worlds returns,
From the beginning and to the last.
For if he wins, the second time,
Our fate, forever, will be cast.

"A fourth verse was missing from your original Prophecy. And, more than that, two lines in the last verse are not the same! Do you see?" she asked pointing to the words on the parchment. All around her had puzzled looks on their faces.

Everyone looked at each other. While it was obvious a fourth verse did exist, no one knew what point Sarah was trying to make other than just a missing part. They couldn't read it!

Sarah huffed, and flopped down into the chair behind her. She rolled her eyes, and shook her head.

When she looked up at them again, all she saw were faces with questions. Lots of questions. She hung her head. OK. She'd try it - again!

"What? Can't you read? It's plain as it can be, and right here in black and cream!" exclaimed Sarah. After all, parchment was a cream color, not white.

Sam put his arm around her. "Sarah, love, it's not in a language any of us can read!"

~ 15 ~
Did I say that Puzzles are relative? Everything is relative!

Sarah's mouth dropped as she stared at Sam. What? What did they mean they couldn't read the writing? She turned back to look at the words. They were clear as a bell to her, and they were written in English.

Sarah was surrounded by puzzled faces. She was totally bumfuzzled as to why Sam would say they couldn't read it! Why were they teasing her about this?

"What do you mean, Sam? What language? It's written in English, right there, plain and simple!" Sarah admonished him tapping the scroll.

"Uh, no it's not," Dan informed her. "All we see are scribbles - runes, if you will."

She looked at all of them in surprise, then back at the scroll.

"Really?"

Nods all around the table made her realize they were not joking.

Sarah dropped her head shaking it in disbelief. She looked back up. In the back of her mind, she wondered how she was able to read the ancient text in the first place. She had no explanation. So, why could she read it, and they couldn't? Runes? She looked at it again. Nope. No runes. Plain English!

"OK. I don't get it, but I'll read it aloud."

After Sarah read it, everyone still looked a bit puzzled. What was this about "the four"?

"Moving on," Lynne said. "How does adding four more lines make a difference?" Lynne asked what everyone else was thinking.

"Don't you get it? The White Wolf Prophecy, the one

you have all known forever? It's a *forgery*!" Sarah's voice went up an octave.

Mouths dropped.

"A forgery?" Cordone yelped.

Sam repeated it. "A forgery? Are you saying that we've been misled all this time?"

"Oh, for goodness sakes! Sam found the original scroll a week ago. We had no time to tell anyone, before I was murdered! The scroll you know was forged. The one who cursed us had the forgery as well. He wanted to curse the entire supernatural world! The person was who translated the Prophecy misunderstood it. He translated the word 'world', but it was 'worlds'.

"Holy fucking hell!" Richard yelled.

"OK. I'll ask it. Who the hell forged it?" Kaitlan asked.

"Dunno. But, two things are clear. One, someone in the distant past manufactured a forged scroll from the original scroll, and there was a conscious thought to hide the original. Although, why we found it fairly easily is a mystery at the moment. Two, the verse that was left out tells what was needed to invoke the curse, who was needed to invoke the curse, what is needed to break the curse, and how to break the curse."

"You've lost me," Richard stated. The others agreed with nods, and uh-huhs.

Sarah read it aloud, and as she read, she interpreted what it meant as she, suddenly, remembered what Tara and Canaan had told her. At last, everything she had assumed was right in front of her eyes. She was absolutely ecstatic as she read the following:

"1) Four there were:
The four elements - earth, water, air, and fire - were needed to cast it.

2) Four were cursed:
These were Elementals - four women from each supernatural race were used

3) Four there are:
The four elements are needed to stop Zanack

4) Four are blessed:
The four Elementals - women - from those the supernatural races must stop him"

More puzzled looks. They still didn't get it? Sarah rolled her eyes for the umpteenth time! She was tired. Strange from someone who had been dead. Well, strange from the point that she had been dead for seven days, but hey! Who hasn't had that happen to them at one time or another? Obviously, everyone still didn't quite understand what she was trying to say. She tapped her chin trying to think of a way to explain it better.

"Look," Sarah tried again, trying to keep it as simple as possible. "It took Four women who were granted the privilege of wielding the four elements of earth, water, air, and fire. Those same four women came from the four races of beings on Earth - Werewolves, Vampires, and Elves."

She looked around. Hmmmm. She wondered who would ask the question.

"Now, all of these were needed to make the curse permanent. Yet, it was flawed. Remember when I told you that it was like old LP's that were scratched? How they 'skipped', and you wouldn't get the entire song? Well, that's exactly what we have. We already deduced that one of the elementals must have been missing during the original curse, keeping Zanack from invoking the curse permanently. It is also an assumption, but a good one, that because of the forged scroll, Zanack may not have known that he needed all four elements, so he proceeded to invoke it anyway. It's obvious that he has realized, by now, that the curse was not as permanent as he thought. That's the reason for all these attacks. But, he also doesn't know about the real scroll - at least not yet - but he will. And, since we know someone on the council is Zanack, well, he will find out fast enough when we show this to the council. By trying to kill at least one of the four of us, he is actually hurting his second chance to invoke the curse again. He needs all the four elementals. And, once he finds out I am alive, well …."

Cordone who had been sitting forward, elbows on the table with his fingers in a pyramid leaned back in understanding, started to speak, but was interrupted by Anita.

"Wait a sec," Anita said. "Elementals? Are you trying to tell us that the four of us are these Elementals?"

"And, Anita gets the golden apple award!" laughed Sarah.

"It's so good to have you back!" Lynne hugged her, laughing.

"Moving on. Sarah, what you are saying is that women from each group of supernaturals - Werewolf, Elf, and Vampire. But, you only mention three? What is the other race?"

Sarah nodded, and rolled her eyes. "And, Cordone gets the 'you paid attention award'! The fourth race is human, of course!"

Suddenly, everyone was talking at once. Sam's pride in his mate was evident on his face. In an instant, she had put together what no one else had done in thousands of years! But, to be fair, no one had the original scroll.

"That's my sexy girl!" he told her privately. *"Wait till I get you home!"*

Sarah grinned at Sam. *"Why do I need to wait? Can't we just do sexarobics in your office?"*

Sam laughed out loud drawing odd looks from

everyone.

"But, humans are not part of the supernatural world." Anita pointed out, and it was followed with nods of agreement.

"But they are, Anita! The number FOUR is all over the place! Four elements, four women, and four races. Besides, do we not live in this world? Do supers not live, and work, side-by-side with humans in this world? Just because humans do not know supers exist, does not mean that humans are not a supernatural race just like us. All races have supernatural powers of some kind, and humans are no different! Look at the facts. We have four women around this table … from the four races of the Earth. I am human and elf; Kaitlan is human, elf, and werewolf; Anita is full werewolf; and, even though Lynne is Elf, and while no longer a vampire, she was. I doubt that all traces have been removed entirely. Anita can confirm if I am right or not. The last Elementals also came from all four races of Earth."

Anita's shocked face was priceless! How did Sarah know that she had found traces of vampire still within them? Anita had never meant that to become public knowledge, but had kept it a secret known only to herself. Well, now the werewolf was out of the bag, and she had no choice but to confirm it.

"Sarah's right. Although both Richard and Lynne were vampires, and aren't now, there is a tiny trace of the vampire gene still within them. It's a disabled gene. But, she's also right about the fact that their DNA was altered. I suspected that the vampire gene became dormant upon their mating. Technically, both are still vampires, but they have no symptoms at all, and they never will again. Well, unless they are bitten, again, that is."

That flat out shut everyone up in an instant.

Anita suddenly realized that Sarah looked, well, different to all of them. What had happened to her? Her eyes were loving and kind as always, but her ability to understand what no one else had been able to in thousands of years boggled her mind. There was something definitely something different about her. And, Lynne noticed, too.

"Sarah? What's with the eyes?"

Sarah looked at her in confusion.

"Huh?"

Kaitlan realized it, too. Sarah's skin glowed with a transparency almost paper thin. Her eyes had speckles of glittering gold within her clear blue eyes. Her hair was a brighter red than ever before. Her eyes looked at you, but appeared to be seeking your soul. Kaitlan's mind struggled to describe her. She snapped her fingers! That's it! Sarah looked Ethereal! That's the word! No doubt about it. Angelic, perhaps? How about ethereally angelic? But, what happened to her?

Sam just stood there, and smiled at Kaitlan when she turned to him.

"Well?" Sarah kept talking pretending not to hear Lynne's question. "Am I not right? There are four races in this world - at least within our known existence. Each with their own unique quality. For thousands of years, they have mated/married with the other species. In other words, our entire species are actually a mixture of all races. Very few are pure-blooded any longer. Lynne is an anomaly."

No one said anything as they continued to listen to Sarah who seemed to know things they did not. But, she was making sense, now. In fact, they realized that she was right.

"I'm going out on a limb, here, but I'm assuming that the first four women were probably pure blooded having no mixed blood. Each one of them was also directly connected with one of the four elements of Earth, Water, Air and Fire. Of course, by now, that would no longer be true. Most of us are a mixture of different races. That means that Zanack, or whoever, cursed all of us."

"Wait. Humans aren't cursed," Lynne said.

"Were they not? Humans have their own abilities that are blocked. Empaths are just an example. They connect with others through emotions, but only ten percent of their brains is used, whereas prior to the curse, they used ninety percent! There are those who do have these powers, but it's only haphazard at best. They only know something is different about them, and they can connect somewhat, but not completely. Empathy, remote viewing, and ESP are what they call it not knowing that those abilities were blocked by the curse."

Sarah heard a plopping as Kaitlan fell into a chair, while the others' mouths dropped open. Humans had abilities, too? Would that mean that at one time, even humans knew about the supers? Maybe worked with them? If so, that would put a whole new twist on the world as they knew it!

"While humans have pretty much lost their history beyond the past three thousand years, the other three races have lost only a small portion. The Prophecy was one of these. Someone in the super world took that verse out to make sure that no one could ever enact it. What they didn't know was that it could still be cast using only a part of it. Doomed to fail from the get-go. If anyone had found one person who could wield all four elements they probably wouldn't need four separate people. But, no one has that power."

"That made a hell of a lot of sense," Cordone thought sarcastically to Kaitlan.

"It does to her. Sarah has obviously acquired the ability to understand things that we can't," Kaitlan answered.

Something was bugging Kaitlan. She remembered one person who could wield all four elements, but she couldn't remember who it was. Man, she hated it when she had a brain fart!

Sarah was still talking. "Numbers are a huge part of our lives. It is the universal language in everything. Other numbers are associated with other things - even creation. I was told by Canaan and Tara that the four of us," pointing at herself, Kaitlan, Anita, and Lynne, "have been granted the powers of these elements. When Kaitlan became The White Wolf on Canaan's death, she was the catalyst that effectively made the curse null and void. When the rest of us mated on Cordone's land, and we still don't know what that connection is, the curse was broken. I'm guessing that his land has some kind of magical properties that we don't understand. Probably upon mating in wolf form would just be another guess on my part."

"The next will be the hardest for them to believe," Sam thought. Sarah nodded without answering him.

"Anita, I keep hearing everyone say that nothing is making sense. The reason is because. it doesn't make sense. It can't! There are missing parts of history. Missing parts of time. With Kaitlan becoming the White Wolf, everything has changed, but everything is still only partial. What we are experiencing is not a break in history, but a break in the timeline."

Anita nodded. "Well, that makes me feel a tiny bit better. And, that is the reason my tests don't make sense."

"The curse was complicated enough, and had to be cast by someone with the knowledge of the darkest of arts. Does anyone here have any idea who might have this ability, Richard? Who has abilities to cast curses?"

Sarah turned her eyes directly to Richard.

The only one older than all of them was Richard. No one had ever asked him his age. Indeed, they were a bit scared to ask. No one wanted to piss off a Viking King. Well, it was time to piss him off, now. Everyone turned to look at Richard.

Richard crossed his arms against his massive chest, and didn't say a thing, but narrowed his eyes at Sarah. How did she know what she knew, he wondered?

"Richard. You are the oldest one of us here. I understand how you must feel, but this is bigger than your hiding from us the truth about who you are, and it is even bigger than all of us put together. We have to know the truth. Who could cast this curse? Please, Richard. Tell us? Tara and Canaan said it was your story to tell." Sarah begged him.

All eyes turned to Richard in surprise.

"Geez! It's beginning to look like a bloody tennis

match!" Sarah said to Sam who laughed silently. *"I mean, all this turning of heads reminds me of it!"*

Now, Richard was out and out glaring at Sarah. His secret had been protected for thousands of years, and this little snippet of a girl was calling him out. How did she know?

Richard pushed his chair back, dropped his arms, and headed to the windows staring at nothing. While he looked out onto the skyline, Dan had another question.

"Sarah? What about the change in the last four lines? What does it mean?"

The one who cursed our worlds returns,
From the beginning and the last.
For if he wins, the second time,
Our fate, forever, will be cast.

"I don't know, yet, Dan. It is as confusing to me as to you. I guess we'll find out when it's time for whatever."

Dan nodded in agreement.

Ignoring that part for the time being, Sarah turned back to Richard. He could feel her eyes on his back. Hell! He had no wish to tell them who he really was. Indeed, he'd almost forgotten it himself. He didn't want to remember. He looked down, and rubbed his neck. He was caught, and he knew it. But what would Lynne say? For the first time in all his thousands of years of life, he was actually scared.

"Sorcerers, of course. After all, they were the fifth race, but were wiped out long ago due to fear."

Everyone's mouth gaped open in surprise.

"A FIFTH race? What the hell, Richard!" Anita exclaimed.

"I know. Well, it's time for truth. Please, follow me." And he strode out of the room with Lynne following behind him.

"Where are we going?" Lynne asked him. He looked at his mate. What would she think of him when she knew the truth?

"Beneath The Hall of Records."

~ 16 ~
Never Judge a book by its cover … or … Just don't make assumptions

Richard led them all to the cavern that housed The Hall of Records. The ones who had yet to see it gasped in awe at the sight before them. A chorus of voices sounded at the same time.

"Wow!"

"Holy Cow!"

"No, freakin' way!"

"What are we doing here?" Cordone demanded of Richard, thoroughly confused.

"Bear with me, my friend, for it is time for you to know the truth," he begged Cordone. "Please, hear me out, before you act."

Cordone stared at Richard, then nodded. The lift took them down to the main floor.

Instead of leading them inside The Hall of Records, he made a detour to a door in shadow at the left of the lift. A locked door to which only Richard had a key. He opened the door seeing Cordone frown at the key. Why did he not know about this door?

Richard continued to lead them to another elevator taking them further down, and beneath The Hall of Records. Richard met Cordone's suspicious eyes.

When the elevator stopped, Richard stepped out, and to the left allowing them full view of what was below them. One by one they filed onto a lift, much like the one in the Hall, only to stop short at what they saw before them with gaping mouths.

Before them, a huge cavern of monstrous proportions, even larger than The Hall of Records, revealed ruins. Ancient ruins of a huge village. No. More like a city! One that had obviously been devastated long ago. Scorch marks of fire were evident. Destructive forces had reigned here. Almost as one entity, they turned to look at him.

"There's that tennis match thing, again," giggled Sarah to Sam who gave her a "shut the hell up" look.

"What is this, Richard?" Lynne asked stunned. "and, how the hell did this get down here?"

Richard took her hand. "This, my dear Linora, was my village, once. And, because of this village, the curse was enacted."

He turned to look at the stunned group.

"And, my name, at this time in history…" he paused, "…was Zanack."

At first, everyone was frozen in place. Then all hell broke loose as the men tried to catch him. Richard jumped, and landed next to a village wall far down below. Richard looked up, motioning everyone to come down to the ruins.

Jumping from the great height to the cavern below, Cordone grabbed Richard's arms, while the rest of the group rode down on the lift. He pulled Richard's arms behind them, his face full of disbelief and anger. Richard did not struggle against him.

"No! You can't be! I killed Zanack myself! What the fuck, man?" Then, he drew back. "Who the hell are you?"

"Please. Cordone, you have always been a fair man. A great man of honor. Will you listen before you act?" Richard looked at his mate with sad eyes.

Lynne was frozen in place with a tear running down her cheek, but her body was beginning to glow with her pure Elf form in reaction to Richard's containment. Dan and Sam had to act quickly. If they didn't, and her power was not stopped, it would be too late for any of them. Before they could do so, though, the other girls put their arms around Lynne to comfort her, and it was working. Lynne's glow dissipated. Kaitlan had no doubt that Lynne would have killed someone. Nope. Never gonna happen on her watch!

Cordone's eyes were blazing black, Dan was on the verge of changing, and Sam looked as if he would attack at any second as he felt betrayed by his friend. They gritted their teeth in anger. It had better be good. Before them stood the most notorious evil I history - the one who cast the curse.

"Please?" Richard asked. "Do you mind?"

Cordone looked at Dan and Sam who nodded, and he let Richard loose remaining close by his side. Richard started pacing as he began to speak.

"I was born in the year - well, the year really doesn't matter. Let's just say I am a bit older than Mount Everest."

Lynne's eyes widened. Just how old was her mate? Did she even really know him?

"Eric, what the fuck is going on? Just who are you?" Lynne yelled at him.

He looked into Lynne's eyes, and shook his head.

"There was, once, a fifth race of beings on this planet. They were known as wizards, or sorcerers. Take your pick."

"Richard, what are you taking?" Dan asked.

Ignoring Dan, Richard continued. "This village held all five races of Earth, and it was, once, the most beautiful place on the planet! All races were long lived to the point of immortality."

He saw the question in Sarah's eyes.

"Yes, Sarah. Even humans. We lived in peace together. There was nothing but cooperation, and great respect for each other."

How was he going to do this?

"I was a very young man. My Father knew that the norm was to offer one's child as an apprentice, and arranged for me to become one with one of the greatest of wizards of all time."

When Anita's mouth started to open to ask the obvious question, he waved her silent. She obeyed, but had no idea why. Richard took a deep breath, and continued.

"His name? Odfrin. I hated my Father for sending me to this primitive village. I hated my own life. It wasn't long until I realized that the physical body was not Odfrin's, but that Odfrin, the wizard, had, somehow, taken the life of a simple human, infusing him with his power." A little lie, but necessary. "The human had been destroyed when Odfrin took it. Other wizards, who had great power, were no match for Odfrin, and they cowered before him. Because he knew that I was incredibly strong, he forced me to learn from him. He was more powerful than any other being on Earth at the time. Even with my great strength, I could not break from him."

Richard looked at Lynne, and tried to walk over to her. Dan and Sam stopped him watching Lynne take a step backward with tears in her eyes. The hurt in her eyes pained him more than anything he had ever felt. All because of him. He hung his head, and was silent for a long time.

He, finally, took a deep breath. He'd rehearsed this for years, just in case.

"Odfrin was an out and out nutcase. He gave me the name of Zanack - the identity of the prior human he had killed, and inhabited." Again, another lie, but needed.

Anita had to ask, "Sure sounds like some form of parasite. It certainly fits the definition of one."

Gasps were heard at the question. What did she mean?

"True. I never thought of it that way. When he discovered that I would not do what he wanted, I was beaten until I was almost dead, and then thrown into his version of a dungeon. I healed quickly, but he never returned. I used that time to rebuild my muscles and my mind. I was not, yet, a werewolf."

Stares just bombarded him after that revelation. Not a werewolf yet?

"How long were you there?" Cordone sighed. Then, "You were turned. How?"

"Honestly, Cordone, I don't know. But, I have a guess. I was fed only once a day, but I don't know who did it. I was there a long time."

"How long, Richard?" Lynne finally was able to squeak words out.

"By my calculations? Maybe twenty years." OK. That much was true.

"Holy shit!"

"No fucking way!"

"Hell and damnation!"

They all thought the same thing. How could a man who looks like Richard, come out of something like that for so long with tremendous strength? How was that possible? If only they knew all of it, but he couldn't risk it.

"Suddenly, out of nowhere, Odfrin returned. Let me explain. I had always been a hothead, always picking fights. And, that is what he fed on. By now, he had another idea. I would be the first of his experiments to create a hybrid being. He overpowered me."

"How did he overpower you?"

"A sure fire way. Like everyone else. Wolfsbane."

More gasps and cussing hit the walls of the cavern.

"It was used to immobilize me. He took me into the forest to a place where he knew rogue werewolves ran, and tied me to a tree." He visibly shook at the memory. "The rogues bite could turn anyone into werewolves in those days. Unlike Dan, there was no one to bring them back, or to kill them. As much as Odfrin despised hybrids, he desperately wanted to create them for his own personal watch dogs. He planned on killing them once they served their purpose. I was to be the first, and leader."

Cordone watched Richard carefully as he leaned against one of the destroyed village rock walls, and crossed his arms. Richard was every inch a powerful being. Cordone wondered why he had never noticed it before, noting the pain and regret on Richard's face.

"I was bitten many times over, and I turned into a were. Honestly, I don't know how I survived that many bites. The consequence for me was to become a far more powerful being. Odfrin waited for my first turn. But, I discovered that my mind was as clear as possible - and even more so in my wolf form, so I skittered off into the forest, and never looked back. I was not going to be used as his tool in whatever his warped mind had planned. Odfrin, however, was obsessed. I know he searched for me, but he never found me. When I discovered this village," sweeping it with an arc of his arm, "I lived happily for many years working my way up to rule."

Seeing their faces, he amended, "It was actually a very democratic society, and we lived in peace. One day, while I was away on a hunting trip with some of my fellow villagers, the destruction occurred. What we found upon our return angered me to the point I craved killing whoever had done it. From the description of a few he left alive, but dying, I recognized the power to be Odfrin's, but it wasn't Odfrin. The physical description didn't fit. I realized that he must have taken over another human body, and was using the name he gave to me as well as the one before him."

Kaitlan's eyebrows shot up as she looked around her. "This? This is the result of the original curse?"

"Yes. I discovered, too late, that the curse directly affected the village. The power must have been massive. There was nothing I could have done. It was at this point that I realized that this world had no protector. So, I decided that it was time to be the protector of all who lived on Earth. I made a vow to do so, much to my Father's anger, and have never broken it. I could not stop everything from happening, of course, because only the Creator has that type of power.

Other survivors of the village, described the destruction as a 'dragon' who used its fire to destroy the village. Next, a massive wind that twirled counter clockwise able to lift even the heaviest of equipment. A tornado, of course, and finally, followed by a flood. I recognized three of the four elements at work of fire, wind and water. But, all I could get out of the last person before he died, was that four of village's women, one his only sister, had been taken from it the previous week. These women were, obviously, the Elementals. I urged the people left to flee to other villages. Since I had learned some wizardry from Odfrin, I used those powers to bury what was left of the village beneath a ton of Earth into this cavern. I wasn't thinking, and used a basic spell using the earth, but it worked. After a few weeks, I encountered other supers, and discovered that their ability to procreate had been stopped - or at least slowed down drastically. It was by using the element of the Earth to bury the village, I realize, now, that it was I who had triggered the curse - retroactively. Whatever I had done, it was very basic, and it was only temporary for a few years, before it was negated. When it did, the curse was only in partial effect, and time skewed and skipped.

For a time, I felt such guilt, I became reckless, and my old self again began courting any excuse for a fight. I would fight anyone, or anything. I kept hoping that I would find someone who could best me. I failed."

"Wait. You wanted to die?" Lynne said in horror.

"I did. I couldn't live with myself." Richard hung his head in shame.

Lynne covered her mouth in horror at the thought that she may have never met her mate! If *none* of them had met him!

He dipped his head thinking. He couldn't bear to see contempt in their eyes, but most especially from Linora.

Everyone was captured by the story, listening intently. Kaitlan was becoming more confused. He was Zanack. Not THE Zanack. Just the second Zanack, of three? She was getting such a headache!

"It was then I realized I was right. That Odfrin had taken over a human body. Before the destruction, I had heard of a new, powerful wizard. This new power appeared to carry even more power than Odfrin. I had not heard his name, but I caught a glimpse of him in his real form, once, and he wasn't …"

He looked at Cordone. "What? What wasn't he, Richard?"

"Uh, the same person." If they only knew! "This is why I believe Anita was right. Parasite. That is the best description I have heard. He must change hosts when the one he inhabits fails. Cordone, what this Zanack showed Teri was nothing! Even as long as I will live, I will never erase the horrors from my mind that I discovered as I roamed the land, and discovered, later, that he was calling himself Zanack. I changed my name, of course, which I had kept until then, and disappeared."

"Must have been about the time we killed him," Cordone said. Cordone's stomach clinched tightly in fear. Wait!

"Richard, did we even kill Zanack?"

"No. It was probably a patsy. I'm betting that he took the body of someone else when you did."

"Who?" Cordone asked. Deep in thought, Cordone was beginning to understand exactly what had happened. He told Kaitlan his suspicion. *"A council member. That's whose body he took over."*

Kaitlan's eyes darted to her mate. *"Who?"*

"I don't know."

Richard shook his head. "Don't know, Cordone. I changed my name to Eric, and founded a Kingdom. My kingdom held the view that everyone was welcome, and again, I found a place to live in peace for many years. Then, the Vampire wars came. After they were over, I had sent my people home. I wish I had not, but I tried to make sure that the rogue vampires were completely destroyed. But, you know what they say about hindsight. I found Linora who had been tortured by the vampires. When we found the rogues attacking Canaan and Sam, years later, well…you know the rest, now."

He looked at Lynne whose face shot up in confusion.

"What do you mean? Tortured?" she asked, scared of

the answer.

Richard walked over, and knelt in front of her. His hand took hers.

"I never wanted you to know this, my love. But, it was wrong to keep it from you. You remembered nothing about what you had told me when I found you. You weren't just a vampire. You were an Elf. Your village had been devastated, and all Elves killed. Many of the rogue vampires had apparently raped you repeatedly, drank from you, and left you for dead. Then, one returned to rape you again, and this time, he turned you into one of them. You told me how you ran like a bat out of hell (no pun intended) as fast, and as far, as you could until you collapsed. When I found you, your turn was complete. You had killed a moose draining it of its blood. You were covered in blood from your hair to your feet, and your mouth was dripping with blood after your kill."

Lynne's eyes widened in even more horror as she listened to him. It can't be true!

"Because you were new, you were out of control, and bit me. Yet, for some reason, you cared for me until I turned. But, it still took me days on end to gain even a part of your trust. You just wanted to forget." His eyes met hers. "Linora, you were terribly close to losing your mind, and your mind must have shut down. Effectively, it was so traumatic, it blocked your memory. A vampire Elf who became crazy to the point of Elven rage would have been among the worse things ever seen. I'm glad we discovered, later, that it wasn't the case. The alternative was too terrifying to contemplate. I couldn't let it happen, and you didn't want to remember."

Lynne was crying by this point. She still didn't remember any of it. Things made so much more sense, now. She was glad she couldn't remember the rapes. Now, she had even more to be grateful for from this man who was her mate. She threw her arms around him holding him tight to her. Even with all of this confession, he hardened for his mate. Looking at everyone over her shoulder as he held her, he finished.

"I had deliberately hid my name of Zanack, and who I was in hopes of finding a way to reverse the curse, but I had no knowledge of The White Wolf Prophecy until long after my own kingdom was destroyed. Lynne and I came to Canaan's Father to protect him. When I found out, I scoured The Hall of Records for years upon years trying to find something. I had every intention of trying to reverse the curse if I could, but I needed a clue as to how to do it. And, now, I know, thanks to Sarah. She is right. The spell will continue, but only with the gaps in time. The rest has been reversed, and for that, we should be glad. Zanack will not take it lightly. That is why, Anita, nothing makes sense to anyone. We are experiencing a timeline anomaly, because of the curse."

He was not done, but his mate was in his arms, and her crying had finally ceased. She drew back, and pressed her lips to his. He kissed her back.

The assembled group was silent for a long, long time. Each person deep within their own thoughts.

Cordone broke the silence first, and stepped forward to shake Richard's hand.

"It is we who should apologize. The one thing I have always prided myself on is to listen to both sides. I broke my own rule. You may rest, now, my friend. As Alpha, hereby absolve you from all transgressions."

Richard released one of his arms around his mate to shake Cordone's hand.

"Thank you, my friend. That's one mystery finally solved. Thank you, Sarah, for helping me heal today," said Richard. He walked over to her, and kissed her forehead.

Everyone looked at Sarah with sad smiles, yet pride in her amazing accomplishment. Kaitlan ran over to her bestie, and hugged her tightly.

"Well, so, now. Where do we go from here?" Anita was asking the question everyone else was thinking.

Kaitlan turned, still with her arm around Sarah. The White Wolf showing in her eyes.

"It's not going that's the problem. It's getting the monster that has plagued the supers for thousands of years. That's the problem!"

To Cordone she thought, *"You know, someone dedicated themselves to the protection of the beings on Earth, but I can't remember who it was?"*

"What are you talking about, Kaitlan?"

Kaitlan shrugged. As they all began to leave, Lynne looked at Kaitlan. Kaitlan knew that look. Lynne needed to speak to Richard alone. OK. So. Maybe not to talk! Kaitlan was so ready to spread her legs for Cordone to take her!

"Stop that thought right now if you don't want me to attack you right here in front of everyone, gorgeous! I'm horribly horny, right now, and your pussy smells wonderful! I wouldn't care if we had an audience!" Cordone thought to her.

"Did you...did you...? Did you SERIOUSLY just say 'pussy'?"

Oh damn! She clinched her thighs together as she came! They were always trying to get the other one to come, and that one did it! She smiled as she considered pushing him! Kaitlan sent him a visual feeling of how she had come, and was intensely satisfied when he groaned with his own orgasm. YES! Finally! She'd done it!

"Watch your pants, mate!" she smirked just to add fuel to the fire!

After they all left the cavern, and especially after the visual she had sent him, Cordone pulled Kaitlan to his office, and locked the door where he stripped them both. He plopped her naked ass on top of his desk, and his hard cock found its way inside of her with one thrust! Kaitlan groaned as he rocked in her tight channel until they both experienced a massive orgasm when he exploded his seed inside of her.

~ 17 ~
Who needs enemies with enemies like this?

Now, that everyone was gone, Richard held his mate tightly. He never wanted to let her go.

"I'm so sorry, I wanted to keep you from the truth. I never wanted you to know what had happened to you."

Lynne stroked his face. The moment his lips touched hers gently, the passion between them ignited immediately. It was like going from zero to one thousand miles per sec in a split second! Richard pulled her to him, grinding his erection against her while she groaned with her need for him. Hands flew as fast as possible stripping each other's clothing. Richard picked Lynne up, and she wrapped her legs around his waist letting his swollen cock slide easily into her wet channel. Their loving was fast and furious. When their release came, his semen entered her with an explosive force.

Lynne laid her head on his chest as their breath came hard and fast.

"Your warmth flooded all the way up inside me, Eric!" She was in a state of ecstasy!

"Really?" he wiggled his hard cock that had remained inside of her, and she laughed. "So, want some more?" he teased her, feeling his balls filling quickly.

"As much as you want to give to me, my love. I love you, Eric!"

That's all he needed to know. He was ready to give his mate anything she wanted. She deserved it for having to put up with him. The others could wait a bit longer for them. They had other things that needed their immediate attention!

"As I love you, my Linora."

He hated waiting. He hated waiting where people could almost see his face. But, the Viper was worth waiting for. The deadliest assassin known, he would kill you if you looked at him wrong. In truth, Zanack could kill him without lifting a finger. Viper would soon know. His hours were numbered.

Zanack was still reeling with glee that he'd killed that bitch, Sarah, and her mutant spawn. Moreover, her mate was now dying as well. TWO down! He'd finally succeeded in something! He hadn't seen Teri since she had killed Sarah, and that bothered him a little, but the important thing was that she had followed his orders to the letter. Maybe he ought to keep her on for more missions? Nah! He really looked forward to ripping her to shreds just as he had done to the other woman. His gut had told him Teri might back out of the deal, so, to teach her not to betray him, he had caught up with her, dragging her back down into his basement. She had thrown up the second she smelled his scraps of rotted corpses. He had tied her up. The other woman was waiting tied to the table with a dirty rag muffling her cries. Ah, yes! That was the best taste of meat he'd had in months! And, force-feeding the woman's blood to Teri was an added plus. In fact, forcing her to watch what he did to the woman turned him on! But, now, it was Teri's turn! She was a pretty little thing. Damn! He had a hard-on thinking about enjoying his prey for several hours before he ripped her to pieces for his midnight snack! Zanack licked his lips in anticipation! She'd probably never had anyone as good in the sex department as he was! Thousands of years had taught him how to pretend to pleasure his prey, before they realized what was really happening. Maybe, just maybe, he'd keep her around for a little bit for his own pleasure before he ate her. A sound interrupted his silent plans. He didn't know whether to be glad, or angry, but he'd settle for anger. At least his hard-on would go away, and given his condition, probably for the best.

Viper did not like the light any more than Zanack did, but getting really good help was hard. So, he kept his temper barely under the surface.

"Alpha?" asked the hooded figure appearing, suddenly, in front of Zanack. He'd snuck up on him? That never happened.

"Vip…" He shut up when Viper held up his hand.

"No names. Better that way."

"Agreed. So, what have you found out for me?"

"You mean other than that you are a fucking jackass? Your so-called accomplice, Teri, was discovered, and they executed her. You know nothing about the subtle art of murder."

Zanack shot up straighter.

"You're a fucking liar! Impossible! There is no way they could have found out about her!"

Viper got in Zanack's face. Zanack reeked of death, but Viper was probably the only person on Earth who could stand to smell it.

"*Do not, ever, call me a liar!* You're fucking up a lot lately, and I'm beginning to think you are a damn, piss-ant fraud!" Viper hissed.

"Do not get me angry! I will not hesitate to kill even you!"

Viper laughed out loud. It was not a nice laugh!

"Only if you can catch me, you bastard! Call me *when* you can prove to me you are competent, and prove to me you can carry out a simple murder!" He shot his glowing red eyes at Zanack. "Mark me! It is *my choice* to work with you. But, I do not work *for* anyone. Get it?" He started walking away, then turned. "Get something done right, and then I might consider doing another task. Until then, do not contact me in any way. When I hear you have succeeded, I will contact you!"

The Viper turned his back on him. Zanack's anger was magnified ten-fold! How dare that snake demand to him! How dare he turn his back on him! He had already planned to kill the Viper when he was through with him. He stared at the Viper's swift moving back, and his eyes narrowed.

"I guess I'll just have to kill him a lot sooner than I

thought." He'd definitely lost his usefulness with that stupid move. Viper's arrogance had just sealed his death warrant.

Zanack started after him, then stopped. No. Not until he fed. He could control the situation much better if he ate. Eat first; kill Viper second. As he looked around for his late night snack, his mind drifted to the past.

His deal with the Evil One, to live forever in human form of some type, came at a price. He took another body when the one he was in had lost its usefulness. With the exception of a tiny little detail that had been deliberately left out of that deal. He was required to devour blood and flesh once a day. And, it had to be a living being of any race, even animals. He had tried all the races, and the supers were much harder to catch. Humans were easier, and his favorite food! So, Zanack chose them most of the time. For a change, now and then, he managed to catch one of the supers for a treat. Few strayed into his territory limiting his choices. He still held the resentment and hatred toward that old bastard for what he did, but the ability to be more than immortal was an elixir that he could not resist. He had sacrificed humans for a long time on plenty of altars in many forms.

He sighed for the "old days" remembering when humans were such uneducated sheep. He, and a few others who held power over them, had denied them knowledge while the select elite had it all. It made it so much easier to rile them up. One voice … just one voice (his of course), preyed upon their stupidity into accepting what he said without so much as a question. He hit them where it mattered most. The old "the elite were causing their sad lot in life" was a classic tactic, and they believed. Worked every time in every age! Always behind the rise, and fall, of many conquerors, Zanack found it was easy to control them. Now, while Hitler was one of his best, the fact was that he much preferred Genghis Khan. Khan was the one who was a hero to some, and a butcher to others.

Long before Khan, though, he had helped develop ritual human sacrifice in South America. They had, yet, to use sacrifices, and Zanack just stepped it up a bit, by adding altars. He, then, urged the priests to cut the living hearts out of the chests of the chosen, and eat it, making sure the people watched them do it, driving fear into their subjects' hearts. And, they were willing to even give up their own children for sacrifice.

When he deposed their high priests, he took over. Until then, he had lived on mostly the blood of humans, and the flesh of animals. But, when he ate the living human heart, Zanack found it gave him a burst of power. It wasn't long before he realized that almost any human organ gave him that boost. He had loved it, but it had to be fresh from the body. Ah, for the good old days when humans were so ignorant!

As the years went by, he had learned to stalk only those who had no family such as the homeless, the drunks, and the whores. He felt tremendous power the younger his prey was, and especially from a woman's organs. He hated women even more than he hated men. No reason. To him, they were nothing but cattle that fed his power and lust, and his source for food. Maybe female was on the menu for tonight? And, there she was - with an appetizer!

"Well, lookie-lookie!" Rubbing his hands together. A whore walking her dog down the street. That was a delicacy he had not had in a very long time! He decided, just this once, to break his own rules, and take a chance that no one would look for her! His mouth drooled with hunger as he streaked to claim his two-course meal!

~ 18 ~
Werewolves, and Vampires and Elves, oh my!
(You knew I was going to say it at some point, didn't you?)

The Master Council, finally, convened in the O'Hara council room, after several delays. The MC, for short, consisted of four supers … Cordone, Kaitlan, Ali'on, and Stefan Rico. Truth was that no one wished to be there, and made excuses not to come until they had to do so. To convene the Master Council, more often than not, was for declaring war. No one wanted war. Stefan Rico, elected Vampire Leader for thousands of years, had his base in Italy … naturally. He flopped in his seat, and crossed his arms frowning while Ali'on, King of the Elves who was one of the very few, pure-blooded males left, sat tall and straight with a serene look on his face. No one ever bought that serenity. Ali'on was known to be highly deadly. His base of operations was in … well, no one really knew. He just showed up when it was required.   Both were obviously uncomfortable sitting in the same room with each other, and it really would have been very amusing to Kaitlan if this was not a dangerous situation. If anyone had told her a year ago that one, her Father would be murdered, two, she was a werewolf, three, mated to her biggest irritation in life, four, discovered a really bad guy was out to kill the females, six, had twins, and now, seven sat across from a real vampire and an elf, she would have called the men in the white coats to cart her away all on her own!

The Master Council consisted only of the heads of each group of supernaturals. Unknown to the other two, Kaitlan was there to represent the humans since she was half-human.

"What's *she* doing here?" demanded Stefan jerking his head toward Kaitlan.

With the destruction of the rogue vampires, no one trusted any vampire. He was skeptical whenever supers met for anything. He'd hated the rogues, but all of his people had been punished because of them. It still irked him that they had been treated unfairly, especially when they were denied access to The Hall of Records.

"First, she is the female Alpha. Second, she is the heir to the entire Clan. And, third, she is half-human, and since the humans are unaware of us, she is representing them. Any more questions?" Cordone asked. He hated this, but there was more at stake than their petty arguments.

Stefan just folded his arms, and glared.

"This *puny,* little girl is the daughter of Canaan? The half-human? The one who died then lived at birth?" He grunted in disgust.

Cordone darted to Stefan pushing his nose right in his face.

"If you *ever,* again, *dare* to disrespect my mate, I will personally see to it that you are buried so deep in the earth, it'll take you two hundred years to dig yourself out! Do I make myself clear?"

Stefan showed no emotion, but just kept glaring at Kaitlan. After a few moments, he nodded once. Kaitlan had to fight to stop from rolling her eyes at the asshole!

Ali'on, however, took the suave approach, stood, and kissed her hand.

"I am most honored to meet you, Kaitlan, daughter of Canaan O'Hara. How like your Mother you are, my dear!" His eyes were dreamy, and very seductive as he stared into Kaitlan's eyes. Oh, man! What a douche!

"Talk about smarmy! I guess he can get anything he wants with that voice and line!" Kaitlan privately giggled at her thought.

She glanced sideways seeing Cordone's mouth struggling to keep from laughing.

Cordone had told her that while she was allowed to sit in

on this council due to her status as heir, she was not to say one word. She had given him hell over that one, but in the end, agreed. Right now, it was all she could do to keep from gagging.

She nodded to Ali'on with a sickly sweet grin, gritted her teeth, but said nothing. Ali'on glided away to sit back down.

"Cordone, it was with great surprise when your Second contacted us to convene. We have been dealing with our own deaths, but did not realize you, also, were suffering from the loss of your females," Stefan said in a dry tone. He didn't act as if he cared.

Nope. Kaitlan could tell he didn't care at all about weres, or anyone else, either. She wasn't sure he even cared about his own females. Well, let him sneer. She had a back up plan. Geez. Vampires made her want to gag. Well, not all of them. Just vampire jackasses! Stefan qualified totally! Childishly, she wanted to stick her finger in her mouth, and make the gag sound! Vampires were just damn creepy all the way around. Yeesh!

"Ali'on, we believe we are dealing with Zanack. He has taken it upon himself to kill off the females of weres and vampires in the same way that the Elven women were so long ago. What can you tell us about how it happened?" Cordone sat down.

Ali'on stood up. "Zanack? I thought you weres had killed him?"

"Apparently not." Cordone was short.

"No need to tell them the whole truth, Cordone," Kaitlan told him.

Ali'on elaborated. "What we do know is that some random Elf was once jealous of my father's mate. He coveted her, and if he could not have her, then none could have a mate. He found a way of developing a Wolfsbane poison to kill our females slowly, over a very long time. Unfortunately, my Father did not realize it until too late. He was not the smartest Elf on the shelf. He was repeatedly told by some council members that there was a plot to kill the female Elves, but he would not listen. I was but a lad at the time, and even I knew something was wrong.   But, when my Father discovered his horrible mistake, and my Mother was killed, he killed himself, and I became King. Since then, our bloodlines have become diluted. If Anita had not discovered that we could mate with humans, I doubt Elves would exist today." He sat down.

"We already knew that! He's hiding something. Don't know what it is, though. What about the Vampires, Cordone?" She saw Cordone barely nod.

"Stefan, what about your situation?"

"What can I tell you? I already told you. The damn Wolfsbane has killed some of our females! What do you expect me to say? Whoever it is, though, has to be a traitor!"

"Well, that's a big DUH! What a dick!" Kaitlan was having to bite her tongue to keep from saying it out loud to this asshole! Hopefully, it would be her last encounter with this jerk!

"Stefan.   That is not helping us.   How?"   Ali'on demanded with the same serene look, and quiet voice.

"Why don't you go back to fairyland, you damn Elf! Why are you here, anyway? Your females were killed long ago!"

Cordone knew this wasn't going to be easy! He was right.

For the next several minutes, all three men traded stupid insults. And, when she said stupid, Kaitlan meant stupid. Even her own mate! Kaitlan was annoyed at all of them. Since she had been told she was not allowed to speak, she leaned back in her chair, gritting her teeth while observing them.

Ali'on was gorgeous. He was extremely tall. Maybe six foot seven? Eight? His skin was a translucent white with a long, sleek neck, and elongated, oval face. His eyes were a medium lavender with silver sparkles in them that glowed, and his hair was almost a lavender white. Unlike the stereotype Elf, his hair was crisply cut short in a wind-blown style, and had the same silvery sparkles as in his eyes. Even though he was very tall, and lean, his proportions were perfect in every way. He was probably as toned as all the other males she was around. Geez! What was it with the super males? Were they all gorgeous hunks of men? Answer. Yes.

His clothing was a light gray, white pinstriped suit, a crisp, lavender shirt. and light gray tie. His slip-on shoes were white, and highly polished. When he smiled, it was almost blinding with his gleaming white teeth. Kaitlan just waited for one of those little star bursts from his teeth like she saw on TV commercials for toothpaste. She snorted at her joke.

Other than a ring she had noticed as he kissed her hand, he wore no other jewelry. It was extremely intricate which reminded her of vines twisting around a tree. In its center was a single stone of lavender. It wasn't amethyst, of that she was certain. The stone was something that she had never seen in her life. In fact, her own Father had worn a similar ring, but with a tiger's eye stone in its center. The last time she remembered him wearing it was when she was small. The rings must have some significance, yet, Cordone wore no ring. She made a mental note to ask him.

She turned to Stefan. He looked nothing like his stereotype, either. Standing at about five-foot-ten, his hair was a dirty brown which wasn't short, but long to his shoulders, neatly coifed, and shiny, and his eyes were hazel. Like Ali'on, he wore no jewelry except for a ring which sported a ruby. No black leather, or tight fitting jeans for him! His solid black suit looked as if it was straight out of a famous designer's top of the line clothing, and was custom fit to his large chest and lean hips. His shirt was black as well, with a black tie and small flecks of red in it. He was the epitome of a narcissistic and arrogant leader. His teeth were snow white as well, and any female within a thousand miles of him would succumb to his incredible good looks. The problem? He was a prick!

Her own mate sported a black suit, and pale blue shirt and black tie. With his black hair, her heart turned over in her chest as she looked at him. He looked good enough for her to eat! He could be arrogant when the situation called for it. But, if she had seen him on the street, his eyes would scream "Danger Ahead"! Women would lick their chops within ten blocks of his presence, and he'd have his choice of them!

Her eyes narrowed as she sat, and listened to them argue. All three of them were acting like pricks. It was getting them nowhere. Hell! They were worse than old lady gossips!

"That's enough. Get on with it, Stefan. Or, do you not care your females are being killed?"

"What's the diff, Cordone? Why should we care about your females? It's too bad Canaan isn't here! He gave us respect!"

Cordone's eyes glowed blacker than Kaitlan had ever seen them. All black - even the whites of his eyes! Whoa! That was a new one, and obviously did not bode well.

"HELL & DAMNATION! So, you want Zanack to make sure we are all extinct? And, for what? Your own self-aggrandized view of your importance? Would you prefer him to rule over you? If he kills all females, he could easily take over not just *our* world. Zanack is back, damn your hide! What the hell part of that do you not understand?"

Cordone banged his fist on the table, and it jumped, startling Kaitlan.

"You want respect from me? Earn it! But, you will, by God, show me respect! I am not Canaan. He is not here, and I am Alpha, now. Pull your head out of your ass, Stefan. However, if you have nothing more to say, then get the hell out of my building, and out of my territory! I have no qualms with your species completely gone, and I'm quite sure that Anita can come up with a way to hasten it. Unless you want another war? Is that you want? You lost that one, remember?"

Stefan shot up out of his chair in anger.

"How *DARE* you speak to me that way, Cordone Valon! You have not been Alpha for very long! We fought to determine the final outcome of that war, and it ended with my people being treated like dirt! However, if you wish, I'll be very glad to accommodate you a second time!"

"Gentlemen, gentlemen," Ali'on interjected calmly. "This bickering is getting us nowhere!"

~ 19 ~
Save Me from Macho Supers - PLEASE!

Kaitlan was surrounded by way too much testosterone! Seriously? Didn't anyone ever tell men that their incessant, arrogant arguing wasn't going to get anyone anywhere? She looked around at the three men with whom she had the misfortune to be trapped, and gritted her teeth tightly. Right now, she wanted to strangle all three of them! Yes. She was having another GRRRRR day!

Suddenly, she had a vision, and almost laughed out loud.

"Clan Leader Kaitlan did it in the council room with a knife!" Thank goodness for Clue! Good thing no one was paying attention to her.

Cordone growled at Stefan. Stefan hissed at Ali'on. Ali'on sat with the face of patience. Seriously? She could practically feel the anger rolling from all three. At least, it was suddenly silent!

Kaitlan's patience ended. The White Wolf was beyond angry. Kaitlan felt the wolf feed its power to her, and she found her anger magnified ten-fold as the power increased. How dare these sons of bitches act this way! Her own female counterparts were being killed, and this was the attitude of these jackasses? She was finished with this macho crap! She shot up out of her chair ignoring Cordone's warning look. If he thought that was going to stop her, well, he had better get over it, because she was done.

"THAT. IS. ENOUGH!" Kaitlan asserted her authority. "I am damn sick, and fucking tired of having to listen to you bastards indulge yourselves in a pissing contest while you show no respect for your females! It ends here! It ends now!"

Cordone grabbed her shoulder to push her down in her

chair.   Kaitlan swatted it away from her, then turned her glowing green eyes on him with a frightening glare.   Cordone took a step back in surprise. Kaitlan's wolf eyes were showing. Kaitlan was The White Wolf, now - in human form. Shit! He had no idea what this meant. He'd never seen anything like it before. Their wolf eyes never crossed to their human form. Canaan was born that way, but this should be impossible with Kaitlan! It must have startled both Stefan and Ali'on as well, because they were sporting shocked looks.

"I have had it!" Kaitlan enunciated. "If this is the way the Master Council has acted every time they met, no wonder you idiots can't get anything done! You spend more time at war with each other in the council room than discussing a plan of action! Each of you is bound, and determined, to try and force your own fucking desire for power. Well, hell! I won't have it any more! This is my Father's council room! Do you understand me?"

"Kaitlan, don't!" demanded Cordone.

Kaitlan whirled on him with her wolf eyes.

"Shut the hell up, Cordone! I won't sit here, and listen to you idiots fight while the women suffer and die!"

She moved to the other side of the room, and turned to glare at all three men in the room with her White Wolf's eyes. Kaitlan had no idea what was happening to her, but she felt a raw surge of physical power feeding her anger.   At that moment, she knew, without a doubt, that she could easily take on all three men in the room, and defeat them with one finger! The feeling was amazingly powerful, and she loved it!

"Reign in your female, Cordone, or I will do it for you!" yelled Stefan, and he bounded to his feet in fury.

Before Cordone could say anything, Kaitlan's power surged, again, and she had Stefan in a headlock faster than any of the supers could see!

Stefan couldn't move at all, and was completely powerless to escape her grip. Her power was such that she could easily tear Stefan's head off with a mere flick of her wrist.

Shock was in Stefan's eyes. In fact, they were all in shock including Kaitlan. Cordone had taught her some things, but where did she learn this trick? How had she become that strong?

She was both elated, and terrified of the power that welled up within her. But, she couldn't stop now. The White Wolf wouldn't let her.

"Listen to me very carefully, Stefan." Kaitlan spoke into Stefan's ear - low with authority, but all could hear her. "I may not be old like you, Ali'on, or even my mate, but you are nothing more than a big mouth with a little dick to me! And, I'll cut it off in a heartbeat! I am far more dangerous than you could possibly know. Do not underestimate me! Either you respect your females, and talk, or I'll make sure every single one of them who are left will know your real feelings toward them! You will find out why females of any species are on this Earth!!"

She let him go twisting his neck slightly making sure that he understood she could kill him. She shoved him into his chair, then swung it around to face her placing both hands on either side of the chair arms. His eyes were wary as their eyes locked. He was afraid of her! A vampire was afraid - of her? Whoa! That might just go to her head if she was as arrogant as he was!

"That's right, Stefan! You'd better fear me!" She told him quietly. "I am not Canaan's daughter for nothing. You cannot fight me, nor do you have the power to one-up me, you bastard! You warn me? By GOD, I am warning YOU! Do not fuck around with me, because I guaran-damn-tee you, I'll break you apart with my bare hands, and throw you in to burn! I'm too tired to listen to you men bullshit each other." She pushed hard on his chair sending it slamming into the wall, then shot to the door so fast the three didn't even see her do it!

Opening it, she waved someone inside. To their surprise, Stefan and Ali'on's mates entered the council room. Each one nodded their heads to Kaitlan who responded with in kind.

They stood by Kaitlan with their arms crossed watching the stunned males. Knowing females, Kaitlan had called both mates of the vampire and elf to stand with her, and after they found out what was going on, had agreed to come in case their mates were stubborn and stupid. She had found she liked both of them, and they became fast friends.

Sandra, mate to Ali'on, stood only five-feet, two inches, and was absolutely beautiful! Sandra was once human, but the years with Ali'on had turned her into part Elf. Her dark brown hair was beautifully woven with silver flecks, and hung far past her waist. It was pulled back off of her face with a high braid, and a silver comb, placed on the crown of her head. Her figure was tiny, with small breasts, a tiny waist, and perfect hips. Her skin was translucent as milk, and her eyes a deep, ocean blue. She was dressed in royal blue flats, a snow white skirt, and a tight, ocean blue, silk shirt, which was the exact color of her eyes.

The other woman was a vampire, but she completely shot the stereotype to hell. At about five-foot eight inches, Jennifer's shoulder length, strawberry blonde hair was curly, and bounced riotously with every movement. It was obvious that it was hard to control. Her figure had perfect proportions. He breasts full, but not voluptuous, her waist thin, and her hips the same proportions as her breasts. Her eyes were hazel which changed to a deep gray color when she was angry. She wore tight, skinny blue jeans, a red shirt with three tiers, along with the highest red stilettos Kaitlan had ever seen. Her skin was pale white, of course. Kaitlan, standing beside these two women, wore her favorite color of green in a long-sleeved, t-shirt knit top with snow-white jeans, and silver sandals. All three women were the wet dream of any man's fantasies - blonde, brunette, and redhead! In fact, any man who saw them would believe they had died, and gone to heaven!

Cordone just stood there stunned. What the shit?

"Kaitlan, what the hell do you think you are you doing? This is a Master Council. Only the heads of each Clan are allowed!"

Kaitlan shot her wolf eyes at her mate.

"Master Council, my ass! Don't use that tone with me, Cordone Valon. I am not who you think I am right now! I love you, and I am your mate, but this goes far beyond the heads of the clans! This monster is targeting *females* - not males! And, I will be damned if I will let you three argue about it! The longer you argue, the more of us could die!"

The other women nodded in agreement. Kaitlan deferred to Stefan's mate, Jennifer, who stepped forward without bowing her head to her mate as was the vampire custom in formal situations.

"Stefan, I love you. You are my mate, but my friends are dying! Yet, you continue to pussyfoot around while more die! No longer will I sit by, and remain silent on this matter. You men had better get a clue, because believe us, we will take over. As of today, we have elected Kaitlan as female Alpha over all clans in order to get this done!"

OK. That was news to Kaitlan, but she tried to keep her surprise under wraps. Hmmm. Maybe that was disinformation. Not bad!

"You men can just sit here with your precious Master Council, and argue like you have *ALWAYS* done! That's why the Vampire Wars were started! Your stupid Master Council sat, and argued over the rogues, till you waged war! If you remember, it started just like this! With a council meeting of supers arguing with each other, or have you forgotten? Pull your heads out of your asses!"

Stefan glared at his mate. How *dare* she speak that way to him! Then, Jennifer looked straight into his eyes. Suddenly, his lips turned up into a wicked grin. He hadn't been this turned on by his mate in a very long time, and it appeared that she, too, felt the same by the snarled grin she gave to him.

Jennifer backed up, and deferred to the mate of Ali'on, Sandra who stepped forward. Her voice was soft, but strong.

"Ali'on. When you took me as your mate, I gave to you

my whole heart and my respect. But, today, you dishonor me! By not telling the entire story, you do all Elves grave damage! Like my counterparts, I will not stand by and let what happened to our females so long ago, happen to theirs." She looked around the table. "What Ali'on will not tell you is something we have kept secret for a long time." She looked at her mate. Ali'on's eyes pleaded with her to stop, but she ignored him.

"There is far more to the story you have heard about the Elven females. When Anita found that Elves were able to mate with humans, like myself, a side effect occurred that we did not, immediately, realize. Within two hundred years, their human mates turned into pure-blooded Elves."

A gasp was audible in the council room.

"We are not sure what the mechanism is. And, this has been our secret for well over several thousand years as I'm sure you can understand. Our pureblooded females have increased in numbers to the point there are almost as many, now, as in our beginning. I mated as a human, but I am now as pure-blooded as my mate!"

Ali'on's mouth dropped at his mate's words. Never had she disobeyed him like this! And, as much as he was very angry at her for revealing their secret, he was just as turned on by her as he stared into her gorgeous eyes so much like his! He'd tell her later how he loved to see her like this! Sandra looked at her mate with smoldering eyes of pure lust.

Not even Kaitlan had been told about humans turning to pureblooded elves when she had called Sandra! Whoa! Now, that was a revelation to everyone!

Sandra continued with shocked faces staring at her as if she was speaking another language.

"Ali'on, my love, our people understood why this secret was kept, but you have to understand. If this Zanack is allowed to continue, how much longer will it be before he discovers our secret, and tries to kill our females again?"

Cordone sat with a plop!

"Well, shit!" he exclaimed aloud.

"Fuck!" Stefan agreed.

"Hell! I never thought of that!" Ali'on shook his head.

Kaitlan held her hand up when she noticed Cordone was going to speak further. His eyes glowed black more than ever! But, no longer with anger. His black eyes glowed with pride for his mate! She gave him a very wolfy, suggestive grin.

She was magnificent! He would take her in front of all these people if he could right now regardless of an audience! He preened, and sat up straight as pride for her grew within him. This was his mate! The daughter of Canaan! She had gained his respect when she put Stefan in the headlock! He didn't know she was that strong. But, then, again, she was The White Wolf. That was such a damn turn on, and he hardened immediately! Maybe there is more to her than either of them knew! He sat back in his chair with a grin, and waited to see what she would do next.

Without looking at him, Kaitlan thought, *"I'm so completely turned on right now for you, too, mate! This is what I am going to do to you."* She sent him the picture.

She had a desire that she had not yet had within her. Her wolf and her human self had somehow combined into one. She sent this to Cordone.

"You and I won't make it out of this room before I take you! That is a promise!"

Cordone was shocked as he came right then! He looked down at himself, and the slight wetness showed through his pants. He felt her wolf eyes look at him as his eyes met hers. Her eyes showed satisfaction with his response. A slow, intimate smile appeared on Cordone's face.

"I'll be so looking forward to it!"

Aloud, Kaitlan continued trying not to smile.

"Yes. You will!" She answered him.

"We will cooperate with each other. Read this!"

She threw three newspapers on the table, then stood with her head held high, arms crossed lifting her voluptuous breasts upward. She was in full Alpha mode.

"Go on! Read it! This monster's hangout has been found! And, if that does not make even vampires sick to their stomachs, I'll walk out that door, and leave it to you!"

Cordone read, his eyes glowing with hatred with each word. Then, he looked up at Kaitlan. "Where did you get this?"

"Dan. Richard brought this to his attention a few days back. They wanted to make sure it was a legitimate source, before telling us. Richard just handed it to me before the meeting started."

Cordone read aloud.

"Captain Randolf Sanders of the St. Louis police department, informed this paper that during a demolition scheduled for a building, workers found something horrific in the basement while setting explosive charges for implosion. The abandoned building, which had been used for apartments thirty years earlier, is located in the red light district. The workers placing the explosive charges discovered remains of what appeared to be mountains of human body parts in the basement.

According to Sanders, there was a pile to the ceiling scattered all over the basement.

Captain Sanders told this reporter that "In all my years on the police force, never have I ever seen anything like this. The coroner estimates that these bodies have been decomposing down there for perhaps thirty years, if not more. We have had numerous and continuous complaints over the years of a horrible smell at times, but were never able to locate its source. It is impossible to identify the parts, and even with DNA sampling, it could still take years to identify the victims. There is evidence, also, that there seems to be what looks like animal parts as well. The coroner believes that the majority of these parts belong to women, and possibly children. What is more shocking is that those that are still identifiable as body parts were apparently eaten. It is unknown who, or what, ate them at this time. It could very well be the source of many missing people."

While police are careful not to create panic, they have implied that there is a serial killer who may be a cannibal. We hope to have more for you as we investigate this horrific crime."

There was total silence, and only one conclusion they could make from the article. The majority of the victims were more than likely humans. It said a lot that most were women - human women.

The men were silent as the grave after reading this. (No pun intended, of course. Right. Sure. Keep thinking that). Stefan had grudgingly found respect for Kaitlan after she had threatened him, and he didn't give his loyalty lightly. Stefan stood without his normal arrogance, and looked at Kaitlan. Ali'on and Cordone stood as well. All three men dipped their head to Kaitlan.

"Kaitlan Seneca O'Hara Valon, heir to the O'Hara Clan, we also defer to you as female Alpha of the Clan of O'Hara, and will endeavor to make sure this monster will be found." Stefan stood, and kneeled to her.

As do I." Ali'on agreed kneeling to her as well.

Finally, Cordone stood before his mate with his eyes glowing black, and kneeled before her.

"My mate, I give to you my heart, my life, my love, and vow that we will not rest until we find Zanack! You are not only my Alpha and mate. I announce to all within the sound of my voice that my mate is not just Alpha, but she is also … The White Wolf!" He bowed his head.

Gasps were heard from everyone in that room. On hearing this, the women, too, kneeled to Kaitlan in awe and honor. The Prophecy had just come true in front of their eyes.

This was so not what she wanted! It was just weird. She wanted to be with her children, and her mate in their home. But, drastic measures had to be taken. The White Wolf had finally emerged, and somehow, had merged with her human side. That was clear by the power she had felt surge in her earlier. It had not gone away. Without her, the Prophecy would not come true. But there was more. All would be lost if they did not kill Zanack. No matter what she wanted, she was The White Wolf, and it was her destiny to kill him. Kaitlan had taken her place as The White Wolf as was her destiny.

~ 20 ~
**A person who desires power will never have it; A person
who does not want power, will receive it.**

As the council filed out of the room, Kaitlan stood aside to let all but Cordone leave. She looked at him with pure, unadulterated lust in her eyes, and stopped him by stepping in front of him. She turned to Lynne, and smirked.

"Lynne, will you see that Dan takes our guests to the corporate apartments, please?"

Lynne started at seeing Kaitlan's wolf eyes, then grinned knowingly.

"No prob at all, Kaitlan!" Then, she whispered to her. "Cordone is such a lucky bastard!"

Kaitlan grinned at her, and nodded.

"Oh, and Lynne," she said, turning to look at her mate, "why don't you go with Dan, and the two of you can just take a two hour lunch at the same time?"

She looked at Cordone who stared at her with a wicked grin. Kaitlan met his grin with her own. She put her fingers to her cheek, drumming them in thought.

"On second thought, Lynne. Why don't you all take the rest of the day off?"

Kaitlan's eyebrow went up in the "secret code" women have when they are telling the other friend they plan on getting some! Men aren't the only ones with a secret code!

Lynne gave Kaitlan a second, knowing smile, and nodded. She grabbed her purse, and ran to catch up with the others.

"Let's find Dan to take you to your ...," Lynne was telling them.

Kaitlan shut the door on her words, and locked it. Then,

The White Wolf turned to stalk her prey.

The last thing anyone would have heard had they been there, was Cordone growling as his mate took him - without an argument!

Richard wasn't happy about this. He slid his glance toward the vampire who was wandering around The Hall of Records for the first time in thousands of years. No. He did not like this one bit. He had been charged with protecting the Earth, and its inhabitants, and lately, he was really doing a really shitty job.

His eyes slid to Cordone.

"I really don't like this at all, Cordone. It's completely against anything that I believe!"

"Neither do I, but it's a step in trust." Cordone agreed.

"Maybe. But, I don't have to like it! Stefan is the last person I want in here!"

It went against everything Cordone believed, too. To let Stefan and his mate into The Hall was testing his patience. But, Kaitlan had insisted. And, right now, with her eyes telling him The White Wolf had merged with his mate, no one dared cross her. He wasn't sure what was going on, but he had to admit one thing. When she had shut the Council Room door, their coupling was nothing he had ever experienced! Just thinking back on what they had done in that room gave him a hard-on. The combination of her human, elf, and wolf that had merged into one being was more erotic than anything he could have ever believed possible, and she had been demanding and tireless! He closed his eyes remembering her body, and the changes he had seen and felt - up.

Her voluptuous breasts, firm and huge, had increased at least one, full cup size. Her nipples were larger, and sharply pointed with desire. Everything about her had been supercharged! He almost hadn't been able to keep up with her.

But, satisfied? Oh, man! Never! He would never tire of her! He wondered if she would be able to do this at will, now? Kaitlan had stripped in seconds, and her entire body was pure sex on legs! He had even had a huge orgasm just looking at her before he had touched her! The front of his pants had been completely wet. She had stalked across the council table with a wicked look on her face, and then, parked her luscious ass on the table in front of him with legs spread. Her sex glistened, and he licked his lips. She "forced" him to drink from her, and he happily did what she asked. In fact, he was enjoying her being physically demanding with him! He was extremely happy to be her "boy toy", as she had called him. While he drank his fill of her creamy liquid, she twisted her hands in his hair holding his face to her entrance until he finished. His face wet, and his mouth full of her delicious taste, he shared it with her as he met her lips in a fierce kiss of passion.

Cordone's balls had been weighted down stretching them to their furthest point. Quickly, he stripped, and she had pulled him on top of her, put her legs on his shoulders, and begged him to stab her deeply with his "huge stick". He had complied immediately! But, it didn't stop there! Something amazing happened to them. While inside of her, just before he exploded, both of them had begun to shudder indicating they were about to change. It was involuntary, and neither of them could stop it. Before it happened, Cordone had pulled her off the table, and they had both fallen to their knees. Her hips had lifted to him, and he plunged back into her, both of them phasing simultaneously. Good thing, because the human and wolf are not compatible, and they had never been. It was disgusting to think about it! But, apparently, nature had taken care of that problem.

When his wolf exploded his seed into his mate, locking him inside of her, they had phased back to human together with him still inside of her! That was the single, biggest turn on they had ever had! When they discovered this, they were amazed about the ability to phase back and forth from wolf to human form during sex! It was as if they connected on a far more primitive level. Or, perhaps, this was the way it had been before. No one really knew for sure what went before. After pulling out of her wet, slick channel, she pulled him up forcefully, and dragged him into his office. What stunned them both, was that they were eager to continue! He had sat down on his chair, and she had straddled him slipping that luscious slick channel over his hard cock bouncing up and down on him with her bouncing breasts in his face that he suckled until they both came again! And, still her wolf had not yet disappeared.

Just as he spilled his seed into his mate, again, Richard had called complaining that vampires were in The Hall! Cordone huffed, and reluctantly dressed in clothing that he kept in his office for an emergency. After what just happened, he decided he had better keep several changes in his office at all times! He turned to Kaitlan who was stretching her naked body across his desk as if she were a satisfied cat. He had filled her body full. The evidence on his desk was proof! He kissed her before he left, and nibbled on her breasts. She would wait at home for him, nude. He told her he wouldn't be long. There was no way he was going to be away from this sexual creature for very long!

"Cordone," Richard interrupted Cordone's thoughts. "When I first built The Hall, I had to use a large staff of people to move all of the knowledge into it. It was a massive undertaking. I was absolutely sure it was the right thing to do. Now, I'm having second thoughts. Is it really right to keep all of this knowledge from everyone on Earth?"

"DAMN!" he exclaimed when Kaitlan sent him a vision of herself.

"It's OK, love! I'm already home, naked, and wet for you!"

Cordone felt another orgasm coming! Kaitlan sent him a picture of just where she was wet! He jerked, then turned back to Richard trying to concentrate, and more than that, trying to keep from coming in front of everyone!

"I don't know, Richard. I understand what you are asking. In the wrong hands, it could be devastating. But, in the right hands? It could be fantastic! Why don't we table this for now?"

Richard just nodded then looked at Cordone. His eyes widened! A small, wet stain was slowly spreading on the front of his jeans. He grinned at Cordone with waggling eyebrows, and told him he had better get to his mate before his pants got any wetter! Cordone had laughed, and dashed away.

Richard just shook his head. He had also asked Lynne the very same question earlier that day.

"I think I'm a bit torn both ways, mate. I could not make that decision. You've lived so long, wouldn't it make it easier for you to make the decision, my love?"

"I have learned in my long life, Lynne, you never find certain decisions to be easy. Long ago, I believed it was important to keep The Hall of Records secret. But, because I have lived so long, perhaps I have overlooked the ability of those on this world to accept the truth."

"Well, some won't. That's very true. But, Eric, I think we are all ready to accept the truth of our past. I know I am."

"Yes. But are humans?"

For that, Lynne had no answer. Richard had kissed Lynne, but then, wondered. How would she feel about one of the biggest secrets of all that he had been hiding from everyone? How would all of them feel when he told them everything. His power had diminished greatly when he became a werewolf. In truth, he didn't have the power any longer. Richard had put it away long ago as mankind and supers left myths and legends behind. It rested right here in this Hall, but no one had ever noticed.

His eyes lifted to the icon that was placed on a shelf over the door leading to the village. It was in shadow. He had thought never to use it again, but now? Truth was, he doubted he could help at all. His had been one of brute force. DAMN! These four women would be receiving the powers of the elements - and very soon. When they did, he knew of someone who could help them develop their powers. One who saw all. Of course, that would call for a trip where he had never thought to go again.

Lynne put her hand on Richard's shoulder, and knocked him out of his train of thought.

"I guess we better get to work, my love."

He nodded to her, and they walked to the section that they had been assigned by Sarah.

Sam pushed the scroll away from him, and brushed his fingers through his hair. They'd been in The Hall for a long time. He was tired, and he knew Sarah was as well.

"Sarah? This is just an impossible task! We only know part of what we might be looking for, and that is almost nothing!"

Despite the fact that his mate was able to read an entire novel in a matter of five minutes with perfect recall, now, wasn't making it easier. Whatever happened to her while she was dead, coming back apparently gave her abilities that seemed to be growing - quickly.

She was frustrated as well. Sarah and Sam were the only ones who spoke of the loss of her life, their baby's, and almost Sam's. Sam would have died in a couple of minutes if Sarah hadn't woken up when she did. At night, Sarah would awake sobbing her heart out. Sam would hold her tightly, and let his tears fall, too. They hadn't even made love since they had awakened. So far, the only thing she actually had was interpretation, understanding, and speed-reading.

"God, I'm thirsty!" Sarah said running her hands through her hair. That's when Sam noticed something very odd.

"Sarah…have you done something to your hair?"

"Huh? No, why?" She asked in surprise. "Well, I did

wash it last night."

"And, you stayed in the shower almost two hours, too!"

Sarah looked at him in surprise. She had?

Sam stood up to look at her hair. He brushed it with his fingers. He dropped her hair, and fell back against the bookcase behind him landing on his butt.

"OH. MY. GOD!" Sam's voice was loud in the hall.

Hearing Sam, those closest to them dropped what they were doing, and rushed over to them. Kaitlan and Dan arrived first, and eyes wide, approached Sarah cautiously. Dan helped Sam stand up where he had fallen on his ass. They both stared at Sarah.

"What's wrong ?" Sarah asked watching everyone staring at her hair. She was getting nervous.

Kaitlan reached out to touch her hair. Her red hair had turned as blue as the Caribbean, and it flowed like water on top of her head, yet no water dripped on anything.

Lynne had arrived, gaping her mouth, and she took a mirror out of her purse handing it to Sarah. Two seconds later, Sarah screamed, and dropped the mirror. Richard caught it before it hit the floor.

"W-w-what the HELL is happening to me?" Sarah cried, and tears burst out of her like a river as she looked upward slamming her fist onto the desk.

"Haven't I been hurt enough? What else do you want from me? I was raped by my own Father till I was five!!! I've had my child die! And, now, you're making me into some kind of a freak! Haven't you taken enough from me!"

In the next instant, all she could think of was that she had to get out of there! Gasps all around stopped her in her tracks. Even though it was stupid, she phased. She froze at the looks on their faces.

"Please, Sam, don't tell me. My wolf's coat is the same color."

"Your wolf's coat is the same color," Sam told her almost hysterically.

"I ASKED you not to tell me that!" It would be a funny line from "Get Smart" - if it wasn't true.

Sarah sighed, and phased back putting her head on her arms. Tears were coming rapidly. Sam sat beside her, and held her hand while he waited for her to calm.

Everyone had frozen in shock as they heard her confession aloud. Sarah hadn't even realized that it was the first time anyone else had heard what happened to her when she was little. It horrified everyone standing there. Sam had quietly told everyone that he had taken care of the bastard a long time ago. Even Stefan, who was above feeling sorry for anyone, gritted his teeth at her confession. He would have gladly taken care of the bastard himself! One thing he could not abide, and he did not allow in his clan, were rapists. And, that went double for this situation.

As Sarah began to calm, her hair slowly turned back to her red. She didn't raise her eyes. Her calm was almost as terrifying as her outburst had been. She was absolutely still.

Then….Sarah raised her head, and turned to Sam.

If what he had seen before shocked him, this was even more so! Her eyes were brilliant gold - just like his when they glowed.

Sarah was in some kind of trance - almost a catatonic state. Everyone followed her as she went to the main floor. She proceeded to walk into the climate-controlled room only to be stopped by a locked door. She needed a key. It was not supposed to be locked! It had *never* been locked as long as Richard knew. Everything was open in The Hall. That was his biggest rule.

Pulling his phone out, he contacted Johnson.

"Where the hell is the key to the climate controlled room, and why is it locked?"

He was silent for a few minutes.

"What do you mean you don't know?" He listened, and his face was becoming more angry by the second. "Well, get the hell on it, man! I want that door unlocked now!"

Since Sarah couldn't get into the climate-controlled room right now, she said, "We must all meet in the village below The Hall."

~ 21 ~
Explanations - Sure

And, here they were again. In this ancient, burned out village. Sam, who was still watching Sarah carefully, perched on a lower rock wall along with Kaitlan and Cordone. In the meantime, Lynne and Richard stood with Dan and Anita leaning up against another wall that hadn't been totally destroyed. They all completed a circle around Sarah who stood in the center.

Sarah walked to Kaitlan, and spoke, her eyes still glowing gold.

"I thought I would need a scroll that is inside the climate controlled room, Richard. But, no longer. Four women have been chosen specifically for their powers - the powers of the elements. I do not need to read the original Prophecy any longer to know what must be done for sure. It is no longer a theory. The truth is in here." She pointed to her head. "In order for the curse to have worked, the one casting the spell could not achieve his goal unless all four of the elements were present at the same time. These are, as I mentioned before, are Earth, Water, Air and Fire. Without these elements, life cannot not exist. We know that one of these was missing when the curse was originally cast."

Nods were seen all around, but Richard frowned. Sarah had already told them that the girls were going to be given the powers of the four elements. So far, Kaitlan and Sarah were the only ones who had showed real signs of becoming their elements. Kaitlan was Earth. Sarah had just become water. He also knew that their change would accelerate exponentially once the change began. Richard was the only one who knew this, and he knew it would be up to him to help them become what they were meant to be.

"OK, and?" asked Cordone.

"We know the curse was not cast properly. One element was missing. Remember the verse:

Four there were, Four were cursed.
Four there are, Four are blessed."

Sarah's eyes were finally back to normal, and she continued speaking as she paced back and forth.

"In order for Zanack to have cast the curse for permanence, he needed the four. Again, we know this. At any given point in time, and only when the elementals are needed, there are born four women - perhaps thousands of years between each group - but always when there is true danger to this world."

Suddenly, Sarah stopped, and changed the subject. "We have had little, to no poisoning from Wolfsbane recently. Anyone else notice?"

Everyone's thoughts were turning. Why, indeed? Anita snapped her fingers. She had it.

"Easy answer!" Anita said. "Zanack must have learned something we don't know, yet."

Sarah nodded. "Exactly! But, is it possible that the reason why is that there are not just two scrolls, but maybe even perhaps a third?"

"Three scrolls? Are you fucking kidding us?" Dan muttered to himself.

Everyone looked at Dan. He was right.

"Oh for the Creator's sake! *Another* scroll? A third one? What's in it? Why stop killing, now? What does he hope to gain?" Kaitlan wasn't really complaining, but hell!

Again, Sarah shrugged. "There is more. Remember. The first two lines of the last four of the verse were altered.

***The one who cursed our worlds returns,
From the beginning and to the last.***

"OK. So, what the hell does that mean? If he's stopped the poisonings, and found a third scroll, then that means … it means … I mean. What does it mean?" Anita's eyes were wide. "Why in the hell can't we get something consistent?"

"Probably because that's the way things work," Dan laughed at her. It was either laugh, or go nuts.

Sarah finished her thought.

"Those two lines that were also re-written have to do with when, and where, the curse must be recast."

Everyone looked at her in silence.

"And, that would be …?" Cordone asked.

"The past. Zanack must return to the past to the original place to recast the curse."

Dead silence.

"Why is it that that actually makes sense?" Anita growled.

"What the fuck? You're telling us that he has to, what? Go back in time?" Lynne asked. "Are you serious? No one can go back in time!"

"No shit!" Richard agreed. "So, he must have found a way to actually go back in time? I would never have believe that to be possible! So, I guess we must conclude that Zanack has found a way to do it! Holy fuck!"

Anita shook her head in disbelief. What would her powers be like? And, what about her baby? She placed her hands on her belly. She was due any time, but now, she was terrified. She complained to everyone and no one.

"Geez! This just keeps getting better and better! Now, we have to deal with time travel, too?" Anita whined.

Richard narrowed his eyes. How was Zanack planning to go back in time? He didn't like how close they were really getting to his own part in it, but this new addition was not good.

He knew it. Even his own people couldn't cross time!

Sarah continued. Her eyes became fixed, again, and her eyes turned gold, again, as she named the element of each girl.

"Moving on. You, Kaitlan, are of the Earth. If any of us had mated before you, we wouldn't be here now. Because you are The White Wolf, your wolf is totally connected with the Earth. Everything about you is about the Earth. We could, quite literally, call you, 'Mother Nature'! But, it's because you are The White Wolf everything changed."

"Obviously." Sam was just being snarky.

"Of course, I am water. There is no life without water. Our bodies are made up of mostly water. Water carves out mountains, canyons, and change the face of the Earth."

"Obviously." Sam was just being snarky times two, now, and Sarah shot him a "shut it" look.

Anita nodded her head. She was grinning at Sam's remarks. Her baby gave her a large kick right then.

"Sarah's right. We are almost totally made up of water. You take that away, and there would be little left over if it was taken out of us." Anita explained.

"Anita," Sarah continued, "is the air. Air is the breath of life. As long as we breathe, we have life. Air can either build, or destroy, given time. It never lets up. It manifests itself in storms, and can freeze, or be so hot, it can take away one's breath. Just like the wind, you continue in your quest for knowledge. You use the air for good."

Only one more element to go. And, everyone's face turned to Lynne.

Lynne muttered, "It figures I'd be fire!"

"And, finally, Lynne. You are fire. You remain dormant until needed to burn away, and cleanse everything - usually that which comes first while the other elements washed it all away. Fire is good, but also can be destructive."

"OK. So. Who's up to teach us how to use them?" Kaitlan asked.

Sarah's head jerked up! Who would teach the elementals

how to use them?

For a while, there was silence. Way too much was going on for them to concentrate on everything.

"Nope. Got nothin'. And, is there a third scroll? What? Does it tell us how to circumvent time?" Again, Sam with, yet, another snarky, sarcastic remark.

"The third scroll is …" Sarah began, "… it's a wizard's scroll. Perhaps a page taken out of a book. It has to do with time."

"And?"

Sarah just shook her head. "Don't know - yet."

Lynne stopped, and thought about what she would become soon. She turned to Richard. She was frightened for a whole other reason. Fire was unpredictable. He put his arm around her.

Everyone looked around them, and shrugged. No one had any answers. And, then, Sarah said something else that truly put terror into their hearts.

"Putting the 'who' aside for the moment. I just thought of something else. What's usually used to make curses work?" Sarah asked under her breath.

Shocked faces stared at each other. They knew the answer. Their horror was apparent. Sam uttered what everyone was thinking.

"And, how do we go back in time?" Kaitlan asked.

"We don't know, and a human sacrifice, Sarah. Blood. Some one, or several, are going to die." Richard answered.

~ 22 ~
The Elementals Begin

Anita spoke first, more to herself than anyone else.

"Then, who were the sacrifices the first time?"

"I doubt we will ever know who it was, Anita," Richard told her.

Richard's mind was running fast. There was something there, but what? It was his own mate who provided his answer.

"Well, Richard already answered that," Lynne said. Then, "or did you?"

Richard just looked at her. His eyes were looking everywhere but any person!

A most amazing thing began to happen. Kaitlan's eyes narrowed, and she felt her body physically change. Her body became covered with White Fur, a small snout formed, and her ears elongated. Her eyes turned the most brilliant, glowing green anyone had ever seen. Her full transformation was completed in front of their eyes. The shock on their faces at the realization that she was the physical incarnation of The White Wolf was not terrifying. This was not what they ever had thought would happen!

Sarah followed right behind her, and changed at the same time, becoming the human version of standing water. Her entire body glowed blue, and her hair flowed from her head like water. Her eyes the same brilliant blue. Again, like Kaitlan, she was not scary.

The first two elementals were completely "born" before their eyes.

Kaitlan, or The White Wolf, laughed. (It was a toss up. Pick One)

"What? Haven't you ever seen a fuzzy white wolf that

walked upright?"

Sarah grinned, and nodded throwing water all over everyone. She gave everyone a guilty, but sheepish grin.

"Ooops! Sorry, guys!" Sarah apologized.

The power both girls felt was amazing!

Richard wasn't paying attention. He was focused on what the girls had just said.

"Where was the fourth woman? Who took her?" asked Cordone. Still, no one had the answer to that one.

Sarah finished the discussion.   She controlled her shaking water this time.

"Again, we will probably never know. But, it still doesn't make sense that neither Kaitlan nor Anita were ever targeted at all even though the traitor had total access? Wonder why?"

"Maybe because Kaitlan is immune, and Anita was needed to help Lynne, and sign off on Sarah's death?" Dan said.

Everyone gave Dan a "what the hell are you talking about" look while Lynne's eyebrows went up as she thought of something else.

Now, everyone seemed to be skipping around the subjects, talking without listening to each other, deep in their own thoughts.

"When Anita sent Eric and me out to force us into admitting we were mates," she turned to Eric, "a huge storm arose. Wind, Lightening, thunder, hail, and a tornado came after us. Remember, Eric? We had to dive to the bottom of the river to wait until it passed over us! It seemed as if it was coming after both of us."

Remember? Richard's face became a mask of shock.

"Come on, Lynne. Tornadoes don't chase people," Dan laughed out loud.

"But, this one seemed to be. We were at the bluff when we saw it."

"Ah, fuck!" Richard said almost to himself. He put his hand on his head, and shook it. He couldn't believe he hadn't seen the signs!

"Eric? Eric? What's wrong?!" Lynne demanded as she tried to touch him.

They were all witnessing something they didn't understand. Why was Richard so stunned?

"Why didn't I see this before?"

"Again, Eric, what are you talking about?" Lynne shook his shoulders.

He just kept shaking his head. Now, how was he going to tell them what that had meant.

"DAMN, DAMN, DAMN, DAMN!"

"Eric? What is going on?" Lynne approached her mate cautiously.

He looked up at Lynne. "I can't believe I missed it!"

"One more time. WHAT, Eric?"

Richard closed his eyes, trying to calm down. Nope. There was no way he was going to get out of this, now.

"Wait with the others, Linora. Please. I have to retrieve something." He walked with Lynne to the others, and left her there. Then, he walked back to the lift. He rode the lift up to The Hall. Stepping out, he stayed in the shadows as his eyes went to the icon he had hidden so long ago to protect his real identity, and had never thought to need again. He held out his hand.

"Lynne? What the hell?" Sarah asked as they all just watched Richard leave.

Lynne shrugged her shoulders. She had known Eric for thousands of years. But, never had she seen him like this. She was as confused as everyone else. So, what wasn't confusing about all of this?

Kaitlan's new form was giving her a clarity that she never had as a werewolf, or human. She was trying to remember something Richard had said in an earlier conversation she had with him while she made him a sandwich. It was on the tip of her tongue. What was it?   Then, snippets came back to her as she felt the fog lifting. He had told them that he had chosen to protect Earth and its inhabitants. Damn, it was starting to give her a headache! Well, she'd figure it out sooner or later. In that same instant, she heard four words popping into her head. The Hall of Records. Why did that sound so familiar? No, it's not just about the archive of all knowledge. It was the NAME of The Hall. And, according to Richard, it had never been in Egypt under the Sphinx as was the current thinking in alternative science. That was it! Richard had told her that he had moved it from a northern country. A northern country ….

The entire cavern lit up with thunder and lightning, blinding everyone.

Turning slowly toward the direction from where it all seemed to come, a man on the lift, his arm raised with an odd object in his hand. From that object came lightening and thunder.

"Who the hell is that?" Cordone demanded to no one.

He was commanding in his very stance. His height? Almost six-foot nine? His bare torso was very broad, toned, tight, and his skin fair. He wore brown leather pants. His arms were massive as were his legs. His eyes glowed with a blue light, and his shoulder length hair was blonde! In his hand he held a what? A triangle? On a stick? Kaitlan almost had it! Her brain started working overtime.

Their mouths open, their bodies frozen with shock at this figure that wielded such massive power. The man stopped his demonstration, and jumped from the lift to the assembly. Where a werewolf had no problem jumping long distances up and down, this man almost flew! He landed directly in the center of all. Then, raised himself to his full height. To look at the women gape, you would think that they were teenage girls with their first crush! Yes, he was that gorgeous!

It was then, Kaitlan realized what he held in his hand, and her white furry legs collapsed out from under her. Cordone caught her before she reached the ground.

"OMG!" she said, almost to herself.

"It's not possible! It can't be! You're not real!" Kaitlan

vocalized aloud. "That would be too crazy!"

The man smiled at Kaitlan with beautiful, snow white teeth.

"I knew you would guess who I am, Kaitlan. Your knowledge, reading and editing skills belong to the only person who could possibly figure it out!"

Lynne's mouth dropped - and so did her legs. Dan caught her before she hit the ground.

"It can't be! This gorgeous man was speaking - with Eric's voice!" she thought.

"Yes, mate. It is I." Eric answered her.

"E-Eric?" Lynne stuttered softly. "How … I mean … why … I-I mean…."

"I'm sorry, Linora. I should have known. The tornado … It was time unraveling."

He held out his arm, picked Lynne up as if she were a feather, and held her by his side as he turned to explain things to everyone. All Lynne could do was stare up into the face of the most gorgeous man she had ever seen.

"Eric, and Richard are only a few of many names by which I am known."

Kaitlan looked at everyone else. Their eyes were questions. Sarah, Lynne, and Anita were just dumbfounded. The men were puzzled. She frowned at them.

"What is it with all of you? Don't you know who this is?" Kaitlan was exasperated.

"Uh … no? Should we?" answered Dan.

"Oh for the love of …. " And, that's when the final piece of the puzzle came forward. Kaitlan put it all together in an instant.

She whispered loud enough for all to hear.

"Hot damn! It's been there … right in front of us all this time, hasn't it, Richard?" He grinned at her deciding to let Kaitlan tell everyone who he was. "The Hall of Records."

"Kaitlan, what the hell are you babbling about?" Cordone asked her grabbing her shoulders, and shaking her.

"The [T] Hall [H] of [O] Records [R]." Kaitlan said it like a cheer. "And, what does that spell? T H O R! How many times have you told us you chose to protect the Earth and its inhabitants? You were giving us clues all along the way, and we didn't even notice."

"Who are you talking about, Kaitlan!" Dan asked.

She pointed to the Norse god who was grinning from ear to ear at her. She really was The White Wolf. What others, and Kaitlan, did not know about herself, well, they would learn later, and soon enough. He was proud of her.

"Thor was, I-I mean, IS, the Norse God of thunder, lightening, storms, and strength!   The Protector of Earth, mankind, healing and fertility!!!! And, that…" she pointed to the triangle on a stick, "… is the Hammer of Thor! Mjölnir is what it is called, and is only able to be wielded by Thor. He commands the elements, and more than that, he …." Kaitlan broke off when she heard Lynne whisper.

"Richard is … Thor?" whispering so low, the others almost didn't hear her.

Thor smiled at Lynne.

"Yes, my gorgeous mate. I am Thor."

Then, Kaitlan spit out the first, dumb thing that came to her mind.

"It doesn't look like a hammer. It looks more like a triangle on a stick!"

Richard threw his head back, and roared with laughter.

"Of all the things you would wish to ask me, and that is what you come up with? Trust me, Kaitlan. Myths were embellished so much over the thousands of years, that the truth became romanticized, yet is far different. While the embellishments are really amazing, the truth at the base of the myth is always much less interesting."

"Asgard? Is it real?" Lynne asked him.

"Oh, yes my love. Asgard is part of the truth. I will answer everyone's other questions as soon as I can, but right now, I think I need to attend to my mate who is about to pass out."

Lynne fainted.

~ 23 ~
Never assume. You will invariably be wrong

With the revelation that Thor was in their midst, they had all agreed that it would remain their secret. He took back his persona as Richard, so everyone could better relate to him.

Lynne kept glancing up at him watching Eric from under her long, black eyelashes as he sat on the jet's bed reading a book. She honestly had no idea how she felt about him, or anything else right now. Richard saw her, and put his book down grinning at her.

Lynne's mind had shut down. Zanack, Eric, Richard, Thor. Who the hell was her mate? Lynne couldn't say a thing. All she could do was just stare at him. He just grinned at her confusion.

"Any questions you need to ask, Linora?" he teased.

"Thor. Why haven't you used your powers to help us?" Lynne asked.

"Fair question. I can do a few 'tricks' like in the cave, but when I became a werewolf, it caused my powers to leave me. Even Mjölnir does not respond to me as it did."

"Oh," was all Lynne could say. And, that was that.

It was Kaitlan who had said they needed to go back home to "nowhere land". After Richard had shown them who he really was, and the shock had worn off, Cordone and Sam had whisked Kaitlan and Sarah to the jet, followed by Richard, Lynne, Dan and Anita. Richard had taken the unconscious Lynne to the bedroom in the jet.

Reaching the house, Richard asked everyone to come into the main room so he could explain what sent him into a tailspin. He also had planned to tell them how they would find it easy to change forms at will as soon as their transformations were complete. However, Richard would not be the one to teach them what they needed to know, but he knew someone who could.

"OK, Richard. You're on," Kaitlan said. She really couldn't wait to hear this one!

Richard started to pace. Where to start? He stopped. The beginning.

"First, when I became a werewolf, as I told Lynne, my powers were virtually gone. I was born before anyone started keeping dates. Wizards in Asgard had their powers limited by Odin for obvious reasons. But, those on Earth, did not. In consequence, many of them left Asgard for Earth to practice their craft. Odfrin knew that his powers would be unlimited if he went to Earth. Most myths about us are not true, however, the ones about how I was rash and young, and had a penchant for war, are true. Odin had been seeking a way to curb my hunger for violence. Odfrin petitioned my Father to let him take me to Earth. Once there, he told Odin that he could teach me what it meant to be humble. Odin granted him the petition, and Odfrin brought me to Earth against my protests. I didn't trust Odfrin, but my Father did not listen.

Odfrin did not hide his face from me long. He wanted to rule, and wanted to use me to do it. He sneered at me telling me that he had taken the name of Odfrin to mock my Father for daring to limit his powers. I refused his 'offer'. After twenty years of imprisoning me, he found rogue werewolves, and tied me to a tree like bait. He believed that if I could be turned, he could force me into helping him gain rule of the Earth. Unfortunately, what he didn't know was that after my turn, and even with Mjölnir, my power was sorely limited. I escaped upon my first turn, and never looked back. I'm positive that Odfrin's body was deteriorating at that point.

When my Father found I had no desire for the throne, he was sorely angered. I was truly afraid he would take his anger out on me by hurting those of Earth. So, I announced to all realms that I was the protector of Earth."

He stopped for a moment remembering how sad his Father had made him.

"Eric, you are a good man, and you are not your Father. You must know that?" Lynne said to him, and he leaned over to kiss her tenderly.

"Odfrin's body was old. He needed a new host just like Anita said. He's some type of parasite. Then, he took your name." Cordone reasoned, and Richard nodded.

"That's as good a guess as any," Richard said. "He also craved the same longevity extended to the royal house of Asgard through our own technology. However, it looks as if Odfrin found another way to extend life."

"I suppose you know what you're talking about?" Sam asked.

"You?" Lynne knew. He nodded.

Her eyes widened. She was mated to Thor, Prince of Asgard, King of the Vikings, and Protector of the O'Hara Clan. Lynne wasn't sure she could wrap her head around that one. Eric was still speaking.

"I am the heir to the throne of Asgard, so yes, I do, Sam. Coming to Earth from Asgard may have hastened his demise. Possibly an innocent victim stumbled across Odfrin's path when he was dying. All wizards pass their knowledge onto their 'chosen one' just before they die, but only their knowledge. None I know had the ability to transfer themselves into another body. But, Odfrin was arrogant, and always boasted he would live forever. Must have been a shock to the human when his very consciousness was being stripped from him."

"Wait," Sarah said. "Are you saying that Odfrin, basically, traded bodies with an innocent, destroying his soul in the process? Did he have that much power?"

"Not trade, Sarah. Took it over. However, yes, Sarah. He did have that much power in his Asgardian form. Hmmm. I wonder if his powers were decreased as well when he took the human body?"

"If so, maybe that's the reason the curse was botched?" Cordone wondered aloud.

"A human body cannot contain his immense wizard powers. Instead, he would be nothing more than an excellent magician. But, he did have the ability to use some magic - enough to cast the first curse. If he plans on trying again after his first failure, he's had plenty of time to get much better. But, by human and supernatural standards, even now, he is very powerful. But, what I don't understand is how he stayed in this human body for so very long? This doesn't make sense to me. What could he have done to extend the life of his human body?" Richard stopped for a minute, and looked at Sarah. "Sarah, you were right. The timeline has been royally screwed up!"

"Ah! That makes more sense as to why he must return to the exact place at the exact time where he enacted the curse the first time, and that means traveling back in time." Sarah squeaked. Then, "Holy shit! If we go back in time, we could meet the original Elementals!"

"That would be really cool, Sarah," Kaitlan said. "Unless …."

"Unless what, love?" Cordone put his arm around her.

He face was blank as a thought occurred to her.

"Unless …," she looked around at everyone. "Unless, those Elementals…."

"What, Kaitlan?" Sarah pushed.

Quietly, "They are us!"

Silence. No one wanted to go there. That was just way too weird.

"Time travel is way too complicated, and is giving me a headache," Dan muttered.

Time was short, and the confrontation was getting nearer. Everyone could feel it. Kaitlan and Cordone's children had been brought to the house from their undisclosed position for a visit. They had grown a lot, much to Kaitlan's sadness.

Canaan and Tara, though, giggled to see their Mom had a furry coat! Every time she held them, Tara petted her Mommy's white fur, and snuggle down into it to sleep. Cordone was amused to see them think of their Mother as a living stuffed animal! His eyes rolled in laughter, and then looked at his mate with great desire. That hadn't changed at all! It was a whole new experience for both of them.

Kaitlan hadn't known the couple who took care of her babies until now. Their names were Milon and Muriel Carter - Cordone's aunt and uncle. Kaitlan fell in love with them the moment she met them, and had no more qualms about their loyalty to Cordone and his family. They were highly amused at her White Wolf fur, yet were in awe of the Prophecy before them. They were even more so by Sarah's flowing water hair, and blue skin which undulated with water underneath. Canaan and Tara giggled when their Aunt Sarah would shake her head throwing water on them. When she wasn't amusing the children, she spent a lot of time in the pool with Sam, reflecting on what their future would be.

After a week, Milon and Muriel had to take the children back to their secret place. Cordone made arrangements for them to take Anita's child as well when it was born. Kaitlan cried when they were gone, but safety was their foremost thought. Both couples were finding a whole new element to making love. But, they figured it all out, and it brought out a whole new dynamic that the men loved.

Lynne and Anita's powers had yet to manifest themselves. Their timing was off by about two weeks. Anita's theory, based upon Richard's estimation, was that they were coming in increments, and probably as needed. Once one received their powers, another would receive her powers. So far, that theory was pretty much a wash. But, her other theory that they would come in the order of Earth, Water, Air, and Fire seemed to be fact. Of that, Anita was sure, and she would be next. She had no idea what that might entail. She was sure that it was going to be an interesting change The only thing that worried Anita was her baby. Would she get her powers before the baby was born? She was due to deliver at any time, now. Dan was prancing like a, well, a wolf! He couldn't wait to hold his baby in his arms!

Lynne was the least excited. She had way too much to cope with right now. She sat in a chair, and brooded. She didn't even know whom she had mated. Richard tried hard, but knew she would have to learn to cope. He was patient. Time really meant nothing to him. But, happy that she knew everything, now, he was sad he had caused her so much pain. Finally, when they were alone, he sat down at her feet, and laid his head in her lap. Her hands automatically came up, stroking his hair.

"Linora, I am so sorry. I hope, someday, you will forgive me. I hope I haven't lost your love. You hold all of my heart forever," Richard told her.

Lynne's eyes grew wide? What did he mean? She loved him to distraction. Then, she realized she must have been acting like a woman who hated her mate. That was far from the truth.

"Lost my love? Eric, you haven't lost my love at all! I'm sorry. I was trying to figure all of this out. I didn't mean to make you think that I didn't love you!"

She lifted his face to meet hers, and smiled.

"You know? It's kind of nice knowing that I can make love to my mate who can transform into different men! It definitely has potential for fabulous sex!"

She leaned down, and crushed her lips to his. Richard hadn't lost a second getting her into bed, and inside her as fast as possible! He had missed his mate. For fun, he changed back and forth from redheaded Eric to golden-headed Thor as he moved inside of her. All it did was make Lynne more excited than ever before! It was fun making love to two different men. Well, technically, one, but who cared? After their initial heat, they continued the rest of the night making slow and wonderful love to each other until dawn came creeping over the trees, and they lay sweating and replete in each other's arms. Now was the time, Lynne decided.

Her fingers caressed Eric's, uh, Thor's chest.

"I love you, Zanack, Eric, Richard, Thor! Whatever your name is!" she laughed gently.

Thor, uh, no, Eric, wait, Richard now, teased and tickled her nipples with his tongue causing them to grow harder as he suckled first one, then the other.

"I love you, Linora. Whoever thought that I would feel this way about anyone?"

"Kaitlan told me that you … ," she hesitated.

She wasn't sure how to ask him this particular question. She had no doubt that he loved her, but she needed to know.

"It's OK. Ask me anything, and I will never lie to you again," he said.

"Well, she told me you had a wife, according to myth. Her name was Sif?"

Eric's body tensed.

"She was."

Lynne jerked in shock. She didn't know how she was supposed to feel.

"Linora, let me explain something. Unlike supers, I have lived a very, very long time. I have been away from my home since I decided to protect this planet. Much to the anger of my Father. That you know."

"What happened," she asked quietly.

He leaned on his elbow to look at her. He would not lie. He absentmindedly, but gently kneaded her breasts as he told her their story.

"Sif was my Father's choice of wife and future Queen for me. Neither she, nor I, loved each other. She loved another, and I loved no other woman. Father wouldn't accept anything less than our marriage, and it was done. Both of us were unhappy. As fate would have it, though, a war broke out between the realms. A battleground was chosen."

Lynne looked at him. "Earth." It was a statement, not a

question.

"Yes. In our arrogance, we had no wish to fight on any of the other eight planets. Earth, then, was sparsely populated, and considered superfluous, and the only planet suitable for war within the nine planets of Yggdrasil. We did not want to ruin our own planets." Seeing her questioning look, he explained. "It's not exactly a tree, but the positions of the planets are lined up in such a way that connecting them gives it the appearance of a tree. It is also known as The Tree of Life. So, we took our battle to Earth. No one I knew cared any more about the races on Earth than I did, until I met a kind, but human couple, who I saved from one of our most powerful weapons. It had hit me, instead. Their kindness, and caring overwhelmed me, and obviously influenced my future. They managed to whip me back into fighting shape quickly, and I went right back to the war. It was a long one, and we lost many on all sides along with a great many humans. Sif was one of the strongest, and most powerful warriors ever. Even though I did not love her, I admired her skills as a warrior. We were friends at that point, but never would there be anything other than friends. At the end of the war, just before we traveled across the Bifrost, Sif was brought down, and killed."

Lynne's face was sympathetic to her mate.

"I'm so sorry, Eric," she said softly. "Kaitlan said you did have children?"

He shook his head. "No. The myths man has written are so far from the truth, it's been quite comical to all of Asgard. Well, save for one."

"What would that be?"

"Humans worshipped us as gods, and we relished in it. Biggest mistake we ever made. It's where most of your myths originated. It's great for movies, books, and TV, but no truth is in them except that I am Thor. Hell. Even some of the names aren't right. Norsemen called me a "god" only because we were far advanced above them. They wrote of us from their point of view."

"Makes sense. You wielded huge powers. Odin was King?"

"Of Asgard? Yes, he is."

"Is? He's still alive?" she asked in surprise.

"Most definitely."

Now, Lynne really was having a hard time with that one!

"And, one day, the throne of Asgard will be yours? Even though you told your Father you renounced it?"

Thor was silent. He never had any desire to be King. He didn't want it. But, he could not escape his destiny. He knew he would be King one day.

"Yes, someday." He pulled Lynne's body closer to him. "I can't get away from my destiny, Linora. And, neither can you."

"My destiny? We will be together until you do become King."

The thought of his leaving her caused her heart to cry, and her stomach to sink. Perhaps his child would keep her from going insane without him.

Thor's eyebrows went up, and his eyes widened. Her emotions were all over the place these past few days.

"What do you mean?"

"I'm not of your people, Thor. I am Elf."

"And? I don't follow you."

Was he that dense? Guess so! Men! Or, in this case, god!

"Do I have to spell it out for you? When you leave for Asgard, I will stay here."

His eyes cleared up instantly. And, he laughed loudly. She didn't find it the least bit amusing, and whacked his shoulder.

"Ouch! What did you do that for?" He ran his hands through his hair. "God, Linora! Is that what you think? By all that is holy, woman! You are my mate, and you will come with me. You will become Queen of Asgard," he assured her.

She flew off the bed, and turned to stare at him as if he'd lost his mind.

"You can't mean that, Thor! Your people will not want an Elf as their Queen!"

"You'd be surprised at the Queens Asgard has had, Linora. Many were not Asgardians. Just more myths. We have had human, Elf, and other queens throughout our history. My Mother was human, Linora."

Lynne dropped back down into his arms, and stroked his hardness gently. He refused to wait another second, and pulled her on top of him, lowering her soft, warm, wet folds onto his cock. He moved inside her slowly, tenderly bringing tears to her eyes.

"I love you, Linora," he told her. "You are my Princess, and will be my Queen."

"And, I love you, Thor," she whispered into his ear.

Her back arched as she took him inside of her deeper, when Richard stopped moving.

"What was that?" he wondered.

Lynne grinned mischievously watching his eyes dart to her stomach.

"What the fuck was that, Linora!"

She began to move on him slowly in and out all the way with each stroke. He felt it again, and then she stopped leaning down to whisper in his ear.

"That was our child moving inside of me, Eric," she whispered.

Richard froze. Then, pushed her up to see her eyes shining with happiness.

"Our child? A baby? Linora? I knocked you up?"

Linora laughed. "Yes, you 'god', you! You knocked me up very well!"

Richard howled with happiness as he released his seed into her, bringing her mouth to his at the same time. He felt their baby kick him, and placed his hand on her stomach.

"He is Asgardian, Linora. No doubt about that! Only

we can kick that hard!”

"Well, I have to admit, SHE can kick hard! And, I love it!"

Richard had never been as happy as he was right now. He was inside of his mate, while their child moved inside her, and against them. Nothing could ever take that feeling away from him! Nothing!

And, Lynne? As excited and happy as she was when she realized she was pregnant weeks ago, she was worried, too. What would happen to their baby when she came into her powers?

~ **24** ~
Two down; two to go

It was the middle of the night, and a scream ripped through the silence of the house.

Anita was in labor. Again, Cordone was called into action to deliver another baby. Seriously! Cordone could make a fortune delivering babies at this rate!

Kaitlan held Anita's hand while Sarah and Lynne helped Cordone deliver a beautiful, baby girl. Sarah used her water element to clean the baby thoroughly, then Lynne wrapped the squiggly little girl in a soft, cream colored blanket. She gave her to Cordone who presented the child to his Third. Anita was beautiful even though she was covered in sweat, her eyes were shining as Dan placed their daughter into her arms, then leaned down and kissed her lips.

"Rachel," Anita whispered. "Her name is Rachel after my Mother, Dan."

Dan nodded, and everyone slipped out of the room to give the new little family a chance to be alone.

Secretly, Lynne was grateful that her powers had not come yet. It just brought the anxiety forward for her. At least Anita didn't have to worry about that any more! Her Elf body would not show changes until just before delivery. She had kept the secret of her pregnancy for a long time due to all that was going on. She hoped she would deliver before her powers manifested, too. According to Sarah, Lynne's power was the most dangerous of all. For the first time in her long life, Lynne was terrified for her unborn child.

A few days later, they all gathered in the main room.

181

Anita had just finished nursing Rachel, then, put her into the makeshift crib, and started to sit down with the others, when she started exhibiting odd behavior. She began to shake, and jerk, then her features softened. Her body was lost in transparency as she seemed to dissolve into a gentle wind, which brushed across everyone. She felt free as the breeze - pun intended. They watched her rise up into the air, and spread her arms twirling up to the ceiling, and back down again. Unlike Kaitlan and Sarah who exhibited physical forms before they manifested, she remained in her elemental form, and would until the transformation was complete.

"How the hell am I going to feed my baby, and do my work like this?" Anita complained to no one, and everyone.

"Well, I guess you'll have to talk me through it so I can do your work." Dan grinned staring up at her. "And, the baby? Well, I guess Rachel will just have to learn to drink from a bottle!"

Anita gave him a furious look, and lifted him up to the ceiling, then dropped him. Dan landed lightly on both feet. Anita would never have dropped a human. Dan just looked up at her, and grinned. He so loved that woman!

Richard, however, was far more serious than the others.

"The transformation process is accelerating. In a few days, Lynne will change as well." He didn't know what would happen to their baby when it did happen. "Each of you must learn to harness, and control your element. Some knowledge of this control may be yours after the transformation process. But, you will need further guidance."

Anita's eyes met Lynne's. Lynne's eyes were full of fear. She had told Anita a few days ago, but begged her to keep it silent. And, she did, until now.

"Richard. What will happen if Lynne's baby hasn't been born?" Anita asked.

"I have no idea. To my knowledge, no elemental of the past was ever pregnant."

His worry clearly showed on his face. Of all the things

he had ever encountered in his long life, he had never felt true terror until now. That's when he realized there was dead silence as all faces turned toward Lynne. Richard looked at everyone.

"Oops. I guess Linora and I forgot to tell you."

There were huge pats on the backs, and laughter all around. Another baby would be born. Lynne just hoped it would be before her change. But, her instinct told her that it just was not going to happen. She would gain her Elemental powers before delivery.

Sarah was very happy for her friends, but sad for herself. The monster had killed her baby, killed her, and almost killed her mate. After congratulations, everyone dispersed, and Sarah stripped off her "water clothing" she had designed, and dove into the pool straight to the bottom where she felt at home right now. She cried so much sitting there, she was dry. Strange for a woman who was made of water, sitting in water, to be dry.

The pool room had been off limits for everyone, but the two of them since her change. Sam came into the room, stripped, and dove in after her wrapping his arms around her as her body shook in silent cries. She'd been through so much. Sam hurt for his mate.

Much later, Sam held her as he thought about the logistics of everything right now. For one thing, Sarah found that she could drag Sam under the water, and he could breathe under water just like her as long as Sarah touched him. Making love had come with some very interesting difficulties, and figuring out how to achieve it was a whole different matter. But, after trying several different ideas, they had figured it out. Sam had decided that making love to her on the bottom of the pool was about the most amazing, and erotic thing ever. Sarah loved it, too. Her element, with her mate inside he,r was amazingly exciting. Even though he was inside her body, her wetness was constant, allowing him to stay inside her easily!

When Sarah tightened her water around his hardness, it stimulated him more than ever, and it caused him to explode his seed inside of her.

She was blue as the Caribbean, but how long before she would finally be able to alter her body from her water form back to her human form was anyone's guess. Anyway, necessity is always the mother of invention, and they had the inventions down to a fine art! As long as he was touching her, he was able to sleep with her, and make love to her on the bottom of the pool. With their minds speaking to each other, there was no need for verbalization.

Anita, though had a more interesting challenge now that she was air. It wasn't that easy to make love to Dan. But, if Sarah and Sam could figure it out, then so could they. After multiple ideas, they hit on the answer. When she was in the air, all she had to do was to touch him, and he would also be airborne. While Anita's outside appeared to be air, inside her she was as solid as normal. Dan's cock really appreciated it! So, when they weren't taking care of the baby, they spent a lot of time on the ceiling of their room!

Cordone sent for Milon. He would take Richard and Lynne's baby, after it was born, to keep safe with his children.

Cordone was taking a shower, when Kaitlan rushed into the room.

"Cordone! Look at me!! No more furry stuffed animal!" She was laughing. "I'm so glad!"

"The children will miss your fur," and laughed as he stepped out of the shower. Kissing her mouth desperately, he added, "And no more fur tickling my cock while I'm trying to make love to you, either!"

He grabbed her, and swung her around. Kaitlan threw her arms around his neck, and laughed in sheer joy. His lips met hers, then he pulled her into the shower where they stayed a really, really long time.

Sam woke up on the bottom of the pool, and couldn't breathe. He turned to see that Sarah was back to normal, and gasping for air! He grabbed her, and jumped them both out of the water. Sarah coughed up a lot of water, before she realized that she was normal again. Her eyes met Sam's. Without a word, Sam scooped Sarah up into his arms, and regardless of the fact that they were naked before everyone, leaped them to their room shutting the door behind him. Like Cordone and Kaitlan, they stayed there a really, really long time.

Lynne and Richard were sitting in the living area when, suddenly, Lynne jumped up, and ran outside without a word. She could feel it building inside her. She knew, beyond doubt, that she could not stay inside, and risk burning. Richard was on her heels.   As he reached her, she flung out her arms to stop him.

"NO! Eric! Don't touch me!"

Her body shook with a terrible force as she felt her insides heating up. Richard tried again.

"ERIC! PLEASE DON'T! I don't want to hurt you!"

Then, her body began to erupt in flames.

Her last cry was heard. "My baby! Oh, Creator!! My BABY!!!"

Richard was thrown backward thirty feet as Lynne's body erupted into a brilliant orange flame. Everyone in the house heard it, and ran outside. Mouths gaped as they beheld the fiery Lynne.

Lynne held her hands out in front of her. They were flames as were her arms, her legs, and the rest of her body. She searched inside for her child. She found no evidence of pregnancy. The pain inside was excruciating, and had nothing to do with fire. She had lost her baby! And, gained a power she did not want! She dropped to her knees, screaming.

Richard knew. His head dropped in sorrow. He knew why she was screaming. Their child! Their beautiful little baby was gone.

By now, Lynne's body was nothing but flame. Lynne rose in the air using the flames to make her rise. If her baby wasn't gone, it would have been an incredible experience. She had to leave. She couldn't face Richard with the fact she had killed their baby! She began to fly away when ….

"OW!"

She doubled over in pain. She didn't know why at first, but then dropped to the ground. Everyone's mouths gaped as her flaming arms reached into her body, and brought out her beautiful little baby. Their son. Her eyes widened as she looked at him crying, but not in pain from her flames. He was just damn mad that he had lost his cozy warm, well hot, home!

Her eyes slowly raised to meet Richard's in shock, and wonder. How could she have given birth as a fireball? Yet, here he lay in her flaming arms. Beautiful and perfect - and completely immune to her flames!

Richard's eyes narrowed. None of the other mates had been harmed touching their mates, he reasoned. He stood, and walked slowly toward Lynne.

"Stop, Eric. I don't know if I'm safe to come near!" she begged him.

She needed to get their child to him, though, and laid her baby on the grass, then backed away.

Richard picked up his first born son. He kissed him gently, and the baby giggled. Then, he turned to Cordone with an unasked question. Cordone approached him, took the baby to Milon who left with both Rachel and Richard, Jr. immediately.

Richard turned to Lynne who knew, instinctively, what he was going to do.

"NO! Eric! Please! Stay away!" She cried.

Richard didn't listen to her, but continued until he reached her.

"The others were not harmed by their mates, Linora. So, reason and logic dictates that you will not harm me, either. You did not harm our son."

Lynne kept shaking her head until Richard reached out to touch her flaming hand, and the flames turned blue. He was fine! Their eyes met in amazement. Richard took her flaming lips with his. The kiss was unbelievably erotic!

"How?" Lynne asked as if to herself. "I don't even feel as if I gave birth!"

"Why you don't feel it, I also don't know. But if the others can figure it out, so can we. The transformations are almost over."

The others noted the way they kissed each other, and discreetly left them alone.

Lynne smiled, and threw her arms around his neck kissing him soundly upon the mouth. It took them no time at all to figure out their logistics for getting around the flames to make love.

"Richard, Jr.," she breathed into his mouth, and wrapped her legs around his waist. There was no pain from childbirth, and her body had already healed to take her mate.

~ 25 ~
When the going gets tough, the tough get going … what a dumb motto!

Richard had been right. Both Anita and Lynne finally completed their transformations, but they were much faster than Kaitlan and Sarah. Now, it was time to harness their powers. Yeah. Right. That was going to happen.

The girls were outside on a daily basis working on their elemental changes. They weren't doing all that well. It was hit and miss constantly even though they were able to change at will - well, sometimes, yes, sometimes no.

"Shit!" Lynne said. "This is just ridiculous! Why give us these powers if we can't even figure out how to use them?"

"I agree," echoed Anita. "Seriously? What is it with these beings, or whoever, giving powers like this without anyone to teach us how to use them?"

The girls all agreed with that one. When they tried to shift into their elemental forms, they didn't. When they didn't try, they did. The mates were at a loss as well. Richard had said they had to learn to harness their powers, and about all they could do was barely squeak out a tiny bit of them.

Cordone and Richard were watching their lack of progress a couple of weeks later.

"If they don't get their powers under control soon, how in the world are we going to fight Zanack?" Cordone asked. He was totally frustrated.

Richard rubbed his chin. He was thinking about that perfect person to help them, but he wasn't sure just how he would react if he asked. He dropped his arm.

"Cordone … Remember I told you that there is someone who can help. But, it's been a really long time since I saw him."

"Really? He would help?"

"Possibly. But, like I said. I haven't spoken with him in eons. I'm not sure how he will receive me."

"We don't have time to waste, Richard. Do what you have to do. I'll explain to Lynne."

Richard nodded, and left.

"What do you mean Richard went to get help?" demanded Anita .

"He said you girls needed help, and he knew of someone who just might be the one who could help you."

"Where did he go?" Lynne couldn't believe he would leave without telling her.

Cordone just shrugged. He wasn't about to tell Lynne where he thought Richard had gone! And, he was getting damned tired of all these females ganging up on him - including his own mate.

"Did he say when he'd be back?" Sarah asked.

"No." Cordone closed his eyes praying for patience. He gave up. Never going to happen.

"Didn't he say where he was going, Cordone?" Kaitlan repeated Lynne's question.

"*Women*! Creator, save me from women!" he yelled. "That is enough out of all four of you! I sent Richard to get help, and he'll return when he returns! I'm going for a run!"

He turned on his heel, phased to his black wolf, and ran like the wind!

Kaitlan started to laugh so hard, her sides started hurting. Did he not think that just because she was his editor she didn't read his books? Seriously?

"Well, that was rude." Sarah stated.

Kaitlan finally calmed down long enough to tell the girls that the "scene" they had just witnessed was directly out of a novel he wrote two years before. Then, she started laughing again. The others joined. They had a really good laugh!

Zanack was furious! He had been unaware that the building he used for his human refuse and meetings had been targeted for demolition! It had brought him up short when he arrived. And, he couldn't do a damn thing about it, either, because he couldn't afford to be discovered. This made him even angrier. He needed what was inside that basement, but they were in the process of removing every single body part he had ever stored in it! He needed all that rotting flesh and bones to gorge before he could cast the curse. Now, they were looking for him! He had no idea how he was going to gorge, now.

He stood looking at the building trying to figure out another way. He'd spent years stockpiling what he knew he would need in order to recast the curse, and now, it was all gone! A second problem was he needed the scraps to maintain his glamour. He was almost ready, and now?

His hands raked through his brown hair as he stared at nothing. Fuck! He'd have to find another way to gorge, now. This would set him back, and Zanack hated to start over again, but he really had no choice! He shoved his hands in his designer Dark Blue suit, turned, and started walking back to Seneca Publishing slowly. So far, no one knew who he was, and it was a good thing he occupied a place on the council, or he wouldn't be able to get away with any of this.

The Elementals needed to gain their powers. That was another thing he had found out as he had read that damned second scroll he had taken from the council room the night before. Something that he would seriously have screwed up, because he hadn't all the information needed the first time. Now, that had been an eye-opener! One dead elemental was all it took to doom his plans! He had cast the curse the first time not knowing he needed all four! And, that allowed the damn Prophecy to come true. Even after all this time, he wondered who had kidnapped the first Earth Element. Oh, he had his suspicions, but nothing concrete.

Zanack stopped at a stop light waiting to cross, and tapped his fingers on his leg. He had one chance, and one only.

Closing his eyes, Zanack pictured what he would do with these weak humans. A food source, yes, but his carnal desires as well. His corruption was almost totally complete. He needed blood tonight! His cock was hard and horny as hell. He desired every carnality tonight. But, he was unable to do anything about it right now, because he had not yet found another building to pile up scraps again. The problem was that his time was running out.

The light turned green, and he walked forward in the midst of all the people working. Reaching Seneca Publishing, Zanack glanced all the way to the top. This is where he would rule. And, the first thing he wanted after he changed this world? Kaitlan O'Hara Valon - if she was in the next world! She was deliciously sexy. Somewhere along the line, he had ceased being disgusted at being inside her body. He thought it might be her new power, but he wanted to be inside her! Feel her luscious breasts under his spiny fingers. He was insatiable, and could fuck her for days on end. He wanted to bury his cock into her body deep until he spilled his burning seed into her. She would be in horrible pain as his seed joined with her egg, and implanted his offspring inside her womb. His cock hardened even more at the thought of her pain. Their offspring would be the epitome of evil. Unfortunately, only one child could ever come from her body since a painful death would follow from birth! He almost rubbed his hands together, and laughed aloud, before he realized where he was. A sneer appeared on his face, and he headed directly to The Hall of Records.

Hours later, Zanack slammed his hand on the table startling others in The Hall. He smiled, and waved an apology to them.

He had still found nothing! It had to be here! The key to getting the two time periods to merge. He knew he had to gorge before he opened it. That was known to all wizards. A blood sacrifice was needed for time travel, but, he didn't have the spell to open up the time barrier. He rose out of his chair to put the scroll back in its place, and started to turn around when his sharp eyes noticed a small cubbyhole where he'd just returned the scroll. He pulled out the scroll, and saw something behind it. He reached into the cubbyhole until it buried his arm to his armpit. His fingers touched something, and he pulled.

It was a scroll! An odd-looking scroll. He put the other one back into its hole, and sat back down. Shaking, he discovered that the seal had not been broken. The seal was unrecognizable. He'd never seen it before. It looked like a rune of some type. He checked around him making sure no one could watch him break a seal he was not authorized to break. He knew the dangers attributed to breaking a seal not meant for him, but he was too close, now. He broke the seal, and rolled it out.

His mouth lifted in a sneer, then a smile, then it took everything in him not to dance about! He'd found the Scroll of Time! He'd found the missing page from the wizards' book of spells on how to merge the worlds and the time between worlds! He covertly tucked the scroll inside his suit coat, and left The Hall. Silently, a figure grinned, and disappeared.

Richard asked his friend to wait while he went inside the house to get the girls so he could initiate introductions. When they appeared, their mouths dropped. A tall man stood, almost regally, in front of them. He was just another one of those "god" type men. He was the same height as Richard, but had a tanned, golden skin that glittered. His eyes were an impossible dark brown with unusual gold flecks, and looked as if they were looking into your very soul. His hair was a rich brown streaked with what looked like real gold! His arms were bigger around than the bodies of the girls. His body was hard, toned, and gorgeous. But, his face bore great age, and ages of battle. One would never want to be on this man's bad side, but almost any woman would want to be under him!

"Ladies, I want you to meet an old friend of mine. This is Dahll."

Richard placed his hand on his friend's shoulder.

"Ladies," Dahll said, then swept low in a graceful bow.

His voice was low, and deep. Mesmerizing would probably be a better description. Richard was tickled to see all four females practically drool over his friend.

"It is a great honor to meet the Elementals."

The girls looked at each other. All of them, and even Lynne who knew where he was from, had this insane desire to curtsy to him!

"Eric tells me that you are needing help conquering your new powers."

All four nodded their heads, and Kaitlan spoke.

"Yes, Dahll. With the elemental powers we have just received, Richard told us that we might be able to control them. Oh, we can 'control' them, alright! Not!"

"Richard, I will work with each lady individually. Until they can master their powers as individuals, it would be most confusing to them."

Richard nodded.

"Then, I leave you to teach them, Dahll."

Dahll nodded to Richard.

"I will begin with The White Wolf, for her elemental will be the most difficult. She is bound to the Earth, and must learn to control all that which exists both on and under it. Each must be in their wolf form to cross the veil. Kaitlan, please phase, and follow me."

Kaitlan's eyes widened. What did he mean, on and under it? Oh, man! This was so not what she had envisioned when she became the White Wolf. Truthfully? She was terrified out of her mind. But, she knew that they all had to become what they should become. She had a really bad feeling about how it would all end.

Dahll was waiting. A gray mist rose up behind him.

Kaitlan looked at Cordone, then back to Dahll. She bent her head and sighed.

"I am ready," then phased into The White Wolf.

"No. You are not," Dahll told her as he walked into a mist with Kaitlan following.

~ 26 ~
Practice, Practice, and Practice Still doesn't always mean perfect !

Kaitlan had to almost run to keep up with Dahll his legs were so long. When he realized she was having a hard time keeping up with him, he slowed his walking. He was one of few words, but he was a bit curious with all that he had been told by Richard.

"I understand that you were the first to gain your elemental, Kaitlan?" He asked.

"Yes, sir."

Kaitlan suddenly had an extreme urge to be more polite to this man than she had ever been in her life to anyone.

"Do you effect the ground?"

She shook her head.

"The plants?"

Again, she shook her head.

Dahll narrowed his eyes.

"What about the animals? Do you hear them?"

"No."

Kaitlan didn't know what to say, but she remembered everyone else's power would do cool things.

"I just turned into a human, fuzzy wolf."

Dahll just looked at her. He looked at her for so long, Kaitlan began to get a bit uncomfortable. She felt as if she was in a fishbowl, and that this man could look through to her very soul.

Finally, Dahll nodded his head.

"Come," was all he said.

A mist began to form around them, so thick, Kaitlan could see nothing around her. In a moment, the mist cleared.

He led her to a bluff, somewhere, that stood so high, the bottom of it could not be seen. Kaitlan had never seen anything like it in her life, let alone heard of anything this high.

"Where are we?" Kaitlan asked.

She was sure, beyond doubt, that this bluff was no where on Earth. It couldn't be! Above her four moons shone brightly enough to light whatever planet they were on at the moment. The stars were blotted out. The ground could not be seen. In fact, it was so high, it appeared to be in the clouds! She saw thick clouds below her.

He pointed down.

"Where is not important. Jump," he ordered.

Jump? She looked over the edge, then back at him. Jump? What did he mean, jump?

"Are you insane?" Kaitlan raised her voice.

"Jump," Dahll said, yet again still pointing. "The only way to gain control of your powers is to do what they do not expect you to do. Now, jump, Kaitlan."

"I already told you. I did not have any powers except being a human, fuzzy wolf!"

"Jump," he ordered a third time.

He hated when he had to explain anything. But, he forgot he was working with someone from Earth. They were totally clueless about things. Very few on Asgard had patience with those on Earth. Luckily, he was one of them. Thor was another. He never understood why Thor decided to live there.

"You must feel the fear others will fear in order to control your powers. You must also conquer your own fear of heights. If you do not jump, I will throw you off this bluff. Do you understand?"

Kaitlan gulped. Yep, she understood perfectly. Richard's friend was a psychopath!

When it looked as if Dahll was really going to follow up on his threat to throw her off, she complied.

"We aren't on Earth. Exactly where are we? If I'm the earth element, how can it work when we are not on Earth?"

He cocked his head at her. Did she really just ask him that?

"The word 'earth' can be used to describe your planet, or the ground on which you stand. Point of fact…it is the ground where you stand, no matter what planet you are upon."

Her mouth dropped. Could he be any more cryptic? He pointed, and started to speak.

"OK. You don't have to say it again. I'm going on a little faith, here, but if I go splat at the bottom, Cordone won't let you go!" She walked off the bluff.

And, she fell. Five minutes later, she was STILL falling? Ten minutes, and still falling! After about fifteen minutes of falling, the ground finally came into view, and it was coming up fast. Kaitlan started to panic, and wished something would at least slow her down so she could think. Something grabbed her left leg and arm slowing her descent. To Kaitlan's left, vines stretching out of the side of the bluff wrapped their arms around her gently setting her down gently on the ground. The vines wiggled as they retracted back into the bluff! They had completely disappeared. No. They weren't vines. They were roots!

"What the hell?" Kaitlan thought.

"Hi." Was that a voice said inside of her head? But, it sure wasn't Cordone's voice!

Kaitlan whirled around. No one was there. Hearing things. She tilted her head up.

"Now, how do I get back up? Climb?" she asked of no one.

"Of course." The voice was back.

No one was there! Now, she was turning into a psychopath!

"No, you're not." The voice. *"Ask for what you need, and it shall be given to you, Mother."*

She darted around three hundred and sixty degrees. Nothing. No one.

"Ask, huh? OK. Uh…voice? Can you get me back to

the top of the bluff?"

The ground rumbled around her feet, and a small sapling appeared. Then, it grew fast, and Kaitlan grabbed a branch holding on for dear life as the tree shot her upward so fast, she couldn't draw a breath! It continued to grow into the largest tree she had ever seen!! It had to be if it had taken her fifteen minutes of free fall!

The top of the tree stopped just at the bluff's edge, and she found herself staring face to face with Dahll who was smiling at her.

"Well, done, Kaitlan. You have mastered the plants that bury their roots deeply into the earth."

Kaitlan stepped onto the bluff, and turned to face the monster tree. She was afraid how far down she had fallen, let alone afraid to realize how big the tree actually was.

"Uh…Mr. Tree. Thank you for the lift," she smiled tentatively.

"It was my honor, Mother. Ask anytime, and we of the plant kingdom will be pleased to serve you."

Then, the tree dropped faster than it had grown until it was gone. She turned to Dahll.

"Mother?" She was puzzled.

"To the entities on, and within the ground, you are their Mother Kaitlan. It will be thus when you return to your Earth."

"Mother Nature? That's what Sarah said."

"Whatever you wish to call yourself. It is your choice."

Dahll looked around at his feet, bent over, and picked up something that looked like a beetle, but was snow white. He handed it to her.

She had never been one for bugs, but one look on Dahll's face told her to take it. She held out her hand, and the beetle crawled into it.

A tiny, but high pitched voice said, *"Hi, Mother! How may I serve you?"*

Kaitlan jerked her whole body. She can talk to animals, now? Like Dr. Doolittle? Whoa! Seriously?

"Uh, hi?" she said to the little bug. It wiggled in her hand.

"Like the plants, you also command the animal kingdom, Kaitlan."

"Uh, no. You don't need to serve me, little bug. You can just go home, now, but thank you."

She felt like a total dork talking to a bug!

He took her hand after she laid the beetle back down, and it scuttled away after thanking her, and promising to be there if she needed him!

"Your power is the most powerful for you command the Earth, and all which is within it, as well as those who live on its surface. You command the plants, the animals, the earth, and even the rocks. You can call forth volcanoes, split the ground, forge the course of rivers. Even the oceans will bow to your will. You also can speak to all animals of the Earth - even those within the oceans.

This was almost too much for her to process. Was she truly that powerful? Her mind couldn't comprehend it.

"But, Sarah is the Water element."

"True. But, she can only command the water itself. You can command the Earth below the water. You can create Earthquakes, flatten mountains, and raise others. This is why your gift is so powerful - much more than the others. Without you, the other three elementals cannot accomplish the destruction of the one of evil. This is why the original curse was able to be broken. Not only must the evil one use all the elements to invoke a permanent curse, but *you* must use them to invoke his destruction. And, only you can command all four elements, Kaitlan. All will be needed before you can destroy Zanack."

Eyes wide, she was having a hard with all of this. No doubt about it, though. If he was telling the truth, she was all powerful. But, should anyone be allowed that much power? Her answer to herself was that no one should ever be given that much power.

"But, if I can command all of them, why give the other three powers, too?"

"Power, Kaitlan, great power is given to only those who are expected to wield it for good. No one can wield all the elements for a long period of time. Think of Sarah, Anita, and Lynne as the 'holders' of the power that you will take when it is time."

"You mean, 'With great power comes great responsibility'?" She loved Spiderman.

"More, or less. But, the power can be used wrong, and there is a cost if they do. Believe me. It is NOT something you want to know about. It's one of those catches. Many have accepted great power, only to misuse that power to the point of their own destruction. Remember this, Kaitlan. What you face will be an evil most have never seen, nor imagined. Everything is being set up as it was before. The evil one has no mercy, and has made a pact with the devil himself. Even his entire body has changed into something - well, even I cannot describe what it may look like. But, what he will become will be hideous! If you let your guard down, even for an instant, it could mean the difference between the existence of evil and death, and the existence of good and living. This has to be played out, and it will be the final act. It's up to you and your friends to destroy him. You, alone, will be most at risk. The last time, the Earth element was ripped away, because she had no idea how to wield her element in order to stop him. She had not been taught before it began. That is why she was taken away. The difference is, you will have an advantage, because you will know how to wield it. The evil one will not know this until you are ready to defeat him. But, beware. You could easily be used for evil. Do you understand?" Dahll asked.

She nodded. She definitely understood. She did not want to dance with the devil with the powers she had been given. Especially, now that she knew what they were. Yet, she also knew she didn't know what she could actually do. Practice makes perfect. Oh, goody. She hated to practice!

"I must go to Sarah, now. I want you to stay out here, and commune with the Earth. See what she has to offer you, and what you have to offer her. Listen to her. Use every single empathic ability that you have, and yes, you do have empathy as do all elementals. Do not fail, Kaitlan. If you do, everything you know will be gone forever. Beware, Kaitlan, for you may be called upon to sacrifice the greatest gift from the Creator. You must be prepared for this."

That did not sound good to Kaitlan.

"You will be returned to Earth when you have mastered your powers, Mother," said Dahll.

"Wait! What did you mean that my friends will keep the powers until I am ready to take them?" Kaitlan turned to ask the question.

Wait! Where did he go? She looked in all directions, and saw nothing. Why did you always think of things after the fact?

It didn't sound good. Taking power from her friends? Sacrificing God's greatest gift? What did all that mean? But, no matter. She would do what it took to get rid of the monster.

Shaking her head, she turned and sat down at the edge of the bluff. How to start? What to actually do? She felt something soft and furry against her leg. It was an adorable gray bunny rabbit. She bent down to pet it, and asked him something expecting no answer.

"So, little one. How do you suppose I should begin?"

"Easy, great one! You must touch the Earth in every way with your skin! That is why you hear me, now. You are touching me with your skin. But, you can also talk to me telepathically if needed."

Kaitlan started, looking into the innocent eyes before her. She picked up the bunny, and gave it a kiss on its little head.

"Thank you."

She put him down, he nodded, then hopped off on his nocturnal errands. Night was rapidly descending.

Kaitlan sat there a minute, thinking what she should do.

Instinctively, she stripped off all her clothing. Her feet touched the Earth, and she could hear something. Skin. Telepathy. That was what she needed to use!

The bunny had hopped back to her, and touched her foot.

"I forgot. You need to bring forth your wolf, too." Then he hopped off again.

OK. Now she knew. She needed to become the human wolf. But, how?

"I wonder. Can I phase to my human wolf the same way I can phase to my wolf and back to human?" It hadn't worked yet, but maybe now?

She thought that if she could call her wolf up to phase, maybe the same thing worked with the human wolf.

"OK. Here it goes!"

She had spontaneously changed before, but this was taking all of her power of concentration. Her body began to shake hard, and she felt the wolf begin to appear.

~ 27 ~
Listening is the key to all things, but understanding is more important

Dahll appeared to the group again. They looked at each other. He had barely left with Kaitlan, and he was already back?

Cordone had started to speak, but found he couldn't! What the hell?

Dahll's eyes met those of Sarah.

"Uh-oh. Guess it's my turn," Sarah thought.

"Indeed it is, Sarah." Dahll answered her thought, and her eyes widened.

She had thought only mates could speak to each other along with Alphas, Seconds and Thirds when necessity arose. Well, that blew that idea out of the water. Yes. Pun intended. It was the only way she knew she would keep sane.

He held out his hand. She glanced toward Sam who was really looking worried. She gave him a little grin, and then she walked with Dahll. Geez she felt like she was Scrooge in 'A Christmas Carol'"!

In an instant, Sarah found herself standing on an extremely high bluff overlooking the ocean!?

"How…?"

Sarah started to ask, then shut up at the look in Dahll's face. She already knew wherever she was she was not on Earth. She was certain of it. Especially with four moons above them, and an ocean of red!

He stared into her eyes for a moment. Good. She has learned to control her voice.

"You are correct. This is not Earth. This is a planet of training for all elementals. Sarah, you command the water. You wield a great power. Water is the basis of life - both on Earth,

203

on other worlds, and in other realities. Other types of life are based upon other elements, but water is far more prevalent than any other."

He stretched his arms toward the ocean.

"You will be able to wield the power of the waves, and the volume under them. Your power will allow you to form canyons, erode mountains of the greatest heights, give life to the deserts if you so wish, and even destroy whatever you wish at will. Water is one of the greatest forces on Earth. With Kaitlan commanding the Earth below the waters, and you the waters, your combined powers will be unimaginable."

Sarah's mouth dropped open. No one, she thought, should have that type of power. It's wrong.

Dahll cocked his head. The same thought that Kaitlan had, he remembered. That is good. Neither girl wishes it for their own selfish purpose. She also had forgotten he could hear her thoughts.

"Sarah, because that is what you feel, and believe, it is the reason why you were given this power. The Creator knows that you will not use your power for evil. Your power is tremendous, and can easily act upon your very emotions. You suffered greatly in your beginnings in life. You suffered, again, with the loss of your child. This was needed for you to be able to access this great power along with all your other powers. Unlike the others who have supernatural powers already, you did not have any, because you are human. Until you were sent back after seven days, you did not have supernatural powers. Your ability to phase to a wolf was given to you by your mate's bite. It was a vast need that you transition into a super, and is the reason all these things in your life happened to you. It was preordained long ago. Humans are weak, and very vulnerable to evil in all its forms. You could have, quite easily, gone that route, and become evil with all the sadness and hatred you experienced. But, you didn't. You accepted what had happened to you, and still turned it into something magnificent - enough to be honored with this power. It was your destiny to become this. You were also given the power of a seer - one who sees what was, is, and will be."

"I just wish it hadn't cost my baby his life," Sarah whispered as a tear rolled down her cheek.

A great roar was heard out in the ocean, and Sarah looked up to see a 200 foot wave coming at them. The bluff was much higher than that, but she noticed that a small village, or settlement, stood on the coast below the bluff. Where did it come from? Her eyes had easily picked it out. How? Her eyesight was unbelievable! Her eyes darted up to the wave. She couldn't let those people die!

"Your eyesight has changed to see not only above the ocean, but below it. The power of one tear created that wave, Sarah." Dahll told her quietly.

Her eyes darted to him in shock. One tear did this? NO!!! She could not let this happen. Her hands came up without her concentrating upon it.

Her eyes closed, then opened. She looked around. She was on the bottom of the ocean??? Everything was so clear to her! She had to stop the wave, and so she gave an order.

"Be calm."

Just as the wave was about to strike the small town, it was gone as suddenly as it appeared! She pulled her hands back to her sides, then found herself standing, again, on the bluff with Dahll.

He grinned.

"Did I forget to mention that in order for you to control the waters you must be IN the waters?"

Sarah took a deep breath. "Yeah. I guess you could say you just forgot to mention that one!"

"You must stay here. Learn to control your powers, and most especially, your emotions and tears. If one tear could bring about a 200 foot wave, imagine what would happen if you let loose a flood of them?"

Sarah couldn't imaging it, and her entire body shook. The idea that she could actually flood the entire Earth was unfathomable to her! Yes. Another pun intended.

"Like Kaitlan. You must learn control. It is the only possible way to help Kaitlan's powers of the Earth, and to defeat the evil one. Understand, Sarah. If something happens to Kaitlan as did the first Earth elemental who was taken before the curse was completed, all will be lost this time like it was the last. You must also be prepared to relinquish your powers to her when it is needed. All of you will lose even more than you have already lost. One second chance is all that is ever given."

Sarah took his words to heart, and she knew he wasn't lying. She nodded, and almost cried, but caught herself just in time.

"I understand, Dahll." She looked up at him. "I know that to fight this evil, life must be given."

Again, he cocked his head, and nodded. She had been given the gift of sight. Looking into her eyes, he saw she knew exactly what would be asked of all four of them. Her eyes were sad. She knew what was ahead, and worse was that she knew that their mates would be involved in something horrible, but she did not know what yet.

"Then, I must now return for Anita. Be careful, and use your empathic abilities. All four of you have them. Practice, and gain control of the waters. Once you have mastered your power, you will return to Earth."

Sarah looked down at the town, then back at Dahll. Her head darted around. Where did he go? Then, she shrugged. How should she start the practice? She didn't want to hurt this village, but if Dahll was right, this town would be seeing things it has never seen over the next few hours. She just hoped she would not cause someone to have a heart attack. Or flood them all into oblivion!

Sarah closed her eyes to find she was, again, on the ocean floor. She raised her arms out from her sides, and up. She thought she'd turn the ocean into a fountain. She smiled. There were ways to do this without harming the town as the waters lifted her upward to shoot up into the air as high as possible as the ocean turned into the largest fountain ever seen. She was truly more powerful than she had thought! It was exhilarating, but it was also terrifying as well. By keeping that last in mind, she was able to not let the power gain power over her.

Anita had decided to just go ahead and step forward waiting on Dahll. As with Kaitlan, he had been gone just a few seconds when he showed up for Anita. Anita didn't hesitate, but walked to his side when he reappeared. She turned, and nodded at Dan, then walked with Dahll to the edge of the forest.

She stood with Dahll on a … *"Is this a cloud????"* Her eyes were about as wide as they could be as she looked down at her feet.

She could see a planet below her as if she were riding in a jet at 40,000 feet! The curvature, and everything was magnificent without anything blocking her view!!! It was cold. Very cold, yet she wasn't cold at all!

"Yes. This is a cloud, Anita. You power is the air. Manipulation of it will allow you to control the weather as well as allow you to fly."

Anita's eyes darted up to Dahll's. Control the weather?

"Seriously? The weather?" She asked. Flying was already second nature to her.

Dahll nodded his head.

"With this power, you can affect many things. Wind and air erode mountains, and even man-made buildings given time. Effecting the weather requires wind, heat and cold. If you have yet to notice, when you are in your air form, sometimes you are hot; sometimes cold?"

Well, now that he mentioned it, she did realize that was true. She hadn't given it a thought. She looked up. Then, did a double take. Four moons were above her! Four? Where was she?

"You are on the training planet of the elementals, and have the powers of the four winds of the Earth - East and West;

North and South. You can bring forth these winds to create tornadoes as well as hurricanes without boundaries. You can focus your power on one small area, or raise the wind to the highest of heights to obtain your goals. It is a power unlike all the others. With it, you can bring sandstorms, dust storms. You can dry up the crops below with a burst of hot wind, while freezing them with an ice wind. It is unlimited power. You can cause famine, or you can bring storms with life-giving rains bringing abundance of crops where needed."

"Whoa! That's unbelievable! But, really? I am a healer, Dahll. I could no more bring that type of damage than I can fly…Oh…wait. I can fly!"

He grinned at her.

"I know. It's hard to realize that you can have that power, and use it for both good and evil. These powers you all have are such that anyone of you can use them for evil. But, beware. Once you start down that path, you will be doomed forever. Trust me. You DON'T want to go down that path! Been there; done that."

Anita wondered what he meant by that statement?

"Each of us must suffer our own growth pains, Anita, and we do not always succeed. Sometimes, we fail, but we get up, and try again. And, we learn lessons. The air is life as well as is water. Water is life; air breathes into life for existence. Without it, none of us would be alive. Two things which no supernatural can effect are the heart and the mind. The heart was made by the Creator to beat as long as one is alive. The mind the Creator gave to us with freedom of choice. They are the two things that have even greater power over us than the elements. It is with the mind that we choose good or evil. And, it's an individual thing. No one can choose for you. That is something that you must do entirely by yourself. It is, quite literally, the only time when you are truly, and completely, alone. Do not let anyone else influence your thoughts, for to do so, you will lose any humanity that is within your heart and mind. Do you understand this?"

Anita nodded. She did know. The power of life, and even death, really was in her hands. She could take it away with a blast of hot wind, or cause the land to heal and yield great abundance. But, to do so, she must be careful of her emotions. If she were angry, she could kill people; if she were happy, she could give them life - just by crops alone. She knew she had always lived with this, but had never really thought about it before. She nodded again. She did not think that anyone should have these powers except the Creator.

"I understand probably better than anyone that the power of life and death is truly in my hands, Dahll."

Dahll smiled with real happiness. Anita was truly the perfect element. She had rightly been given the air element.

"Then, I leave you here on the cloud. Below you is a small farm. You will be learning to control the power here. Those who live here have agreed to allow you to take your powers to the utmost. They cannot be harmed, but everything around them can be. Once you master your powers, you will be returned to Earth."

Anita nodded. She knew she had to control it. She just didn't want to hurt their home.

Dahll disappeared into the cloud.

~ 28 ~
Great Power demands Great Control

Lynne stood before Dahll. This was the one person about who he had doubt. Lynne was an Elf. Their emotions were tied to their powers to begin with, yet she was given the most deadly of all. Elves were known for their quick tempers and actions. Her elven power, though, could easily contribute to a deadly combination. He did not understand the Creator's reasoning in this one. But, that wasn't his decision, and it was his duty to help the elementals to succeed in the use of these powers. Even Richard knew not what Dahll had been charged to do.

Lynne stepped up to him.

"I am ready." She said simply.

Dahll's eyes narrowed trying to read her. It was difficult. The hardest of all elements to read was fire. And, Elves.

"Then, come."

She and Dahll, like the others, walked toward the swirling mist. The men were worried sick about their mates. Even Richard. They wanted to go with them so they could protect them, but their feet had been "glued" to the floor of the deck. They had not been allowed to move. They were released as soon as Lynne was out of sight.

"What the hell, Richard?" Cordone demanded.

All three men turned to him.

"I have no idea what's going on. Dahll, I know, was given to me as the one to make sure they developed their powers."

"Yeah, but where did it say we couldn't go with them?" demanded Dan.

"I think I know," said Sam. They all turned to him with frowns. "Dahll is the teacher of the elementals. He has always been the teacher."

All four men looked at each other. That actually made sense. They had to have someone to teach them, but none of them could do it.

"Hmmm…." Richard began. "The original curse did have one less elemental. We figured this one out. But, that begs the question…did they know how to use them? And, my guess is they did not have help developing their powers. Don't know why, though."

"Didn't we read that the Earth elemental was taken before the curse was finished? If that is so, what is to prevent someone from taking Kaitlan?" Cordone said. "More than that…who has the largest power, Richard?"

Richard stared straight at Cordone.

"The one who wields the most power is the one who can affect the most. The one who would be the biggest target is the one who wields more power in her little finger than all the other three elementals combined. And, I doubt, even with the practice, she will not understand this until she is forced to use her full power. Just as the first Earth element, it is so now. I, once, commanded all the elements as well, but frankly, even with Mjölnir, I am not powerful. In fact, I pale in comparison to all four elementals. Being a werewolf also diminished most of my powers except for a few fireworks. But, Cordone, Kaitlan is the most powerful of all."

Cordone collapsed onto one of his overstuffed, leather chairs. His head found his hands, and there he stayed for a very long time.

Richard was worried about Lynne. Her power would be awesome. But, could her Elven temper be used to make it worse? He had no answer to that. He just prayed that she could control her emotions.

Lynne stood in an active volcano, inside a crater, in the lava!!! Dahll stood with her. And, yet, they were just fine!! She couldn't believe it! She turned her shocked face to Dahll who smiled.

"Lynne, your power is, without doubt, the most deadly of all. It can be instantaneous. It manifests anywhere at any time. It comes at the strike of lightning, and even just a butt of a cigarette can cause devastation unmatched when it catches a forest on fire. It can even be caused by simply striking a flint for a campfire. It can start anywhere, and can spread faster than almost anything else on Earth. It has been destroyed completely more than once by fire."

Lynne knew this to be true. She'd seen enough of it in her life.

"But, you are also an Elf. We all know that Elf emotions are explosive. But, combined with this element of fire? It could cause the entire world to erupt in flame."

"I know that, Dahll. That you need not tell me. So, why give this terrible power to me?"

"I do not know the answer to that, Lynne. It is not for me to know, nor you. You, more than the others, must focus your emotions when you use your power. You will be able to destroy with a thought. Your thoughts will be able to move things at will. You will be able to burn anything from the inside out. You must divorce yourself from your Elven emotions. Emotions are what will create a firestorm if all of you cannot control them. The very use of all your emotions combined with these four elemental powers can easily destroy your planet's existence. Listen carefully to what I am saying."

Lynne frowned. He was telling her something, but what? What was Dahll trying to tell her?

"So, in order to destroy Zanack, we must control our emotions in order to do so. Do I understand that right?"

"Yes. But, also remember. If your emotions and powers are loosed upon Zanack, and all who follow him, all that you know now will be erased as if it never existed."

Well, that was totally…*un*helpful! Lynne was totally confused by this time. Yes. He was definitely trying to tell her something. Why such a push about emotions when he told her they needed to be controlled?

"Lynne, you must stay here, and learn to control your power and your emotions for the next day. You must see the difference in what can happen when you do, and do not, use them. This will truly be the biggest test of all." He looked straight into her eyes. "Do you understand what I am saying?"

"Truth? Not really. But, I can tell you this, Dahll. I know of no single being in the universe who should ever be given these powers. I accept it, only because the Creator wants us to have them, but in truth, if I had a choice, I would have refused!"

Dahll's mouth pulled upward into the first, true, happy feeling he had about all of this since it began. None of the four girls wanted the powers. And, he believed them. They were preparing for a fight that may, or may not be, totally won, but he knew they would do anything to save Earth. Their trial would be a hard one, and he did not envy them. But, if they did succeed, none of them realized that the Earth afterward would not be the same, and truth was, they might not even exist! Why couldn't he see what was supposed to happen? Why was his mind being blocked from it?

"I am truly glad to hear you say that, Lynne. You will understand what I am saying when it is time. You will be returned to Earth when you have mastered your power."

Dahl left. With a short stop to tell Richard and the other mates that their mates would return when their mastering of control over their powers was completed, he told them that his teaching was over. He left them to return to Asgard, and to their own future - if there was one. These four women were the second chance, and the last one. If they did not learn to control their emotions and their powers, it would all end. For the first time in his existence, he was unsure of what the outcome will be. His ability to see the past, present and future had always served him well. But, this? It was the only thing he could not see beyond. And, that had bothered him for a very long time. Even he did not know the outcome of their fight. If they succeeded, then it was possible that everything might change, but that there was a very high probability that those who were here, now, would not be, and the future would be completely re-written. However, the option if they did not succeed, scared him even more. He still could not see anything beyond the final battle. Whatever happened, it would not just effect the Earth, but the entire universe! He was handicapped by his very nature, and the powers that had been given to him. Dahll's head was bowed with the sadness of a heavy heart as he crossed to Asgard via the Bifrost.

~ ~ ~ ~

For the next hours, Kaitlan, Sarah, Anita, and Lynne spent their time practicing their powers on the people of on the Planet of the Four Moons. Well, that's what Sarah nicknamed it. As cliché as it sounded? Practice does not always mean perfect.

~ ~ ~ ~

Kaitlan connected with the Earth, and everything on and below it. What shocked her was that the Earth actually talked BACK to her. Another amazing thing was that if Kaitlan wanted to "see" what was under it, all she had to do was visualize it, and she saw whatever was her desire. She found she could influence the tectonic plates if she so desired - which she didn't. She only practiced that a tiny bit - not even enough that would register on any scale, but only enough for her to feel it. She practiced growing things, and her first, permanent growing was for her little bunny rabbit friend who showed up every day. She had named the little creature Libby after a little stuffed, pink bunny she had when she was little. A friend's mother had given it to her for a birthday gift. It just seemed to fit. Truth be known, while it looked like a rabbit, it wasn't exactly a rabbit. It was gray, but to her surprise, it changed colors like a chameleon does with its background. It's fur was softer than the softest down, and its little ears were just that…tiny. Much smaller than a normal rabbit. In fact, it was smaller than one, too. But, it was sweet and kind. No malice ever passed its thoughts, or its mouth. It had taken her a little while to realize it was female, and not male, so when Kaitlan had asked what she called herself, she just looked puzzled. She had no concept of names. But, she loved it when Kaitlan had given her a name, and Libby was excited about it. She told Mother that she would give each of her babies names as well. Kaitlan had also learned where her little "cubby hole" was for her tiny little babies who were growing quickly.

"Hi, Mother!" the adorable little rabbit would say to Kaitlan when she saw her. Libby was lways cheerful, but had wise words.

Kaitlan would pet the little creature on its head. She was such a help! Just before Kaitlan felt that her practice was coming to an end, she wanted to do something for the little thing and her family.

"Hi, Libby! How are you and your adorable little family?"

"We are all fine, Mother. I'm off to find our daily food!"

"I do," "she grinned at her tiny, furry little friend." She had already come to not think of the ground, flora, and fauna as creatures, plants, or inanimate objects, but they were her friends.

A sudden idea came to Kaitlan.

"Libby, have you ever eaten a carrot? It's a long, orange vegetable, and the rabbits on my planet love them!"

"What's a carrot?" asked Libby who had never heard of one, but was suddenly curious. Mother had some very strange ideas and thoughts, but Libby loved to learn. "It's long and orange and a vegetable? What did you call them? Krots?"

Kaitlan smiled. She kept forgetting that some people believed that animals only saw in black and white. So, the best way to show Libby what a carrot was? Grow one. Kaitlan placed her hand gently on the dirt, and in seconds, the leaves of a carrot appeared. Kaitlan pulled it out, and laid it in front of Libby.

"This is a carrot, Libby. It's yummy, and even I eat them.   They are great for your eyes, too!" She pulled up a second one, and started nibbling it to show Libby it was alright to eat.

Libby approached it cautiously.   She had never seen such and odd looking thing to eat. She looked up at Kaitlan in question.

"It's OK. Taste it! It's one of my favorite veggies!"

Libby licked the odd looking vegetable carefully, and it tasted almost sweet. She drew back, then took a nibble on it.

"YUM! This krot thing is really good, Mother!" Libby started nibbling faster.

Kaitlan grinned at her. Libby couldn't say the name right, but what did that matter? It was, after all, another planet. Let her name the carrot what she wanted.

"Would you like some help getting it home?"

Libby tried to lift it, and found she could.

"No, thank you, Mother. I think I can handle it. My little ones are going to absolutely love this! Thank you so much!"

"You are welcome, Libby. Have a great day, now!"

Libby had hopped off dragging her prize with her. Kaitlan decided what she would do for Libby and her whole family as long as they were in the area. She placed her hand onto the Earth, and asked that a tiny patch of carrots would always be available to Libby, and her descendants for as long as they lived there, and that they, and their tiny crop, be protected against any other predator.

"As you wish, Mother. It shall be done," she was told

by the earth.

"Thank you, she whispered."

Kaitlan breathed a sigh of relief. Libby would never go without food, nor would her little family. As long as she had descendants in the area, food would always be available.

That was it. She was done. She'd practiced everything she could think of, but she also tried to do it without her emotions which had been exceedingly hard. She honestly didn't know if she could keep her emotions in check when they battled Zanack. She did not understand why Dahll had been so adamant that they suppress their emotions. Did he not know that suppressing something only built up until it was let loose? Especially emotions?

She thanked the Earth, the trees, the vines, and the animals. She also thanked the rocks for giving her a comfortable place to sit - and until now, it was always rather uncomfortable sitting on rocks. They had, somehow, bent to her when she sat just as if she was sitting on a sofa cushion. Go figure!

Kaitlan started for the house. She couldn't wait to see Cordone. She planned on letting her emotions get totally out of control with her mate! She began to shoot pictures to him of what she wanted when she got there. Cordone's sigh of relief at hearing from her, he shot pictures right back at her, and she had several orgasms before she even reached the house! And, that spurred her on faster! She entered the mist, and found herself back home.

Sarah had been practicing for a long time as well. She had figured out how to control the waters, and yet protected the small town against them. They had volunteered to be her guinea pigs, but they also knew that they might die from it. But, Sarah would not do a thing until she discovered that it wasn't just the water that she could control, but she found she could actually produce bubbles with air inside. The outer layer of these bubbles were hard as stone, and clear as crystal. Sarah blanketed the town with one, large bubble to protect it as she practiced with all kinds of tidal waves, tsunamis, and one, grand thousand foot wave! The town's people were so grateful that she could protect them with the bubble. They actually thought it was fascinating as they watched waves of water flood and bombard it overhead.

A little girl by the name of Gem'a had become her companion, giving her all kinds of ideas for which Sarah was grateful. Children had an amazing imagination. Sarah learned much from her, and stored her ideas in her head for the battle to come.

Like Kaitlan, Sarah wanted to give these people back something that they didn't have. After all they had trusted her implicitly, she was determined to find something. So, Sarah asked Gem'a if she could have anything in the world she wanted, what would it be?

"Well, we are a fishing village, of course, my Lady Ninhursag. Our people would love to have an abundance of fish - enough to eat and to trade for a good price yearly." She sighed. "It's not been good over the past few years which is one of the reasons we agreed to help you, Sarah. We needed the money for food."

Sarah smiled, yet again, at the name she had been given. Ninhursag was the goddess of waters in Sumerian Mythology. She continually wondered why another planet would have the same gods as Earth. She decided when she had time, she would try and research it. But, then again, as she looked at Gem'a's face, maybe it didn't really matter all that much. After all, Asgard was real, and Earth had adopted their gods and goddesses. But, she filed it away for later. She had plenty of time for research.

Getting back to the problem at hand, Sarah refused to let these people ever go hungry, or without fish to trade and sell ever again. She stood on the bottom of the ocean, again. What she had discovered that Dahll had not told her was that she was allowed to communicate with the advanced sea life. She asked them how she could help the town to keep them in fish for their food and livelihood.

"We will promise you, Ninhursag, that you need not worry about this village."

The more advanced sea life agreed that they would make sure that for the town's sacrifice, and their bravery before the great lady, they would ensure that there was enough food for them as well as enough for their livelihood - of all kinds - making sure this town would never suffer again. Sarah thanked them, and she told Gem'a to tell her people. She hugged Sarah, and thanked her.

"No, Gem'a…it is I who should thank you! Without your imagination, I would never have thought of all the cool things you did for me! I shall miss you. Perhaps, one day, I'll be able to return to see you!"

"I shall keep that dream to see you again, my lady!" Gem'a had answered.

Sarah had given Gem'a a kiss on the forehead, and she had run back to her town to tell everyone the great news!

Sarah had decided she needed to see Sam, and also like Kaitlan, sent images to him as she phased into her wolf to run home faster. Sam's relief was visible when he heard from his mate, and couldn't wait to see her He had all kinds of plans for them! Sarah streaked through the mist, and found herself back home, and safe in Sam's arms!

Anita was still in awe at the power she could wield! She had whipped up tiny tornadoes, and gentle, cool winds. Storms with lightning and thunder, and even dust storms were at her whim. Anita decided to keep it only in the country, and not near cities and towns. She had felled trees (dead ones), and destroyed really old, broken down buildings that were abandoned long ago. At the same time, she had also made sure that all her damaging winds skipped over houses and barns that were below her making sure no one lost their homes. She just knew they had no idea what was happening despite what Dahll had told her. Anita was ashamed that she had put them through terrifying things, while not close to their homes, they were certainly close enough to frighten them. So much so, that she heard their name for her on the wind - Aura. Yet, they held no animosity, or hatred for her. So, she decided to make sure that those who had unknowingly participated with her powers would always be protected from all violent storms and winds while still receiving just the right amount of rain and breezes for beautiful crops for their lifetime. The land would remain fertile.

Anita had also discovered that the air could be concentrated in one, small area, or she could make a tornado the size of half the country if she wished! That was way more than she ever dreamed she could do! But, trying to keep one's emotions from these powers was extremely difficult! She honestly just did not know how that would ever be possible in the long run.

Finally, she'd had enough practicing. Like Kaitlan and Sarah, Sarah told Dan she was on her way home, and he'd better have his motor up and running by the time she got there! She couldn't wait to use her powers with him - again! She'd learned some new "tricks"! She entered the mist, and found herself back home. Dan ran toward her, scooped her up, and sped inside like a bullet!

Lynne stood in the middle of a violent, and destructive, forest fire. Her power of fire gave her a tremendously dangerous element. But, what if she could not just dish out fire, but stop it as well? That's why she came here. Thousands upon thousands of acres were already burning out of control advancing onto a neighborhood on the edge of a great city on the Planet of the Four Moons. If left unchecked, the fire had the potential to destroy the entire city. Great place to try out her theory.

Standing in the center, Lynne's hands rose over her head with her hands outstretched each finger acting like a vacuum as her body turned faster and faster and faster as she pulled the fire into her body, taking away all the oxygen from the fire, and extinguishing it. She stopped, breathing hard for a moment to see if it was working. It was! She closed her eyes, and continued her "vacuuming" of the fire. However, while she was doing so, she made sure that all dead brush and trees were completely consumed clearing off the biggest problem that feed fires. Clearing deadened brush out of the way always helped to keep fires from getting out of hand. Unfortunately, these people didn't realize that by not clearing out dead brush from a forest, it was the very thing that fueled a fire to huge, destructive levels.

It took her a matter of minutes to end the fire. She stood at the beginning of the fire to see what had started it. Someone had dropped a cigarette butt. She crushed it out with her foot. She heard firefighters whooping it up as the fire died, giving thanks to their Lady Chantico. She was awed that she had been named for such an ancient Aztec deity, but puzzled how they knew a name from Earth mythology. And, right now, they were a bit too close to her. She did not need to be seen, so she lifted herself out of the forest the same way she had gotten there. By closing her eyes, and reappearing into the volcano where Dahll had dropped her. She was tired. Really tired. It had taken everything within her to not let her emotions get out of hand. She was angry at what was coming. But, she managed to keep it under control.

Lynne had had enough of it, and sent Richard a message telling him she was on her way back. Richard had felt her anger, and exhaustion. He sent her a visual of what was awaiting her when she returned, and she had multiple orgasms of what she did see from him! She couldn't get back fast enough! She entered the mist, and found herself back home with Richard's arms awaiting her.

~~~~

If the four women had but stopped to think, they would have realized that the fact that another world thought of them as great Mothers of their world, how much more so would the people of Earth think of them since they were born of the Earth if they only knew?
~~~~

~ 29 ~
The Enemy Within

The Council poured into their room for their weekly meeting. Cordone was already there. He had a sheet of paper in his hand, folded, and he was tapping the edge on the table over and over in an apparent daze. He didn't even look up when the council sat. He considered the note he held in his hand. He was angry, but cautious as well.

After about ten minutes, the council was starting to be nervous at Cordone's apparent lack of acknowledgement that they were even there when he put the paper down, and rubbed his hand against his chin.

His eyes rose. Cordone looked at each member, one at a time straight in the eyes. One of these sitting her was a traitor. One of them was Zanack. After a moment, he had to add Lon McClain to that list. Six werewolves who sat around him, and one who had sat around him for a great many years was Zanack.

From his left, and going around the table, he observed the Council members with piercing eyes. For the first time as Alpha, he truly wished that Canaan was still alive and Alpha so he wouldn't have to deal with this whole shit! Cordone wondered if he were even up for this. But, it was his lot, now. He had to deal with it, and find the traitor.

1. Samuel James Knight
2. Ceasar Stefan Cecchi
3. Roland Millard Tanner
4. Wayne Daniel O'Kelley
5. Richard Morton O'Malley

One of the six was Zanack. But, which one? He did not

believe either Sam nor Richard were Zanack. He already knew it wasn't Richard, for sure. But, Sam? Cordone stared at his friend, then decided it definitely wasn't Sam.

That left three: Caesar, Roland or Wayne. After a couple of minutes, he added a former Council member, Lon McClain, again. McClain's obvious hatred having been black-balled from the Council made Cordone discount him completely. Lon McClain was open in his denouncements of the Council. Also, it was just too obvious. So, that left him the other three. After a moment, he decided to call Lon into the council meeting as well.

"Keep your friends close, and your enemies closer", as the old saying goes. A quote from Sun-Tzu. Yeah, but was that really going to help?

Cordone allowed each of the council members to read the only note they had. After they read it, their faces showed shock and anger. This had been a bold move for Zanack, especially since the council already knew he was one of them. That was when Cordone began to entertain a trap. One of these would step into it. So, his idea was very simple. Beginning with Lon, he would give each of them a false task. He would be the only one to know which task was assigned to whom. On second thought, he decided to include Kaitlan. Always safer in numbers.

He debated whether, or not, to tell them what he had found on the council table when he walked into the room. He considered it for a moment, then decided against it - right now.

Kaitlan opened the door, and apologized for being late. She had been finishing something that had been extremely important in The Hall of Records. Her eyes met Cordone's. He had already told her what he held in his hand. She was not at all happy about it, either.

Kaitlan took her seat, and the meeting began with the updates of the clan's business.

Lon McClain was furious! How dare Cordone "order" him to go to the council room! He hated Canaan, and he hated Cordone even more for kicking him off of it. He arrived in Lynne's office, and she just waved him into the council room without even looking up. Even though he was furious at being black-balled from the Council, he still had been gaining a grudging respect and honor for his new Alpha.

Kaitlan stood up from her chair when Lon McClain opened the door, and moved behind her mate. At this, Lon frowned. This was not usual. Regardless of whether Kaitlan was the heir to the clan, she shouldn't have been there with the Alpha at a private meeting. This was not normal, and Lon became wary as he shut the door.

"You ordered me here, Valon?"

"Let's just say it was a strong request, McClain. I needed you hear when the rest of the council was gone. Please, sit down." After McClain had settled into the chair in front of the desk, Cordone continued. "I know this is highly irregular…" he began.

"Irregular, Valon? It's downright inexcusable!" McClain raised his voice.

Cordone nodded, and then looked at Kaitlan. Kaitlan came around the table, and handed McClain the paper that Cordone had shown the council just minutes before. He didn't take it immediately, but looked up into her eyes. He was going to say something, but his eyes narrowed at her face. Something was wrong. Terribly wrong, and he knew it. He glanced at Cordone, then back to Kaitlan who was still holding the piece of paper he had yet to take.

"Please, Lon?" Kaitlan asked.

McClain pressed his lips together, and for once, keeping his mouth shut. He accepted the paper from her, but still didn't open it.

"Please, McClain," Cordone asked. "Read it. It says more than I could."

McClain was suddenly on edge as he unfolded the paper

slowly staring into Kaitlan's eyes. His hatred, his arrogance, and even his demanding nature disappeared in a split second after his eyes read what was on it. Was he reading this right? In something resembling the letters from an old typewriter, he read aloud.

I killed Canaan. I poisoned Lynne. I poisoned and killed Sarah Knight, and that mutant bastard she held within her womb. I poisoned Anita, but somehow, she was unaffected. I was too late for Kaitlan and your bastards! But, in the end, I will win, Cordone. I'm sure, by now, you have figured out that I am here at all times - watching all of you. Council members are the only ones allowed into this room. Our fight is close, but it will not occur here in this building, in St. Louis, or in this state. When I am ready, you will appear where I decide, Kaitlan. And, finally, the war between us will begin. I have devoured enough flesh, now, for the strength I need against you. You will not find me - not yet. Be assured ... it will be fast. All of you - the four women and their mates - will die by my hand. Then, a new world will appear where we will breed humans for food, and the supers that are left will be our slaves. Your time is at an end. Watch your back! I am right behind it! - Zanack. The New Earth Age will begin!

McClain just sat with the words swimming before his eyes. This can't be true! No! To be able to have put this paper on the table in the Council room? The implication was that someone on the Council was Zanack!

"SHIT! Zanack is someone on the council?" McClain almost yelled.

"Exactly. As it is now, McClain, I am assigning you a high-priority mission. Secret only to the three of us. I want you to watch everyone on the council with absolute impunity. Including myself and Kaitlan."

McClain looked at Valon. Was he kidding?

"Why me, Valon?"

"Because, McClain, you are the only person who I can completely trust not to be Zanack. Only four of us know about this action I am taking in using you. Zanack, you, Kaitlan, and myself."

Lon McClain threw the paper back on Cordone's desk.

"How do you know I am not Zanack?" McClain asked.

"Truth? I don't. But, then how do you know that I am not Zanack?"

McClain nodded.

"Touché." He said. "The Council will not be happy about this."

"I know. They do not know. But, for the time being, I need a spy. Canaan wrote that you were the one person, above all others on the Council, who he trusted completely."

McClain blinked his eyes in shock. Canaan? Trusted me totally? The thought gave him a grudging happiness.

"I don't understand."

McClain was really confused. Canaan and he had fought like cats and dogs. They never really even liked each other. This was a revelation for which he was not prepared.

"Canaan admired you, Lon. You never bullshitted him in any way. He always knew where he stood with you - even though the two of you argued about everything. You disliked each other intensely, but when it came down to it, Canaan would pick you to be on the side of the clan no matter what. And, nothing, and no one, would ever be able to sway you into going against it."

McClain fell backward until the back of the chair hit him. He never knew this. He had felt the same way, but they fought way too much to ever have a mutual admiration society. He had admired Canaan as well, but he would never admit it to a living soul - werewolf! His eyes shot to Kaitlan who was looking him in the eye.

"Lon. My Dad respected you. If you think you are surprised, you can imagine how I felt when I found Daddy's diary, yesterday. I would never have guessed it at all. But, if my Dad trusted you implicitly, then so can we."

They were right. While he and Canaan had had so many differences it caused them to argue constantly, they were both absolutely loyal to the clan no matter those differences.

Cordone and Kaitlan waited for his response. Finally, McClain's head came up, and he nodded.

"OK. I'll do it. But, I can immediately discount you and Kaitlan as well as Sam and Richard. That leaves three on the Council."

Cordone's eyes narrowed.

"Why would you discount us, McClain?"

"Easy. All of you have proven your absolute loyalty to the clan many times over. The other three, though. They have not over the years. All three of them have tried to change the clan rules at one time or another. The rest of you never even thought about it let alone tried to do it."

Cordone stood, and walked around in front of his desk holding out his hand.

"So, then, we are definitely on the same page, McClain. Do whatever it takes, but find out what you can. The end is coming, and we need information - as much as we can get."

McClain grasped Cordone's arm, and the men shook arms in ancient agreement.

"May I keep this paper?"

"Yes. But, don't lose it. It's the only one."

"I will make sure I find something out for you, Alpha. As of right now, any past grievances that were breached are gone. I am honored by your trust in me, and even more, by the trust Canaan placed in me even though I did not know of it." His eyes traveled over to Kaitlan who smiled, and nodded to him.

"I expect regular updates directly from you," Cordone

asked.

"It will be done."

McClain walked out of the office madder than he had ever been.

As McClain left, Cordone and Kaitlan knew that he would do his best to find whatever he could. He would not leave his clan until he did find something!

Well, that was suspect number one. Three more to go.

Cordone punched the button.

"Lynne? Send in Wayne."

He turned to Kaitlan.

"That's one, Kaitlan. Three more to go. Do you have the note?"

She smiled as she turned to her purse, and pulled out three more sheets of paper all with the same note on it. She put the other two back into her purse, and gave one of them to Cordone.

"Where's the original, Kaitlan?"

"Where else? In Daddy's secret safe! Where else would it be?"

Cordone grinned as Lynne buzzed them to tell them that Roland was waiting.

"OK! Same Bad time, Cordone. Same Bad channel!" She paraphrased from the old Batman series.

Cordone rolled his eyes, and Kaitlan laughed.

~ Epilogue ~

Preparing the Present for the Past for the Future
(When you figure that one out, will you mind telling me what it means?)

Zanack was deep in thought as he sat in his black leather wingback chair. He remembered his own teacher telling him about the curse, and it had been relayed through the ages. The scroll had disappeared, and his teacher only had his own memory from yet another. He had relied on his memory of that teacher. Finding the Scroll of Time gave him the chance to commit the ultimate revenge by granting him a second chance! And, he would not make those same mistakes again! He had been going about the destruction in the wrong way by killing females with Wolfsbane. He counted himself very, very lucky he discovered the scroll, as well as Sarah coming back from the dead. If she had died, he would have been up shit creek without the proverbial paddle! Now, he had no doubt about his prowess to recast the curse with the scrolls guiding him. He almost could not contain himself when Cordone and Kaitlan had shown the real scroll to the council.

The writing on that scroll combined with the Scroll of Time not only gave each absolute step in detail, but also confirmed his theory why it didn't work the first time. He glanced at his notes. He had condensed it into a smaller list of what he needed to have, and do.

1. The Four Elementals (He'd have to trick them)
2. A wizard must cast the curse (No problem)
3. The curse must be cast at the original time and place, which involved time travel. (Difficult, yes. Impossible, no.)
4. Four blood sacrifices were needed to open the time portal. (Had them, or would)
5. Four blood sacrifices were needed to cast the curse, and it required three drops of blood from each (The Elementals blood, of course)

Time travel just added to the complexity. With the loss of a great amount of his own power, only one place on Earth existed that would give him the power for the time spell. It's where the original curse was broken. Cordone's land would allow him to draw on the Earth's energy by using its unique properties. It all should be easy enough, yet he knew he still had to be careful. Timing was everything when it came to time travel. He snorted at that joke. One wrong move, and they would all end up in an alternate world.

A wizard had to cast the curse. But, he would have to revert to his real form to do so. It had been a very long time since he had been in that form.

Magic, black magic, always came at a high price. He needed not only three drops of blood from all that went with him, but also an equal blood sacrifice for each. This meant if he took two with him, two others must die in blood to equal the two that he took. He needed four to die. Their mates. Problem solved.

The next part had been non-negotiable. The Evil One had declared that in order to cast any curse, he was to gorge himself on blood and flesh first. Then he was to fast until after it had been cast. If he ate, or drank, anything at all, no matter how small, the curse would destroy him. Zanack's gorging had been ravenous over the last week. His hunger would continue to grow until he was ready. In his current form, he was able to change to his human appearance, but it was getting much harder with each day. He had been building his scraps up, again, and he was able to keep his glamour. Once he opened the time portal, the glamour would end the second he crossed the time boundary. He would revert to his true form. If it was done right, the O'Hara Clan would never have been!   No big loss. His plan would come to fruition within the next week. Nothing could go wrong!

"I see nothing," Dahll said quietly to himself.

Since he had returned home, his vision was blinded. He could see nothing. No matter how Dahll tried, he saw only blackness before him in his effort to see the future. Did this mean that there would be no future?

While he had awaited Richard to introduce him to the Elementals, he had been overcome by an odd feeling - one he had never had.

"Creator? I do not see the future past the end of this week! You have withheld it from me.   Should I not see something? Or is the end of all ends? Please, if it be thy will, show me something! Anything?" he asked the Great Creator.

This feeling? What was it? He struggled with a description of what he felt. His emotions were truly on edge. And, then, stunned, he darted his eyes into the sky.

"Oh Creator? Is this … is what I am feeling?" he whispered in astonishment. "Could this be … fear?"

He was fed a vision. Only a handful of beings in the nine realms knew of the Scroll of time. Dahll watched as Zanack found it. It was his destiny to find it. Dahll saw all of time. It was his job, his privilege, his gift. He saw not just the past, but the present, the future, and then end of all things.

But, now, for the first time in his long life, as the vision left him, he saw nothing. Dahll was hampered by the loss of his own ability. He saw - nothing! As if … as if the future had deliberately been withheld from him. And, perhaps it had. Perhaps the Creator did not want him to see. But, why now? The moment he asked was the moment he knew the answer. Because the future was not yet written. Perhaps it was because it had been screwed up the first time? He froze at this thought. No matter how much he tried to look through the veil of the portal of time, he could not see beyond it. If he, the only immortal who had been given the gift to see all time - past, present, and future - could see nothing, it was obvious that the Creator did not wish it. He fell to his knees, and asked the one question no one is ever supposed to ask the Creator.

Why?

**End of The White Wolf Prophecy
~ Hall of Records ~
Book 2**

Sneak Peak - Following is an excerpt from the final book in
The White Wolf Prophecy Trilogy:

The White Wolf Prophecy
~ Scroll of Time ~
Book 3

The White Wolf Prophecy
~ Scroll of Time ~
Book 3 - Excerpt

" 'NO!' " his Father had yelled.

" 'I'm not asking you, Zoar. I'm TELLING you what you are going to do!' "

Cordone began to speak aloud softly.

"My Dad's voice was so damned angry. But, I don't know who it was. I don't know who the other voice belonged to, but I do remember it was a man."

He continued with a frown as he tried to drag up a memory of thousands of years ago.

"Wait. It was Johnson? Johnson was there?" Cordone said in surprise.

He began to tell the others what he was remembering. "My Dad was angry at Johnson."

" 'Johnson, you go too far! This is my land, not yours! I will not allow you to take anything from me, or my family! And, most especially, my son!' "

" 'You have no choice! You agreed to it when Ter'act built this house! You gave part of your land to me!' "

" 'No, I did not agree to any of that! Ter'act only oversaw the building! Marta and I designed it, and the Elves agreed to build it. The Agreement was with the Elven clans that once the house was built, the Elves would be given the right to use this land on occasion, because of the magical properties which enhance any supernatural person! Never did we make an agreement with you alone! But, I certainly did not sign anything over to Ter'act, or to you!' "

" 'Then, I will take it, Zoar!' " screamed Ter'act as only an Elf can do.

What Cordone had not seen, or heard, was the rest of the argument. They both watched, Cordone's anger rising as he saw what happened through his Father's eyes.

Zoar had noticed that Cordone was watching them. His eyes full of terror.

" 'My son does not need to see any of this, Ter'act!' "

Ignoring Zoar's pleading, Ter'act forced Zoar to his knees using her Elven powers telling Johnson what she was going to do.

" 'I will take care of Zoar and Marta, and then, Cordone! I will kill all of them! Go get the little whelp!' " She ordered.

Johnson started toward the lift.

" 'Cordone,' " cried Zoar obviously in tremendous pain. " 'Go to your room, son! Lock the door, and don't let anyone in!' "

Amazingly, Sarah was able to merge the two of them with young Cordone's mind at the same time.

Cordone started to turn, but didn't obey his Father. He dropped to his knees to keep out of sight as his Father told him to do should he ever encounter something bad to witness what happens. And, no matter what to report it to Canaan. Cordone could still watch, but not as well as he would have been able to had he been standing. But, he could hear, too. He knew that his Father was in danger. He kept out of sight, but his Father knew he was watching.

Zoar felt his son's eyes on him, and it killed him to know he was watching, and he knew that he and Marta, his mate, were dead. Never had he ever wanted his son to see death. But, he would watch his Father and Mother murdered. There was a reason that he told Cordone to report to Canaan. He did not have the strength against an Elf. Silently, apologizing to his son, he turned his face to Ter'act.

" 'You will never get away with this, Ter'act. Johnson. I will hunt you down. Do you understand me? And, if you kill us, my son will come after you! But, not before I kill you, Ter'act!' "

" 'You will *never* touch my mate!' " Johnson told him.

" 'Keep thinking that, Johnson. I do not threaten anyone without cause.' "

" 'You think that your threat means anything? It does not!' "

Suddenly, a silver wolf appeared from no where, and jumped Ter'act. Ter'act threw the wolf against the wall, breaking her neck instantly. Zoar watched Marta die. He knew that either he fought back and died, or he would die within days without Marta. He chose the former. Even a minute without her was too long. He apologized silently to his son for what he was about to do.

Sarah was horrified as she watched all this unfold. Cordone's eyes refused to move away from the scene before him. She wanted to stop, to pull them away from Cordone's memories, but she couldn't tear her eyes away from what she was seeing. She knew if she did, she would miss all. That was not an option. They needed the truth. But, worse than that was that she could tell that Cordone, while having seen it all happen, was just far more horrified! He was watching his parents die! Why did he have no memory of this? Sarah could feel his desperation to know why.

She could see that Zoar knew his son was there. Neither Johnson nor Ter'act had heard him above, and had no idea their actions were being seen.

So, Sarah continued to watch while bile rose in her throat. This was why she was born. This was what she had been meant to see. The birth of evil incarnate. Zanack.

Zoar phased immediately, and lunged at Ter'act taking her head off of her body in vengeance for killing his mate! Sarah almost threw up right then. The blue blood of the Elf sprayed all over the room. Her blood covered Zoar and Johnson! Johnson's face showed shock, and then his face grew in hatred before her eyes. He almost started to attack Zoar, but stopped as if someone had pulled him back. Instead, he issued a threat against the clan.

" 'Everything is because of Dillon O'Hara, and his life is forfeited as of now. It will continue to his son, his son's sons, until all their line is dead! As for yours? Your line ends here. Today. Your life is over, and then, the life of your son will end as well!' "

Johnson spoke as if he was speaking for someone else, now. Zoar phased back into his human form. Zoar sniffed. There was someone else there. No. Some - thing.

" 'My son will live, Johnson! And, you will pay the price for this one day. I pray that it is by his hand! But, it appears you have entered into something else. Something evil. Maybe that will be your death. Perhaps you take my life tonight. Perhaps it will not be you, but another. But, your time is limited, Johnson. Your life will be taken by The White Wolf when you return to this land. You will be ended forever! Your horror is only beginning. May the great Creator serve on you justice from now until your death!' "

"Oh, but it WILL be me!" screamed Johnson.

Zoar darted out the glass door phasing back to his wolf as he ran. He had to get whatever he could smell away from the house. Away from his son!

Through Zoar's eyes, Cordone and Sarah watched as Johnson ran after him at a speed Zoar had never seen! He was faster than Zoar, and caught up with him. How was he able to do this? Johnson was human!

But, now, Sarah and Cordone could see what Zoar saw with his last breath of life as he was sliced to pieces - slowly, his skin was carved from his body in an instant. The pain, excruciating, he turned his head, and saw Johnson standing several feet away looking at him with a sneer on his face. It wasn't Johnson? Johnson was not his killer? Then, who was shredding his body?

Sarah and Cordone got a brief glance at what killed Zoar, and then she yanked her hands away from Cordone crying uncontrollably!!

Sam gathered her in his arms. Cordone just stared

unblinking. He had seen what Sarah had seen. Cordone began to howl with pain, and tears flowed from his eyes. In horror, Kaitlan ran to his side as he collapsed, and pulled his head to her breast. What they had seen must have been so horrible, it would effect them for the rest of their lives. Whoever had taken his memories away had to have done so to protect his mind from all of this horror! Of that, she had no doubt. But, now, with Sarah, everything had been opened up, and whatever the two of them saw was so horrific, it collapsed both of them to quivering beings.

No one spoke for a very long time as they watched two of their own suffer horrendously.

Finally, Sarah slowed her crying, and Sam, very gently, asked her what she had seen.

"I don't kn-know!" Sarah stuttered between sobs. "It was horrible! *HORRIBLE*! I-I've never seen anything like it!" she cried as her tears began to flow harder.

"I thought they had died in the Vampire Wars," he whispered. Kaitlan knew he meant his parents. "I don't understand? Why did I not remember this? I saw part of it, yet didn't remember? Why? I saw my Mother murdered before my eyes by Johnson's mate! And, that THING that skinned my Father! Oh, GOD!"

Anita bent to hold Cordone's hands with tears streaming down her face.

"You were a little boy, Cordone. Sometimes, our minds have to protect us from seeing things that are so horrific, it shuts down to protect us. Your mind could not process the truth, therefore it shut you down. Whoever found you realized this, and took you into his care. "

"I remember, now. Dillon took me in, and that's how Canaan and I came to be the best of friends." He looked at Kaitlan tears streaking his face. "Kind of what you wanted to happen with Sarah so you could be sisters. But, he told me they had been killed in the Vampire Wars." He looked back at Anita. "Why? Why would he lie to me?"

Anita shrugged. "Easy, Cordone. He must have realized your mind had shut down, and you didn't remember most of it. They must have found you, and then your parents' bodies. How is not important any more. He kept you in the dark, because your own mind 'erased' it. Dillon must have figured it out, and played along. The alternative may have set your feet on another path that could have ended in your own hatred driving you to kill.   Perhaps you would have turned rogue, and had no one to bring you out of it before you did. We'll never really know, but that would be my biggest guess."

"No," said Lynne softly. "That's not what happened."

Everyone looked at her in puzzlement.

"What do you mean, Lynne?" Cordone asked.

"Dillon saw the aftermath. Many of us did. Did you know that I have the ability to block one's mind when I was a vampire?"

Cordone's eyes narrowed, and shook his head.

"He came to me, and asked me to use my mind to block your memories, and give him a false one that his parents were killed in the Vampire Wars." Her head came up to look him in the eyes. "He was my Alpha, Cordone. I had no choice. He truly thought it would be best for you."

Cordone drew in his breath in shock while Richard pulled Lynne into his arms. Then, nodded.

"I should be angry with you, Lynne. But, I am Alpha, now.   And, I understand Dillon. I wouldn't have if I had retained my memory. What I might have become if you hadn't blocked them, may have been worse than anything. My life would have been spent in revenge. My feet were set upon a different path thanks to Dillon." He looked up at her. "Thank you, Lynne."

She smiled at him through her tears.

"Sarah? Did you see who killed his Father?" Kaitlan asked.

"Not all of it. But, it wasn't Johnson. He was standing to the side sneering, and the 'thing'! Zoar had no idea who killed him. But, his face showed a horror I have never seen on anyone's face. It was … Oh, God! I can't describe what I saw!!! It was so fast!"

Cordone covered his face with his hands. If only he didn't remember, now!

Dan knelt by Sarah.

"Try your best, Sarah. Cordone, you too. We need to know, because if what you saw is still around, then we need to know what we are facing."

Sarah nodded her head, and took a deep breath.

"I didn't see all of it. Just a glimpse. But, it's eyes were," she shuddered at the memory. "It's eyes were a burnt orange in color. They were elongated. The face was very large - the size of a massive lion. And, it was long! Really, really tall, and stood upright. It had no hair that I was able to see. Scales. Yes. Scales is what it had. It's color was charcoal gray with a hint of olive, and it was covered in … I'm not sure, but it looked like tiny white spikes. But, its teeth! Oh, Creator! Its teeth! The mouth opened just before it killed Zoar. It reminded me of a shark's teeth. Row upon row upon row of nothing but sharp and pointed, rotten yellow and black teeth!"

Sarah really wanted to throw up again, but she was determined not to let that happen.

"What was it's size, Cordone?" demanded Richard.

"It was too close for me to tell. I just know it stood tall. Sarah has given a rough estimate of its size as best I could see, I agree with her. I can't believe what we saw through my Father's eyes. But, that thing was …. I just know one thing."

He looked at the faces staring at him.

"What is that?" Sam asked him.

"It wasn't from Earth."

Mouths gaped with astonishment. Not from Earth?

"What does that mean?" Kaitlan asked her mate who just shrugged. He sure didn't know.

Richard felt as if a boulder had crashed into his stomach. It couldn't be! Sarah's description had thrown him for a loop.

The race she had described was long since extinct! There couldn't be one here. Yet....

"Ignoring that for the moment, since none of us can possibly wrap our heads around it," Lynne fumbled, "Sarah, what you have been given is an amazing and powerful gift. The kind of power which is only given to one who is completely worthy of such powers. What a great honor!"

"Yeah? Well, as cool as that sounds, it ain't!" Sarah complained.

Kaitlan held her mate tightly against her breast as he, again, broke down in tears. His memory had released the floodgates as it returned to him. It's so hard to watch people you love break down like that, but to watch a male Alpha do so caused everyone to cry. His emotions were so overwhelmed they reached out to those closest to him.

There was silence for a very long time. Not from Earth. Then where was it from, and more importantly … was it still here?

It was Tim's voice over the intercom that shook everyone up. They had all forgotten they were even on the jet.

"We will be landing in ten, everyone. Time to buckle up!"